THE ACHILLES HEEL

Reg Gadney was born in Cross Hills, Yorkshire. He was educated at Cambridge and Massachussetts Institute of Technology. He lives in North London.

The Achilles Heel

REG GADNEY

faber and faber
LONDON · BOSTON

First published in Great Britain in 1996
by Faber and Faber Limited
3 Queen Square London WC1N 3AU
This paperback edition first published in 1997

Photoset by Parker Typesetting Service, Leicester
Printed and bound in Great Britain by
Mackays of Chatham PLC, Chatham, Kent

A CIP record for this book
is available from the British Library

ISBN 0–571–17939–8

2 4 6 8 10 9 7 5 3 1

For Fay with love

My government is committed to the eradication by all means possible of the evil trade in pornography.

HM The Queen
QUEEN'S SPEECH, STATE OPENING OF PARLIAMENT

SECRET

HM Customs & Excise

Chairman H M Customs & Excise
Ms Drew Franklin , CB

INVESTIGATION DIVISION
NEW & PROVISIONAL RANKINGS

Chief Investigation Officer
Richard Gaynor, CBE

Deputy Chief Investigation Officer
Assistant Chief Investigation Officer
permanent appointments vacant

Customs Teams A & B
Arms & Explosives
names restricted

Customs Teams C & D
Agricultural & Tariffs Fraud
names restricted

Customs Team E
Indecent & Obscene Material
SIO Alan H. Rosslyn

Customs Team F
Computer Micro Team
Supplies & Data Retrieval
SIO J. Thornley-Miller

Note: 1996–97 – The Investigation Division will absorb the
Collection Investigation Units to form the HM Customs
Investigation Service.

The new world order has created conditions which encourage the growth of what is called 'organized crime'. This phenomenon is comparatively new. Countering the threat will require those same methods which will have been developed to deal with the more familiar threats such as terrorism. There seems little doubt that crime of this sort will grow, feeding on those same modern trends that I have described – the increasing spread of communications and travel and the weakness of controls. This means the same strategic approach, the same investigative techniques. But above all it means the same close national and international co-operation between security intelligence and law enforcement agencies.

Director General, MI5
Lecture to the English Speaking Union

Thursday 20 July

75°F/24°C. Sunny P.M., cloud clearing to leave hazy sunshine.

12.30

'Straub smells money like a shark smells blood,' said Rosslyn, watching the café clock that advertised Tuborg lager. 'And he hasn't picked the scent up.'

'Hang about, Alan,' said Celeste Quinceau. She looked across the street to the grey brick façade of the Hotel Heelas. 'He's only thirty minutes late. He'll be there waiting if money's his Achilles heel. If you were giving me ten thousand dollars in readies I'd just keep you waiting. Like, to show you who's got the upper hand.'

'Straub isn't one of us,' said Rosslyn. 'You don't know him. He's different.'

'That I'd guessed.'

A waiter set two cappuccinos on the table. Rosslyn stayed silent until the man was out of earshot.

'Straub may not be my favourite person. But given that he's a grass he's been reliable as a timekeeper.'

'He's only thirty minutes late,' said Celeste. 'You did tell him Hotel Heelas?'

'I didn't,' said Rosslyn. He twisted the straps of the canvas money bag tighter around his wrist. 'The meeting place is Straub's choice. And if he's already in there he didn't go in the front way, Celeste.'

She followed his gaze to the hotel across the street. 'We'd have seen him.'

'You don't have to tell me.'

'Don't sit here getting edgy then. Try again. He may have phoned. Left a message at reception.'

'I don't like this,' said Rosslyn. 'Something's wrong from the off. This isn't like him at all.'

'Why don't you try reception again?' said Celeste. 'They may have heard something. I mean, he's reserved a room, hasn't he?'

'All right.' He handed her the canvas bag. 'You take care of this. I'll be two minutes.'

At the exit to the café he looked round at Celeste.

He saw her give a look that said 'Get on with it.' She was toying with the small crucifix on its gold chain around her neck. Probably touching it for luck.

He thought: *I shouldn't leave her guarding ten thousand US dollars. UK government money. We're supposed to stick together at all times.*

12.36

The foyer of the Hotel Heelas smelled of roasting coffee-beans and there was a different woman behind the reception desk.

'I have an appointment with Mr Straub,' Rosslyn told her. 'The representative of Eurotel Guides of Tokyo.'

The receptionist keyed Straub's name into the computer on the desk. 'Room 43,' she said. 'Shall I tell him you're here?'

'No. I'll speak to him if you don't mind.'

'The internal phone is in the kiosk,' she said. 'Over there.'

He made his way to the kiosk past the rubber plants and the racks of pamphlets advertising tours of museums, the Carlsberg brewery, a lecture series on Søren Kierkegaard and special visits to the Erotic Museum in the former brothel at 31 Vesterbrogade.

An American voice said, 'Yes?'

Rosslyn gave the first of the two agreed codewords to identify himself. '*Little.*'

'*Mermaid*,' Straub replied correctly. 'How are you?'

'Fine.'

'You didn't tell me you'd have some black woman with you,' Straub said.

'Do you have a problem with that?'

'Look, we've always done business between ourselves,' Straub said. 'Why do we need a third party?'

'Don't make a bloody issue of it, Straub,' Rosslyn said. 'New rules.'

'Since when?'

'Since recently.'

'Who is she?'

'A colleague. She's with me. What's your worry?'

'I need to know who's who.'

'I've told you. She works with me.'

'Okay,' said Straub. 'Come on up in thirty minutes.'

12.45

Rosslyn gave the waiter an order for two more cappuccinos. Celeste handed the canvas bag back to him. 'The prima donna's there,' he told her. 'Now he's suffering from paranoia. He saw us together and didn't like the idea of meeting some third party, a woman he doesn't know. We do the business in about half an hour. According to the book, this is the moment, in case anything goes wrong, I give you the details.'

'I've never understood,' she said, 'why you're not allowed to tell me from the word go.'

'Because it's a question of need to know. If he hadn't shown up you'd have had a background and an identity that you *didn't* need to know. That's the thinking.'

'Who is this Straub then?'

'Ostensibly, he's a small-time publisher of tacky guide books. You won't often find any of them on the shelves next to *Fodor*, *Michelin* or *Frommer*. His main business is international currency dealing and laundering under the name of

Morton Damm. As Jack Straub, he sells me criminal intelligence direct.'

'When did you find him?'

'Two years back. Straub was recommended by Aiko Holland. US Customs at the London embassy. An American-Japanese. She says Straub's a source we'll find useful. If you must know, I think Aiko Holland has more than just a professional admiration for Straub. I even wondered whether Straub's her lover. Anyway, it turns out that Straub's got things right.'

He waited a moment for the waiter to leave the coffee.

'To contact Straub, I call an answering service registered in the name of EGT at its Tokyo address. Nothing's down in writing, right? You have to remember the details. Like his address is 8–9 Shibaura, Minato-ku. Straub then phones me back from untraceable numbers wherever he may be in the East or West. We fix an appointment at a mutually agreed rendezvous. Say Hamburg. Amsterdam. Or, like now, Copenhagen. Straub says he has a big name to offer. I tell him, "Better be worth it." He says, "I'm not about to waste your time. This is the big one. Ten thousand dollars up front. Ten thousand on delivery. At twenty thousand dollars it's a steal." There's some haggling. I win. I have to get special authority for anything more than three figures in pounds sterling. Straub likes to be paid in person. Cash. We like to think we have a personal relationship. There's some clandestine intelligence you only get face to face. And a seller like Straub only risks parting with it when he's certain the buyer has cash up front. Each side has to trust the other. At least for five minutes, or however long it takes. There you are. Now you know.'

'About bloody time,' she said. 'This little operation is named after me.'

This current operation was *Operation Celeste*.

Rosslyn didn't need reminding. It wasn't so little either; it was big and very nasty and it was his baby.

13.05

Crammed into the small hotel lift with Rosslyn, she looked at him. He was inserting a new Maxell tape into his two-speed Panasonic microcassette recorder. The dark, unruly hair needed combing. His face looked haggard. Paedophile Porn Pallor they called it at headquarters, Custom House in Lower Thames Street. PPP – the result of too many hours spent watching the videos and CD-ROMs. An occupation only for men and women of considerable psychological resilience. However tough you were, they said, you could only take so much of it. PPP came with the territory.

As undercover officers of HM Customs & Excise Investigation Division's Team E, their mandate was the prevention of paedophile pornography imports into the United Kingdom. In these days of strict security and financial accountability, when it came to paying informants like Straub, they operated in pairs.

· In Copenhagen, as in every European capital, the manufacturers of paedophile pornography pursued their trade with a frightening degree of ruthlessness. The informants paid by the law enforcement agencies threatened profits, and anything that threatened profits had to be eliminated. If the lives of their child victims came cheap, the deaths of these informants came even cheaper. Nowadays a contract killer was easy to hire. Easier to hire than a reliable chauffeur or domestic plumber. Many of them, drawn from the innumerable and redundant agents of the old Soviet bloc, were ready to do the business. The half-dozen dismembered corpses recovered from the Rhine, the Seine and the Thames during the last six months were ample evidence. The bloated human remains shared one thing in common. They were all informants. Like Straub.

Celeste was pleased to have been Rosslyn's personal choice for the Copenhagen mission. He'd told her she was a natural. She had the intuition, common sense and curiosity of the born undercover officer. She remembered hearing someone

saying much the same about Rosslyn back in the canteen at
Custom House.

He handed her the tape recorder. 'Get him down on tape.'
He watched her check the machine. He noticed that her
fingernails, bright red and polished, were longer than ever.
'Are those nails real, Celeste?' he asked.

'Scratch me,' she said. 'And you'll find out. By the way, is
this battery flat?'

'You tell me,' he said.

She pressed the PLAY button. 'It's all right,' she said. 'It
works. More than you can usually say for Thornley-Miller's
computer and data retrieval department.'

'Thornley-Miller's a shit,' said Rosslyn.

'The world's full of shits. What makes Thornley-Miller so
special?'

'Because he's after Gaynor's job.'

'Think he'll get it?'

'Not if I have anything to do with it,' said Rosslyn.

On the fourth and top floor they found the American
waiting in the open doorway to Room 43. Straub wore a
crumpled linen suit. Six feet tall, with the eye of a startled
turtle, Straub the informant lived in constant fear. A thin and
haunted figure, he seemed to have his eyes focused somewhere behind you, and his darting smile, like his thoughts,
elsewhere. 'Good to see you, Duty Man,' he said. 'Good
flight?'

'Not bad,' said Rosslyn. 'You?'

'Okay,' said Straub. 'Come in.' He closed the door. 'Came
in from Lillehammer and Oslo.'

He showed Rosslyn and Celeste to upright chairs in the
narrow room. Its only window looked across neighbouring
roof-tops shimmering in the haze of the afternoon. Rosslyn
noted with approval that Straub had booked a room with a
short drop to a nearby roof. An emergency exit, Straub's
getaway if he received an unexpected visit from a dissatisfied
colleague. The American was a professional.

He handed Straub the canvas bag. 'Ten thousand dollars now. And the other half if and when he's banged up.'

'I can give you the name by Saturday evening,' Straub said.

'How will you get it?'

Straub hesitated. He seemed to be weighing up how much he could reveal. He was staring at Celeste. Rosslyn read his thoughts.

Straub said, 'And who is – ?'

'I've told you,' Rosslyn interrupted. 'She's on my team. What do you want, her ID or something?'

Straub seemed satisfied. 'How?' he said. 'Look, I've always come up with the goods, haven't I? I can't tell you everything. But what I can tell you is this. I came through here when – last month, was it? I take a look at a porn warehouse from where this guy operates. My person tells me about codes and names and bank-account numbers in Geneva, Lugano and Chiasso. It looks like the main dealer is using Swiss francs. And down the line there's some connection with the Netherlands Antilles. It seems to be some kind of offshore operation. That's all I know. Then there's this guy, a Russian.

'Don't tell me they are involved too?' Rosslyn asked. 'The Russians?'

'You'd better believe it.' Here Straub showed a set of very white teeth. Shining evidence of expensive orthodontic treatment. His sole concession to vanity and conspicuous extravagance. 'Sometimes I wonder whether you guys really know how big this business is, for Christ's sake. This is megabucks. And they have to be laundered.' He tapped his hollow chest. 'That's where I fit in. And you know what?' The smile really was too flashy. 'It's kind of neat to be taking money from secret policemen. But, of course, I don't include you, Duty Man.' He flashed his teeth at Celeste. 'Or you, honey. I have to be very careful with the Russians, though. I'll need to be careful with these people too. They don't mind who the hell they kill.'

'We can't call on the embassy for help,' Rosslyn said.

Straub laughed. 'If I thought you might call your embassy I'd tell you *forget* it.'

'You're on your own.'

'You don't need to tell *me* I'm on my own.' He smiled in the direction of a flat leather case on the bed. 'Smith & Wesson.' He turned to Celeste. 'You want to see it?'

'I'll take your word for it,' she said.

'Good,' said Straub. 'That's how I like it. I heard what happened to Gustavsen in Hamburg. Plastic bag. Minus one head. Who did it, the Libyans?'

'Who knows?' said Rosslyn.

'I heard the German cost you a lot of money. That he was buying here in Copenhagen. A breakaway porno publisher from Lund & Sondergrad Color, right? You shouldn't have made out he was Salvation Army.'

'Matter of fact,' said Rosslyn, 'that's exactly what he was. A Christian.'

'Now he's with his Lord and Maker,' said Straub, eyeing the crucifix at Celeste's neck. He added, still fishing for her name, 'No disrespect to you, Ms – ?'

You never stop trying, Rosslyn thought.

'We're all on first-name terms,' said Straub. 'No offence meant. Ms – ?'

'None taken,' said Celeste. 'My name's Investigation Officer.'

Straub showed his white teeth again and made a kind of snake's hiss.

'Lund is bad enough,' said Rosslyn. 'You do know how bad the new stuff is? We're not talking *Lollitots. Sweet Patti.* Or *Sweet Linda.* It's far worse than that.'

'I heard,' Straub said. 'What's the latest on your current operation?'

'These people are making snuff movies. Child executions. It'll be flooding the Internet. They even send the instructions as to how to use encryption as a safeguard. It could take ten years to crack. We have a data base of over three thousand known paedophiles. You have to see it to believe it. Total filth.'

'Nothing surprises me these days,' Straub said. 'Its a virus. Like a plague.'

'The new people are sharp operators,' said Rosslyn. 'I want the name of the backer. The person who's really making the big money –'

'I've told you,' Straub said, 'that's what I'll give you.'

'We're deep in the shit if you don't, Straub. You realize we had to go to the top to get authorization for your fees.'

'I appreciate that. But I'm doing this at bargain-basement rates anyway. Twenty thousand bucks is cheap for nailing child-killers, isn't it?' Straub was unfolding a street map of Copenhagen and the outlying districts. 'See this?'

Rosslyn and Celeste joined him at the table. 'I meet my friend in Hvidovre. It's a light industrial area outside the city. It's close to Lund & Sondergard's warehouse. And this is where we meet. Saturday. Sjaellandsgade 12. Public baths and sauna. I'll be there at five. They close at six-thirty. You pay your twenty kroner and you find me in the last cubicle on the left. The Vietnamese attendant is Phan Van Quan. Ask for Phan. He's okay.' He grinned at Celeste. 'You'll have to wait in the street. New rules there too. No women allowed in the sauna on Saturdays. Men only.'

'I don't like saunas,' said Celeste.

'Me neither,' Straub said.

Rosslyn memorized the address. Sjaellandsgade 12. 'Five o'clock. Saturday.'

'By the way,' said Straub, 'Phan needs a tip.'

'That's your problem,' said Rosslyn. 'He's not in the budget.'

'Too bad. A hundred bucks. For his sister.'

'She your girl?' asked Rosslyn.

'I don't mix business with pleasure, Duty Man,' Straub said. His eyes were undressing Celeste from head to foot with approval.

I want to get out of here, Rosslyn thought.

'Make it seventy,' said Straub.

What a cheapskate you are, thought Rosslyn. He handed him fifty dollars. 'Okay?'

'Fifty. You're welcome.'

'If you need to contact me in an emergency you can reach me at our embassy,' Rosslyn said. 'Just ask for the Visa Office.'

'Let's hope it doesn't come to that. I don't like embassies and they don't like me. Furthermore, I like your secret service even less.'

'Good luck, Straub.'

'I don't need luck. Not even the money. I'm doing this for the sake of the children, Duty Man. The only good paedophile is a dead fucking paedophile.'

Rosslyn never ceased to wonder at his informant's craving for respectability. *Paedophilia*, he thought, *is about the only thing you haven't engaged in, and I wouldn't even be sure about that.*

Straub took Celeste's hand. 'Excuse the language.'

'Don't worry,' she said. 'I'm used to it.'

Straub smiled his bright can do/no problem smile. 'Have you seen Aiko recently?'

'No,' said Rosslyn. 'Are you still in touch?'

'From time to time,' said Straub. 'You know she's temporarily based out at the old air base at Alconbury near Huntingdon. She's FBI–NSA liaison now. A big shot. Computers. Surveillance. The New Age. Everybody knows everything. The eyes and ears of the world, they tell me. Nothing she doesn't know. Say Hi to her when you see her next. She the nearest I have to next of kin.'

Rosslyn thought he saw a look of regret or pain in the turtle eyes.

'If I don't get a result,' Straub said. 'I mean, if anything were to go wrong, would you speak to Aiko for me?' He produced a business card from his wallet. 'Here.'

Rosslyn looked at the card.

Aiko Holland
US Customs Senior Special Agent
United States Embassy
24 Grosvenor Square
London W1A 1AE
tel. 0171.499.9000
ext. 7899

'I know where to find her.' He pocketed Aiko Holland's card. 'Keep it to remind yourself to say Hi to her for me,' said Straub.

'And you remind yourself that London needs a result,' Rosslyn said. 'This name, Straub, it'd better be a big one for twenty grand.'

The turtle eyes bulged. 'It's big all right. And it's under your noses. In London. A name that's going to hit you people where it hurts. The porn goes on. But you'll get your name. Infected filth.'

'Whatever it is,' Rosslyn said. 'Get it to us.'

'I will,' said Straub.

Once back in the lift, Celeste handed the tape recorder to Rosslyn. 'I had the feeling he knew we were recording him,' she said.

'He'd be thick if he thought we weren't,' said Rosslyn.

He removed the tape. 'Here, you keep this. Make me a transcript when we get back to London.'

'My God, he's a nasty specimen of humanity.'

'Just about average,' said Rosslyn.

14.00
The Radhus or City Hall's lift makes three daily ascents of the bell-tower for tourists to take in the view of the city. They paid ten kroner each for the trip.

Celeste stood close to him. Rosslyn could smell her

Dioressence, the trace of garlic on her breath. Her lips were moist. She liked to ask questions and made little secret of the fact that what she really wanted was to return to her roots in Jamaica on a Customs secondment to Kingston. Celeste liked to ask questions and she wanted to be an interrogator.

She had asked him once how he'd managed to deal with Mary's death. And Rosslyn had found himself telling her more freely than he had imagined possible about the murder of his lover Inspector Mary Walker, the woman police officer shot down before his eyes by a terrorist in London. In the months after Mary's death he had found himself unable to accept the well-intentioned expressions of sympathy that his colleagues at Custom House had offered. The counselling provided to help him overcome his grief had proved fruitless. So had two love affairs. But with Celeste he found himself for the first time for many months gradually able to relax, even to be playful. And given her success at handling what for him had been unbearable, he felt sure that she was going to make a fine Investigation Division interrogator. Her ability to gain information from an unwilling subject was instinctive.

'Why doesn't Straub sell to the Americans instead of us?' she asked.

'Because if it isn't on their doorstep it doesn't interest them.'

'It might if they were involved.'

'The point is,' Rosslyn said, 'they aren't.'

'Not yet,' said Celeste. 'Do you seriously think he had a relationship with your friend at the US embassy?'

'Who knows?' said Rosslyn. 'I wouldn't blame him if he had.'

'Why?' she asked. 'Do you fancy her?'

'Full of questions, aren't you?' said Rosslyn.

'What's she like, Aiko Holland?'

'Bit deep. Never figured her out.'

'So you don't fancy her then?'

'She's married.'

'Hasn't stopped you in the past, so I hear.'

'All lies,' Rosslyn said. 'That's all you hear, Celeste. They were divorced.'

'They. How many were there?'

'Ask no questions, get told no lies.'

'Who's Aiko's husband then?'

'I've no idea,' said Rosslyn.

He found her curiosity endearing rather than irritating.

Looking across Copenhagen, she said, 'The view doesn't interest you, Alan, does it?'

'Not much,' he said. 'When I'm in London, I wish I wasn't. When I'm abroad, I wish I wasn't.'

'Why don't we look at that Jens Olsen thing?' she said.

'What's that?'

'A clock. Jens Olsen's astronomical timepiece. It contains a five hundred and seventy thousand-year calendar.'

'You should live so long, Celeste. I'll skip it if you don't mind. I have my report to deal with.'

'Don't forget we have our friend to see at the embassy,' she said.

'Yes. At six-thirty,' said Rosslyn. 'Do you still want to see this Olsen thing?'

'It's okay with you?'

'It's fine by me,' he said. 'We've seen the view. Let's go back down.'

'Are you always like this on an operation?'

'Like what?'

'So edgy.'

'I didn't know it showed so much,' he said.

'It does show. Why are you so worried? You said Straub's always done the business before.'

'Well, when you've been in this game a few years,' Rosslyn said, 'you realize that however long you've known a grass like Straub, there's always a first time.'

15.00

At the Absalon Hotel on Helgolandsgade he bought two postcards to send to the two women in his life. No matter that the affairs were really over. In different ways he'd stayed friends with them.

He chose cards of the Gefion Fountain near the Kastel. The picture showed Bundgaard's sculpted figure of the goddess Gefion with her four sons. Small print on the card's reverse side explained that Gefion had struck a weird deal. In exchange for turning her four sons into cows, she'd be rewarded with as much land as she could plough in a night. Big butch Gefion ploughed up a lump of Sweden, leaving an ugly hole which becane Lake Vänern and dumped the landfill into the sea which became Zealand. He hoped Straub could work similar Viking magic and get the big name.

He'd write the cards showing Gefion after he'd checked the draft of his *Operation Celeste* report. He was reluctant to return to it. But it was no use deferring the reading. However much its contents nauseated him, he just had to face up to it. In a strange way he was pleased that he continued to feel that sense of revulsion. It told him that at least he wasn't becoming case-hardened.

<u>SECRET</u>
<u>DRAFT REPORT</u>
OPERATION CELESTE
SIO ALAN H. ROSSLYN
CUSTOMS TEAM E
INVESTIGATION DIVISION
HM CUSTOMS & EXCISE

<u>Names of Suspects</u>
James Martin MINTO
Kim Sang PARK alias Jeong-Kyu HANG
Mr and Mrs Frederick LORD
Jadallah A. WATIYAH

(1)   On the basis of secret intelligence received
from Amsterdam, Copenhagen and Frankfurt via
paid informant (code name: STRAUB) Customs
Team E officers:
   (a)   raided a flat at 05.30 hours on 21 February
last at 239 Bolingbroke Road, London W14,
owned by a man now known to be James Martin
MINTO, aged 35.
   (b)   recovered letters addressed to men and
women (see also: 396) whom we had been led to
believe by STRAUB to be regular purchasers of
pictures of adult male and females engaged in
acts of gross indecency with male and female
children between 5 and 10 years, also bestiality.
   See also: Record of Meetings with STRAUB and
SIO Rosslyn, Amsterdam, Copenhagen and
Frankfurt; plus Audit/Budget of Fees and
Disbursements)

(2)   One address obtained from MINTO's flat was
that of a woman named Kim Sang PARK, part-
time bookkeeper to Mr and Mrs Frederick LORD,
proprietors of an old people's home, Windsor
Lodge, 3 Bury St Edmunds Parade, Felixstowe,
Suffolk.

(3)   Windsor Lodge was raided by Officers of
Customs E at 05.00 hours on 22 February. A
quantity of paedophile material was recovered
from behind water tanks in the attic/roof space.
Between 05.45 and 08.00 hours the proprietors of
Windsor Lodge, Mr and Mrs Frederick LORD, and
PARK were interviewed separately. They
disclaimed all knowledge of the existence of this
material (see: Inventory)

(4)   During the course of their interviews the

above-named interviewees seemed genuinely
appalled that they had unwittingly given house
room to a substantial quantity of child
pornography. Team E has not yet been able to
establish:

(a)   who had actually hidden the paedophile
material in the roof space at Windsor Lodge.

(b)   who manufactured the paedophile
material.

(c)   the origin/distribution point of the
paedophile material.

The delay between the recovery of the
paedophile material and the subsequent arrest
of a purchaser or receiver (WATIYAH: see below)
may have allowed the distribution ring to either
cover its tracks or temporarily close down.

(5)   Among the photographs and magazines
discovered was a home-made video (see also:
Inventories – Item 76 (B)) showing:

(A) Sequence 1 of 4 minutes 45 seconds
CHILD X, a naked female, about 10 years of age,
is tied up with nylon cord on a small divan
covered with a green rubber sheet.
CHILD X is being subjected to vaginal
intercourse by an unidentifiable masked
WHITE MALE, aged about 40. Various pieces of
what would seem to be torn flannelette/gauze/
paper towelling are to be seen on the green
rubber sheet. Also, CHILD X's vaginal area is
bloodied as is the penis of the WHITE MALE.

(B) Sequence 2 of 6 minutes 3 seconds
CHILD Y, a female, about 7 years of age, clothed
in a white cotton vest is being forced to
masturbate the masked unidentifiable WHITE

MALE seen in Sequence 1. The WHITE MALE is also operating the video camera. The soundtrack is identified as part of Tchaikovsky's Dance of the Sugar-Plum Fairy.

(C) Sequence 3 of 8 minutes 12 seconds
CHILD Z, a naked female, about 6 years of age, is being penetrated by the masked unidentifiable WHITE MALE seen in Sequence 1. Sequence has been filmed in a vehicle identifiable as a Volkswagen camper bus. In its opening section of 8 seconds the exterior of the vehicle and its registration number BVV B82 is visible.

There is a MALE VOICE, probably superimposed, on the sound-track speaking in various modifications of a drawling educated accent, sometimes part Welsh, sometimes Scots, which suggests the voice to be deliberately disguised.

The unidentifiable masked WHITE MALE is subjecting CHILD Z to both vaginal and anal intercourse. There are some signs suggesting the use of fluid or lubricant in the vaginal and anal areas of CHILD Z.

Note: In all above instances no use of contraceptive protection is in evidence.

(6)   Team E urgently required to identify and apprehend the man/men/women responsible or associated as soon as possible on the basis of the evidence of:

(a)   the voice and accent. (On 23 February last Team E undertook a voice analysis. It was established that the voice in sequences A, B & C belonged to the same man.)

(b)   the vehicle's registration plate E347 TRS.

(7)   On 23 February, from the DVLC history of the Volkswagen camper vehicle and from the Police National Computer Bureau (PNC2) report, Team E deduced the need to concentrate the investigation in the Heathrow area.

(8)   The vehicle had first been registered by LBM, a car-hire firm, of 61 Gratton Villas Road, Reigate, Surrey; then to Finzil Partners, an electronics company of 45A Hammersmith High Road, London. Subsequently, it had been auctioned at Park Royal Auto Sales Ltd to Sommerling Fitch, car dealers of 21 Bruton Avenue, Maidenhead, Berkshire.

(9)   Sommerling Fitch sold it to its most recent owner, a purchaser in Felixstowe who had failed to register the vehicle. When Sommerling Fitch checked their records they found the name of the purchaser identified as Jeong-Kyu HANG.

(10)   No staff at Sommerling Fitch were able to offer Team E a visual description of Jeong-Kyu HANG.

(11)   Though Kim PARK was not a suspect and there was no record of either the person who had bought the illegal material or any of the people on MINTO's list having stayed at the boarding house, it was decided to mount a surveillance operation in the Felixstowe area on Kim PARK led by Ms Celeste QUINCEAU.

(12)   In addition, with a view to gaining a visual description of anyone answering to the name Jeong-Kyu HANG, a prolonged search of hospitals and doctors' records was undertaken in the East Anglia area.

(13)   After more than half a dozen persons answering to the name had been eliminated from the inquiries, a local doctor, Dr Arvind PATEL, produced the health records of a patient called Jeong-Kyu HANG who had asked for referral to the Gender Realignment Unit of Charing Cross Hospital in Hammersmith, West London, which specializes in predominantly male to female sex-change surgery and counselling.

(14)   From medical records Team E established that Jeong-Kyu HANG and Kim PARK were the same person.

(15)   Jeong-Kyu HANG/Kim PARK was interviewed by CIO GAYNOR, SIO ROSSLYN and Ms QUINCEAU between 14.15 and 16.25 hours on 2 March last in the lounge of Windsor Lodge, 3 Bury St Edmunds Parade, Felixstowe, Suffolk.

PARK stated that a MR X, PARK's homosexual lover whom he/she refused to name,abandoned him/her after surgery to effect gender realignment.

PARK had refused to make good a long-standing loan of £25,000 (twenty-five thousand pounds sterling), most of it spent on his/her treatment at the Charing Cross Hospital.

MR X had taken PARK's vehicle, the Volkswagen.

At one stage during the interview, PARK grew progressively agitated and having twice threatened violence he/she lost control and began, systematically, to break glasses, a mirror, a flower vase and a glass-topped table.

CIO GAYNOR and SIO ROSSLYN made an effort to restrain PARK and during the ensuing struggle

PARK cut his/her cheek and mouth on broken glass and had to be treated for lacerations at the local hospital. As a result, PARK remains scarred. For reasons which remain unclear, PARK held that SIO ROSSLYN was solely responsible for the injury sustained.

(16)   Subsequently, Team E officers obtained a list of the vehicle's service records from Volkswagen UK and extended enquiries to Holland and Germany.

(17)   Mr X had serviced his car at several garages in the Fulham area, West London.

(18)   His identity was established as Jadallah A. WATIYAH, a Libyan diplomat, who gave his address as 139 rue Malherbes, Neuilly-sur-Seine, Paris, France.

(19)   CIO GAYNOR, SIO ROSSLYN and Ms QUINCEAU were present when WATIYAH was arrested by police officers on 4 March last at 238 Sloane Street, London SW3.

(20)   WATIYAH did not deny the charges of possession of paedophile material recovered at Windsor Lodge on 22 February last, which he claimed had been 'given to him in return for certain political favours of significant use to both British and American intelligence services'.

He refused to specify the identities, adding that his conduit to both MI6 and CIA was a non-serving intelligence agent/contact 'of very considerable influence known to both Colonel Gaddafy and the President of the United States and the United States Secretary of Defense'.

Subsequently Team E officers made inquiries of:

(a)   Ms Elizabeth ROBERTSON-JONES, OBE, Middle East Desk Officer, SIS, New Century House, Vauxhall Cross, London.

(b)   Mr Andrzej SZUNIEWICZ, Deputy Station Head, CIA, United States Embassy, London.

(c)   Ms Aiko HOLLAND, US Customs, US Embassy, London.

They confirmed that neither intelligence service had knowledge of WATIYAH.

(21)   WATIYAH maintained he did not know either (a) the identities of the children, or (b) who was responsible for making the videotape/s.

(22)   Subsequently WATIYAH admitted the allegations and was informed that he was persona non grata. He was escorted to the airport and allowed to leave the United Kingdom of his own free will.

Notes:

I   On 21 May last, STRAUB (see: Supplement A. OPERATION CELESTE Informant) passed SIO Rosslyn a CD-ROM disk (see: CELESTE Inventory 2 OPERATION CELESTE Item CD-ROM 87/1).

In addition, STRAUB confirmed that WATIYAH's original supply source had commenced large-scale manufacture and reproduction of similar material, some of which also involved the 'live murder' of children whom STRAUB believed to have been sold for paedophile purposes to the manufacturers under the auspices of various international child adoption agencies and child welfare and charity agencies operating throughout the Far East and Eastern Europe.

The pornography was being manufactured in several suburbs of Los Angeles, then being air-freighted into Western Europe to meet the substantial and growing demands of active paedophile rings in all major European centres.

II   STRAUB was requested to continue covert surveillance of currency laundering conduits known to him which might expose the source of manufacture of this newly expanded aspect of paedophiliac material.

STRAUB indicated he would in probability make this intelligence available to SIO Rosslyn either in Oslo, Copenhagen or Helsinki in the June/July period.

III   It was AGREED that (see: Minutes of OPERATION CELESTE Audit/Budget Meetings):

(a)   SIO Rosslyn pay STRAUB a sum not exceeding US$20,000 (twenty thousand US Dollars) in respect of this intelligence.

In accordance with practice INVESTIGATION OFFICER MS CELESTE QUINCEAU was appointed to accompany SIO ROSSLYN to make payment to STRAUB at Hotel Heelas, Istegaade, Copenhagen, on Thursday 20 July.

(b)   Formal permission for this payment was given by the offices of the Paymaster-General and Home Secretary, who received a summary of OPERATION CELESTE operational details.

References:
Obscene Publications Act (1959) supplemented by Obscene Publications Act (1964).
See also: Inventories, Interview Transcripts, Permissions, Budget/Audit, Related Investigation Summaries (386).

Minutes of Liaison Meetings Division E/SO1(4),
Obscene Publications Squad, Metropolitan Police,
New Scotland Yard.

OPERATION CELESTE remains Code RED ACTIVE
SIO A. ROSSLYN
TEAM E, HM CUSTOMS & EXCISE

18.30

Rosslyn and Celeste kept their evening appointment with the
Secret Intelligence Service's local station head, a third
secretary, nominally the Visa Officer, at the British Embassy
on Kastelsvej.

The new policy governing liaison between SIS and the
Investigation Division of HM Customs & Excise demanded
that Rosslyn report his presence in Copenhagen on a secret
mission overseas.

The overweight third secretary sat on the edge of his office
desk. An outsize photograph of the Queen dwarfed one of
his wife, children and dogs having a rainy June the Fourth
picnic at Eton. 'So you're Rosslyn, are you?' He fidgeted with
a gold watch-chain dangling from the worn buttonhole of his
lapel. 'When's your RV with the American?' he asked,
glancing through the window at the garden fountains in the
Spanish ambassador's neighbouring residence.

'Saturday,' said Rosslyn. 'Seventeen hundred hours.'

'Really?

The Visa Officer brought glasses to his desk with three
bottles of Black Gold Tuborg and an almost-empty bottle of
Red Alborg Akvavit from his refrigerator. 'Help yourselves,'
he said. 'And where have you arranged to meet him?'

'At Sjaellandsgade 12.'

'What's that?'

'A public sauna.'

'Really? A sauna. Dear God.' He raised his thick and wiry

eyebrows. 'In this heat. Rather you than me.' He poured himself a large glass of Akvavit. 'By the way, do you know –' He paused and held the frozen glass of spirit to his sweating forehead. 'Do you know what Straub's real name is?'

'No,' said Rosslyn.

The Visa Officer stared at Celeste as if she were simple-minded. 'Do you, Miss Quinceau?'

'No.'

'Neither do we. I gather the FBI use him too. The rogue adventurer.' He cracked his finger joints. 'Oslo considered running him. So did Helsinki. But there's his insistence that he carry a gun. Rather too dangerously wild for us. How do you rate him?'

'One of the best we've got.'

'Out of ten?'

'Out of ten? Nine, possibly.'

'Really? Nine. That's a very high mark. Mind you, I suppose you're a bit short of reliable intelligence at present.'

'What makes you think that?'

'Your team did rather cock up in Germany, didn't they? That poor decapitated informant bugger Gustavsen. And he isn't the only one you've lost, is he?'

I know I get subsistence and foreign travel allowance, Rosslyn thought. *But there ought to be an aggravation allowance for dealing with prats like this*. 'It's unfortunate,' he said. 'We've lost too many.'

'Head in a plastic bag. I'd no idea the child porn industry played quite so dirty.'

'Those people are dirty.'

'I don't doubt you. Do you mind my asking a personal question?'

'No.'

'Do you two ever get terminally pissed off with it, Rosslyn?'

'With what?' Rosslyn said.

'The kiddie porn.'

'I try not to let it get to me.'

'What about you, Miss Quinceau?'

'You never get used to it,' said Celeste. 'Never.'

The Visa Officer drained his glass of beer, then his glass of Akvavit. 'If Straub lets you down, don't hesitate to call me.' He breathed out as if his mouth was on fire. 'If you two need a helping hand, just a nugget of advice – don't bother our American cousins.'

'What makes you think we might?' Rosslyn asked.

'Straub. Your man. American, isn't he? Pity we couldn't have kept this in the family. Just a thought, Rosslyn. Just a thought. That's what one's here for. To help. Talk to me first if there's any kind of awkwardness. One's always on the end of the blower. Still, needs must. Can't always pick and choose.'

No thanks, Rosslyn thought. *Your sort give us nothing. Yours is an unreal game played out from bloody embassies by toffs. My game's low life. Death in the narrow streets lit with flashing neon where blood looks black, the floating corpses in the canals. Your world's smoothie politics. Ours is rough trade. Bad sex. Abused and even dead children.*

The Visa Officer was saying, 'I suppose you two can find your own way back to your hotel?'

Rosslyn tossed an empty bottle into the standard-issue Foreign Service wastepaper basket. 'Yes, we can handle that.'

'Just a quiet word of warning about this little jaunt of yours,' said the Visa Officer, 'as an undercover footman of Her Majesty's loyal Customs & Excise to wonderful *København*, dirty old queen of the sea. London asks me to let you know that it does not, I repeat, does not want anything that might be construed as an embarrassment.'

'What embarrassment?'

'You go home on Saturday or whenever, Rosslyn, after your business with the bloody American, not having put a foot wrong either with the Danish police, Justice or Foreign Affairs Ministry, the Americans or anybody else. It's not a little important, *qua* Brussels, that our Viking friends in particular are not in any way upset if and when.'

'If and when what?'

'If and when you uncover the identity of investors in and manufacturers of kiddie porn. In words of one syllable, don't make waves, Rosslyn. Tread VCI.'

'VCI?'

'Very Carefully Indeed.'

'I hear what you're saying,' said Rosslyn. 'We aren't here to waste your time unnecessarily.'

'I never said you were.'

'I did,' said Rosslyn. 'For the record. Thanks for the beer.'

'My pleasure,' said the Visa Officer, showing Rosslyn to the door. 'By the way, how's your girl? Your single parent Verity?'

'I can't see what this has got to do with anything,' said Rosslyn.

'Still an item, are we?'

'We don't see very much of each other nowadays, if that's what you mean.'

'Sorry to hear it. Busy lives, I suppose.'

'Our work keeps us apart.'

Verity had said that this Visa Officer, her SIS colleague, was an IPA: idle piss-artist. Seemed too kind a view. Running scared of embarrassment, the desk man was living on another planet. Bland, bored and arrogant. He had the hide of a rhinoceros. Another time, another place, Rosslyn might have told the white rhino to stuff himself.

'What's she doing?' the Visa Officer persisted. 'Still living with – what's the daughter's name? – Rosie on that ghastly boat in Little Venice, is she?'

'The daughter's name is Daisy,' Rosslyn said. 'And the boat's a barge in Camden.'

'Didn't mean to offend, old chap. We like Verity.'

'So did I.'

'Sorry to have touched a nerve. Still, all good things come to an end, I always say.'

'Perhaps you're right.'

'Really? Doesn't pay to be wrong in my job. Well, good luck with the sauna RV. Don't envy you your afternoon. Ghastly places even in winter, let alone in a heatwave. You've got my number. Don't hesitate to call me. 35 26 46 00 extension 512.'

Rosslyn thought: *I certainly do have your number*.

SIS officers are the same the world over. They live vicariously. Feeding on other people's failures. Hard for them to find novel solutions to problems created by idle hands.

Like policemen. Always there when you don't want them. Never there when you do.

19.30

Back at the Hotel Absalon he made two telephone calls. The first was to his immediate superior, Chief Investigation Officer Richard Gaynor, the head of the Investigation Division. Gaynor, the Sea Captain, was on pre-retirement leave at Lapwing End, his house in Suffolk. This evening he was out.

Lucky bastard. Gone fishing, playing golf, strolling on the beach at Aldeburgh.

So he left a message on Gaynor's answerphone saying he had made contact with 'our friend, who says he's delivering the goods on Saturday. I think it'll be okay. So far so good.'

His second call was to Drew Franklin, Chairman and Chief Executive of HM Customs & Excise, at her flat in Holland Park.

Just before last Christmas, when Gaynor was unwell, Drew had asked Rosslyn to stand in for the Sea Captain and accompany her to a two-day conference with their American counterparts in Boston. There were awkward questions being asked about the Americans using HM Customs' secret intelligence. Somebody had asked why we are giving it to

them. *Quid pro quo*. They serve deportation orders on the
Paddies, let us have them back, we give them information in
return. The Americans warmed to Rosslyn, and what might
have become a thorny issue was resolved amicably enough.
It was on the overnight flight home that Rosslyn and Drew
discovered they would be spending Christmas alone. She
had suggested to Rosslyn that he spend Christmas Day with
her. 'I'll buy you Christmas lunch at the Four Seasons,' she
offered. Rosslyn accepted Christmas lunch with Sister, as she
was known behind her back at Custom House.

Over the Christmas lunch she had said after several glasses
of champagne, 'When a woman reaches forty, she either
changes her house, her job or her husband. I changed all
three.' It seemed that her much older husband had taken
unkindly to being what she called 'my handbag carrier'. 'But
in my old man's case, the problem was . . . no money.' The
bottle of claret that followed loosened her tongue. 'So much
money – my money – on his little girlfriend's bijou flat.' Mr
Franklin had left her for a much younger woman. 'She's
rather common,' she said. 'Big tits. No bra. Blowsy. Wears
floral dresses. And a gold stud in her nose. She probably has
a tattoo into the bargain. Owns a successful flower stall in
Chiswick. You know how they met? The shit was buying
flowers for his mother's *lousy* grave in Chiswick. He had the
bloody gall to tell me all the sordid physical details. They
actually kissed, touched each other up. Know where? In the
cemetery. Would you believe it?'

'In the midst of death we are in life,' Rosslyn said. Another
trip down the memory lane of failed marriages. What you
will do for a lunch. He raised his glass. 'Absent friends.'

'Talking of which,' she said, 'what about *your* friend Verity.
SIS, isn't she?'

'How do you know about her?'

'Don't forget who's buying you lunch. I do my homework.
They tell me she's a tough cookie. Are you still sleeping with
her? Any more you-know-what? How's-your-father?'

'If you mean what I think you mean, then the answer's no.'

'Did you practise safe sex?' she said.

Rosslyn said nothing.

'Sorry I asked,' she said with a laugh.

Later, during the early hours of Boxing Day, they became lovers.

By the New Year they had reached a tacit agreement that they would maintain the same level of formality in the office as had previously existed. He still referred to her as Chairman or Ms Franklin; she still referred to him as Mr Rosslyn. They had been alert to any sign that their relationship had become common knowledge. As far as they were aware, no word or gesture had betrayed them. It had been a sort of Christmas present from one solitary person to another.

There was no reply from her telephone.

Just her answering machine.

He left a message for her saying he had made a successful initial contact with our 'friend'. He added, as he had said to Gaynor, 'We'll get a name. I feel it in my bones. I think we're on to a winner.'

After a shower he wrote the two postcards:

Dearest V,
Saw your friend today. Your're
right – what a pompous shit.
Things are looking good here.
Am getting to the heart of Cel.
Still in with a chance of
succeeding the Sea Captain if I do.
Love to Daisy & you. Tell her to
keep our secret very secret. Hope
you're fine.
Best, Alan ♥

Dearest D,
Feel sure money well spent on Cel.
Should be fine. Met a prat from 6
today who should've disappeared
up his own arse at birth.
Arse was big enough.
Hope you're fine.
Best, Alan ♥

He went to the reception area to wait for Celeste.

There was a message from Drew waiting for him at the desk. It said she'd meet him at Heathrow on his return. *'Be discreet about this,'* she had dictated, *'with your companion.'*

Drew wasn't giving up.

He added a postscript to the postcard to her:

Will have bust Celeste by the time you get this.

Ms Quinceau is a first-class officer.

21.30

They began the night out with supper at Bornum, next to the Royal Theatre on Kongens Nytorv. The long weekend had been designated He/She Carnival and had already started.

Said Rosslyn, 'Seems like most of Scandinavia and Germany's come to Copenhagen on a gender bend.'

Settling the bill, he asked the waiter to recommend a club.

The waiter sized Rosslyn up. Then Celeste. Her loose white cotton trouser suit seemed to have persuaded him that she was a boy. Perhaps he thought Rosslyn's ordinary white shirt and trousers were a disguise.

The waiter suggested, 'U-matic in the basement of Kranspolsky. Your *Time Out* called it a poseur's paradise.'

'That's us,' Celeste said, nudging Rosslyn's thigh beneath the table. 'You should've worn a frock.'

22.45

They sat at a table in the U-matic, near the He/She band.

Whether the almost-naked black singer was male or female was hard to tell. Either way, Rosslyn couldn't care about the story of 'My Little Bimbo'.

Tapping her feet to the music, Celeste squeezed up close to him. 'Stick with me,' she breathed in his ear.

The sound was deafening:

> *Sailor Jack McCoy*
> *Was a dashin' sailor boy*

> *His ship got wrecked a while*
> *On a Fiji eee-jee isle.*

'Do you want to go back to the hotel?' said Rosslyn.

'Later,' Celeste said. 'I want to see if it's really a bloke. When it turns round.'

> *He led a savage life*
> *And hunted with a knife*
> *He says to tell you about it*
> *'But PLEASE don't tell my WIFE.'*

A Chinese boy/girl asked Rosslyn for a dance.

'No thanks.'

'Go on, dance with him,' said Celeste.

'Your boy doesn't know how to treat a girl,' said the Chinese.

'So they tell me,' said Rosslyn as the Chinese tripped off to another table.

Celeste looked at Rosslyn uneasily. He was drinking too much Akvavit. She put a hand over his glass. 'I'll be okay, Alan.'

'You think so?'

'I know so.'

'If we fuck up, it fucks us.'

'There'll be another day, Alan.'

'But I'm tired of this. Look around you. Who the fuck are these people?'

'Just kids having a good time.'

'They seem sad to me. Poor sad bastards a long way from home.'

'Maybe they don't have homes.'

'They look more like they've drowned in misery.'

She held his hand for the first time and he let her squeeze it gently. 'Finish your drink and we'll go when the song's done.'

> *Say, I've got a bimbo down on a bamboo isle*

> *She's waitin' there for me*
> *Beneath that bamboo tree.*
> *Believe me*
> *She's got the other bimbos beat a mile*
> *She dances GAILY*
> *DAILY*
> *She'd make a hit with Barnum Bailey.*

The singer was peeling off a very thin rubber leotard.
Said Celeste, 'She's got good legs.'
Said Rosslyn, 'It's a boy.'
'I think she's an it.'
'You want to bet?'
'No', said Celeste.

> *I'll build a bungalow on a bamboo isle*
> *And when I go again, I'll stay a while.*
> *I've seen dancers, plenty of dancers, wear a string of beads.*
> *Give this gal a good jazz band.*

Slowly the singer turned to face the audience.
Rosslyn and Celeste watched in silence.

> *Say boy, that's all I needs*
> *'Cos all I wear is a great big Zulu smile . . .*

The lights went out.

> *My little bimbo down on a bamboo isle.*

There was an outburst of applause.
'I don't want to spoil it for you,' said Rosslyn, 'but let's go home.'
The MC was shrieking, '*My little bimbo down on a bamboo isle! Put your hands together for DAISY.*'
A vivid spotlight came on and, to the accompaniment of a drum roll, harshly illuminated the singer's crotch and hands. Finally it settled between the legs and focused on a writhing rat.

23.30

They walked back to the hotel in silence through the heat of
the night. It was unusually still and humid. Rosslyn
wondered where Straub was. He remembered the American
showing him the handgun with the pride of a boy. It was the
first time Straub had done something like that, and he
wondered whether the American was losing his nerve. *Or am
I losing mine?*

What favours was Straub calling in from his sources?

Money?

What's he trading?

Could he, God help us, be working for the other side?

Near the Hotel Absalon, Rosslyn said, 'I'm sorry, I'm so
preoccupied.'

'You're telling me,' she said.

He drew her close. Then kissed her.

He tasted the faint tang of garlic on her tongue.

23.57

He went into his hotel room and closed the door, standing
still in the darkness.

He had, he felt sure, a bead on the people behind *Operation
Celeste.*

Had the targets in his sights. His people back home had
worked day and night to trap the enemy. They saw it as a
war, and sometimes a few of them spoke, perhaps a little
pompously, of honour and their conviction they were
committed to the protection of the weak. The children. A
few, mostly those with small children of their own, spoke of
revenge. Blood for blood. A life for a life. They tended to fall
back on the old maxims of violence and retribution. Others,
even as they'd viewed the filth, had cracked up altogether. It
was as if they'd been haunted by it, infected as if by a virus,
weakened and brought down.

23.59

When he turned on the bedroom light he noticed the note beneath his door. It had been hastily scribbled on a card of the Little Mermaid.

I don't mind being your shadow. I believe in going on. I am not going to tell you. But I am inordinately in love with you. I will tell you that all I'm wearing is a great big Zulu smile and I'm at the end of the corridor. If it's still Thursday, try the door. It's unlocked.

But it was already Friday.

Friday 21 July

86°F/30°C. Sunny, wind north-westerly, mainly light.
Hot.

09.45
The visitor showed his card to the Crown Estate gatekeeper
at the south entrance to Kensington Palace Gardens.

It read:

> Major G R D Angell
> Chairman and Managing Director
> GRDA Associates
> Box AAA
> 1 Savile Row
> London WIX 4BA

'I have a *pwivate* appointment at Palace Mansions,' he said.
His Rs came out as Ws. 'With Lady *Vwatsides.*' He glanced at
his watch. 'At ten o'clock.'

'If you don't mind waiting, sir,' the gatekeeper said, 'I'll
call the porter to confirm you're expected. This won't take
long, sir.' Odd, he thought, for an officer and a gentleman to
have shown up here on foot. Most toffs arrived by cab or
chauffeur-driven car. Nonetheless, he cut an elegant figure in
his tailored double-breasted suit, cream silk shirt with Prince
of Wales collar and blue silk tie. You could count your teeth in
the polished toecaps of the black hand-made shoes. But the
gatekeeper doubted Major Angell's manicured fingers
polished his own shoes.

There was something familiar about him, thought the
gatekeeper. The stack of dark hair combed back from the
high forehead was reminiscent of a former government
minister. His opaque skin was unblemished, soft and
feminine; his complexion pallid, like a gambling lounge-
lizard who surfaces mostly by night. When he glanced again
at those fingers he saw the visiting card had vanished,
presumably into the wallet with a gold and silver regimen-
ted crest embossed in its snakeskin leather. It was a touch
vulgar, that wallet. A bit flash. A minor concession to
vulgarity. The hand that held the wallet, he noted, had its
thumb missing.

Angell gazed into the distance, his keen eyes with long
lashes narrowed against the morning sun; he seemed to be
inspecting the plane trees and the spray from the water
sprinklers forming miniature rainbows in the formal garden
of pleached limes and hedges of clipped yew. He was at one
with the calm orderliness and exclusivity of Kensington
Palace Gardens.

From inside Palace Mansions the duty porter confirmed
that Angell was expected.

'Sorry to have kept you waiting, sir,' said the gatekeeper.

Angell's loping progress through the morning sunshine
might equally have belonged to a courtier at Kensington
Palace; or perhaps, had the business card not shown he was
Chairman and Managing Director of GRDA Associates, the
inquiry agents, a senior official from the Foreign Service
bound for an appointment at one of the heavily protected
local embassies or ambassadorial residences. At the corner of
Palace Mansions he passed a police officer from the Royal
and Diplomatic Protection Group in shirt-sleeve order, who
saluted him. The high steel gates opened automatically to let
him pass.

Once inside Palace Mansions, he signed the visitor's
register in a spidery hand for the benefit of the hall porter.

'If you wouldn't mind emptying your pockets, please, sir,'

the hall porter asked him, 'and then proceeding through the
metal-detector arch.'

'Not at all,' said Angell.

He produced a Ventolin inhaler from his jacket pocket. He
toyed with it languidly, rolling it across and through his
fingers before taking it to his lips and squirting it twice inside
his mouth. He inhaled the spray deeply.

He followed the hall porter across the Italian marble hall to
the scanner.

Angell left the inhaler, a black and white silk handkerchief,
his snakeskin wallet and a bunch of keys in a leather pouch
on the counter.

His chest wheezed.

'Pollen, is it, sir?' asked the hall porter, watching the visitor
walk through the gate.

'Mild asthma,' said Angell, retrieving his belongings. His
eyes took in the entrance hall surveillance systems. Japanese
infra-red and tilt-and-turn cameras. Guard wires. The closed
circuit TV monitors and sophisticated recording system
housed in a plain pinewood cabinet beside the hall porter's
reception desk.

'The wife's a sufferer too,' said the hall porter. 'Asthma. It's
the heat, the pollen, stress. If you wouldn't mind while I do
the body search.'

Angell spread his legs apart and raised his arms. His throat
and chest gave out a reedy whistle. He hated the pressure of
clumsy fingers on his clothes and his flesh.

'All clear, sir,' the porter said. 'Did you know the Princess
of Wales has developed asthma?'

'Is that so? I didn't notice it when I saw her last week at
Launceston Place.'

'Not a lot of people know that, sir.'

'She has my sympathy as a fellow-sufferer.'

'No end to her troubles,' said the hall porter.

'So one gathers.'

The hall porter called the lift. 'We all have our crosses to bear, sir.' He stood stiffly to one side.

'Yes,' said Angell as the doors hummed shut. 'Indeed.'

Immediately the lift began its ascent, he turned his back on the lens of the closed circuit television camera and opened his wallet to look at three small photographs.

They were no more than mug-shots of three men. One photograph showed the face of Leonard Slaemann, the Mayfair solicitor who had recommended his services to Lady Vratsides. Another showed the face of Morton Damm, the launderer of dirty money and trader in criminal intelligence. The third one showed the face of Senior Investigation Officer Alan Rosslyn. Angell's information was that Rosslyn was currently in Copenhagen.

He stared up into the lens of the surveillance camera and smiled.

Then he returned the three small photos to his wallet, and the wallet to the inside pocket of his tailored suit.

He enjoyed knowing the images of the potential murder victims were close to his body. Close to his heart, he believed, was where the soon-to-be-dead belonged.

10.00

Lady Giselle Vratsides was waiting for him in the silence of her cool apartment.

She watched the eyes, distorted by the camera lens, staring at her without expression from the flickering black and white screen of the closed circuit television.

So this is Major Angell in the flesh. Her solicitor, Slaemann, had told her he was the best in the business. Inquiry agent to the international rich and famous, the society of the great and good of which 'you, the Vratsides,' Slaemann had told her, 'are exemplary pillars'.

10.05

Following Lady Vratsides across the marble floors into the chilled climate of her apartment in Palace Mansions, Angell was reminded of a spider in the shadows.

He thought: *the ex-model on her private catwalk still seems to know the effect she has on a man at first meeting.* Her black hair, as dark as her silk dress, was thick and shining, with no trace of the grey strands a woman of fifty might expect to find.

The heavy scent of lilies filled the mahogany-panelled drawing room. Most of the furniture was lacquered. Through the tinted windows there was a view of Kensington Palace and the Royal Gardens. The door to her bedroom was ajar. He saw her huge four-poster surrounded with woodwork which seemed to have been taken from an Indian temple.

He imagined she had probably never known a life outside the circles of the rich and powerful, like the men and women in the photographs in silver frames on a pair of Chippendale mahogany commodes: the President of the United States and his wife, the British Prime Minister and his wife, His Holiness the Pope, President Nelson Mandela, Mother Teresa, Yasser Arafat, the last but one Prime Minister of Israel, and princes from several Arab kingdoms shown with racehorses. In pride of place, in royal-blue leather frames embossed with gold, were photographs of the Royal Family: reminders, if you didn't know it already, that the Vratsides enjoyed a degree of social intimacy with their royal neighbours and moved in a different world of privilege and ease.

If here in her lair of luxury that occupied some six thousand square feet in the London sky she tired of staring into the faces of these friends and acquaintances, or grew bored of gazing down at the royal residence across the way, Lady Giselle could dream away her time contemplating the value of the paintings on her drawing-room walls.

In pride of place in adjoining alcoves, gently illuminated against heavy black velvet drapes, framed in gold and silver like two matching Greek icons, were the two mid-1490s Michelangelo egg tempera and oil sketches on poplar for *The Madonna and Child with Saint John and Angels*. Their surfaces were smooth as alabaster. In both sketches, pretty and mostly naked infant and adolescent angels clustered round Mary, Queen of the Angels, Mother of God, with her right breast exposed.

On the other walls hung the sleek Klimt of a young tart, *Halbakt von vorne, die linke Hand am rechten Fusgelenk,* with a slim and stockinged leg raised sideways to expose her moist vagina; the Schiele of an angular adolescent girl in frilly silk knickers; an early Picasso of a blind girl-child and dove; three sloppy Jasper Johns; the two Monets of Giverny; and a Seurat, a small version of *Les Poseuses,* three nubile artists' models. Above the fireplace filled with flowers was an enormous and sickly Pre-Raphaelite of a peasant child weeping over a dead sheepdog. Beside it was a row of erotic woodblock prints by Kuniyoshi.

Seated opposite, he noticed the hem of Lady Giselle's black silk dress rise when she crossed her long slim legs. Her thighs were more like those of a woman twenty years her junior. She wore no stockings and he noticed with approval that her pale legs were very smooth. With no need of protection from the sun, she slowly put on a pair of large dark glasses. 'What have you got to tell me?' she asked him.

'One can't, I'm afraid, disguise the gravity of your husband's problems.'

She looked at him with a kind of fascinated resentment. 'Please don't speak to me in riddles,' she murmured. 'My lawyer said you'd provide me with the facts.'

'I know. Mr Slaemann and I both share the view that your husband is heading for a catastrophe.'

This was how he always began with a client who seemed to have more money than sense. With the confident announcement of impending disaster. Scare them with the diagnosis. Keep them waiting, needing to know the worst but almost too frightened to ask, *'Can you help me, please?'* Have them beg for help. Make them ache for my helping hand. Say to me, *'Money no object, Major Angell.'* Keep them hungry. Know that I am the master of your pain. His voice was saccharine.

'I suspect,' he said, 'there are several distasteful aspects of his situation of which even you may be unaware.'

'You do?' she said.

He glanced at the ranks of photographs of the smiling high and mighty on the Chippendale commodes. The royals looked quietly pleased with their loyal and not so humble servants: the beaming Sir Achilles and Lady Vratsides at charity premières and soirées at Christie's and Sotheby's in London and New York. A rather younger Bob Geldof with an arm around Lady Vratsides at the Wembley Live Aid concert.

He thought: *First the good news. A touch of eulogy. Gain your confidence. Tell you a few things you already know in my best bedside manner.*

Be fluent. No 'ums', 'ers', 'I means', 'You knows'.

'The name Vratsides,' he said, 'means the welfare of the world's children. The helpless and deprived to whom World Child Survival offers succour and hope. AVI investors have total confidence in his skills and in his decency. I quote from *Time* magazine: "The moral rock of Achilles Vratsides Investments is a rare example." I hardly have to tell you that the name Vratsides is arguably your family's most precious asset.'

'I leave the technical side of business to my husband,' she said. 'My world revolves around the houses and the gardens.'

Now prepare her for the news that her world is about to crumble. 'Your husband's on record as having said – I quote – "I hope my epitaph will be that this man's vision served the world's children and mankind."'

'Correct,' she said. 'To UNICEF. His speech to UNICEF.'

'And he has been an adviser to the United Nations Committee on the Rights of the Child? Let me remind you that Article 34 of the UN Convention on the Rights of the Child says that all children under the age of eighteen have the right to be protected by government against sexual abuse. We have to assume that your husband has not been, shall we say, completely frank with you about his personal difficulties.'

She gave him the flicker of a smile. 'Does that surprise you?'

'You wouldn't expect me to comment on his private affairs, Lady Vratsides, would you? It's not my job to pass judgement, is it? But let me assure you that, wherever possible, I make a point of carefully researching my clients' psychology in some detail in advance. One is careful with one's inquiries. I know the record,' he said slowly. 'I hope you won't object to my asking you very frankly whether or not it's true that your husband has sexual preferences which most civilized people find abhorrent.'

'What do you mean?'

He leaned forward in his chair. 'Is it true,' he asked, 'about his weakness for children?'

'Slaemann told you then?' she said slowly. 'About the anonymous letters I've received?'

'No. Someone else told me,' he said. Casually he produced some folded photocopies from his snakeskin wallet. 'Slaemann asked me to discover, on your behalf, what I could about your husband. He wants me to be entirely frank with you. This won't, I'm afraid, be very pleasant for you. I have an old friend, a director of your bank, who's provided me with these.'

He produced two photocopies for her to read.

sir achilles vratsides is a paedophile

the girls are 8, 9, 10 years old

Once she had read them she stared into the distance, at the sky outside, through the windows. 'What sort of person is sending these?'

'How would I know? Probably some paedophile ring who knows of his involvement. They probably have blackmail in mind.'

He saw the flesh of diamond rings on her fingers. *Must be worth tens of thousands*, he thought. *Like the ruby on the black silk band around her neck, they'd be more at home in a museum display case.*

'What involvement?'

'Slaemann asked me to provide you with facts about your husband, Lady Vratsides. To make certain there isn't a shred of substance in the accusations. And I asked him why you hadn't taken the matter to the police.'

'Because I don't want a police investigation into our affairs.'

'May I ask why not?'

'Because it would become public. Create press attention. Destroy confidence in our lives. I would prefer to put a stop to this persecution myself.'

'Yet, Lady Vratsides, I'm afraid some paths, as it were, have crossed your own. I gather from a banking contact that there seem to have been any number of irregular payments into your Swiss and London bank accounts.'

He produced a sheaf of photocopies from his jacket pocket. 'Bank statements,' he continued. 'Of accounts in your name. From Barclays Bank in Piccadilly, another from one of its Swiss subsidiaries and others from Credit Suisse in Zurich, Lugano and Chiasso. They show deposits made by your husband.'

'What deposits?'

'Proceeds from the Danish manufacture and sales of CD-ROMs showing paedophiles engaged in sex with their victims. I'm afraid your husband could be identified in them. Remember, there are people who can very easily destroy you. The police. The undercover investigation agents of Customs & Excise. Their Team E that investigates the illegal importation of paedophiliac pornography. Their officers will be formidable opponents.'

She was pointing to the row of telephones on a side table and speaking so quietly, almost in a whisper, he had to lean towards her. 'Why don't we stop now and call my lawyer?'

she suggested. 'Speak to Slaemann.'

'Yes, I think you should. And I think you should put the matter in the hands of the police as soon as possible.' He looked at his watch. 'I'm afraid my work for you is now finished,' he said, getting to his feet. 'Please forgive me.'

'Wait.' She reached a hand towards him. 'Slaemann said you'd help me.'

'I know. He's a decent man and a good lawyer. A friend to most of the major world players. I don't know if what I've done for you has been of much use. Much as I would like to assist you further, I'm sorry, I can't. I'm committed for several months ahead throughout Europe and in the Gulf.'

He produced the Ventolin inhaler from his pocket, flipped it through his feminine fingers like a conjuror preparing a sleight-of-hand illusion. 'As far as I'm concerned, these matters go no further.'

She looked at him in silence, following him out of the drawing room.

The door to her spacious kitchen was open. Angell glanced with apparent approval at its design.

'You use impressive knives,' he said.

'My cook prepares Japanese food for me,' she said.

'So I see. I approve of Shoudai Masayoshi's blades.'

'So does my husband. They were a gift to the AVI Tokyo office.'

'How generous,' said Angell, heading for the lift. 'I've enjoyed meeting you,' he added. 'I suggest you to speak to Leonard Slaemann as soon as possible. That's my advice, for what it's worth.'

11.00

She watched his departure on the closed circuit television monitor by the lift.

The screen showed him fidgeting with his fingers and the knob of flesh that remained of his thumb, and she was sure he smiled.

There was something self-invented about him she couldn't fathom. Something missing. Like that thumb.

Once he was out of sight she returned to her drawing room and telephoned Slaemann on his direct line, at his Brook Street office.

'You can always elect to go to the police,' Slaemann told her. 'Or indeed to the Customs investigation officers who are, we gather, involved in the case. That's one choice.'

'I don't want to take it.'

'I know you don't,' Slaemann said. 'So you're left with the alternative. Enlist Angell's services for protection.'

'What do you advise me to do?' she asked. 'Can I trust him?'

'Absolutely. He's the best in his field. He's not unfamiliar with the sort of territory we've strayed into.'

'Is it really as terrible as he says it is?'

'I've no reason to think otherwise,' Slaemann said. 'I imagine you know Angell's services won't come cheap. You must be prepared to pay for it, or –'

'Or what?'

'Take the consequences,' said Slaemann. 'Now, please forgive me, but I am a little late for a meeting in the City. If there's anything else I can do to help, please don't hesitate to telephone me.'

11.16

She made a second telephone call.

Afterwards, in a Venetian mirror, she caught sight of her reflection.

She gave herself an approving smile. She said to herself, 'I hope, little Mr Slaemann, you haven't forgotten who pays the bills. I may do the shopping. But it's my husband's money.' Moving to a large Indian cabinet, liking what she had seen of herself in the mirror, she unlocked a hidden drawer. Inside, wrapped in a yellow duster, was a Smith & Wesson.

13.05

'For a start, there is the evidence of those bank statements,' Angell told Leonard Slaemann in his Brook Street office. 'They prove that she's substantially profited from her husband's involvement in child sex. I don't have to tell you that as a defendant, she could of course always stand up in court and say, "My husband deceived me. I haven't a clue where the money came from. I never asked." The media will have a field day.'

Slaemann was a small, thin and prematurely balding man who wore what was left of his hair short. 'Where should she start?' he asked.

'Damage limitation, I suppose,' Angell said. 'Get a stop put to the authorities investigating her husband's private life. There aren't any other options available.'

'Are you quite certain he's already a suspect?'

Angell sat opposite Slaemann, his legs crossed. 'My sources tell me yes,' he said. 'Customs & Excise's investigation team doesn't need to collect much more evidence before they arrest Vratsides. Just enough to secure convictions. Most of it depends on what the usual run of informants tell the investigators. From a personal point of view, Lady Vratsides has to ask herself if she can handle the disgrace of being married to a man with form as a paedophile. His activities are pretty clearly demonstrated in child porn CD-ROMs. Several of the children, tiny defenceless girls, have been hideously abused.'

'Is there any conceivable way whatsoever,' Slaemann asked, 'that this could be kept out of the public view?'

'Only if we could gain control of the informants,' Angell said. 'It's possible. And I suppose the investigators could be sweetened.'

'I very much doubt that Customs & Excise would play ball,' said Slaemann. 'I wouldn't be too hopeful about the police either.'

'I suppose you're right,' said Angell. 'We'll just have to do it another way. But it's still going to be expensive.'

'Money's not a problem here,' said Slaemann, clearing his throat.

'If you're asking me to do it for her, it could be pretty expensive.'

'How expensive?' Slaemann asked.

'To abort this operation? This is going to come very dear. We'd be running an enormous risk. Several people are going to have to be taken out.'

'What's your estimate?'

'At least one million pounds sterling.'

Slaemann winced. 'She won't wear that,' he said.

'Then I'm afraid she'll have to lump it,' Angell said. 'Unless she and her husband are prepared to do time.'

'I think I ought to telephone her,' Slaemann said.

'Fine, go ahead. But tell her from me, the price isn't negotiable.'

'I'll tell her.'

'And also tell her that, to be effective, I've got to start now.'

'What do you need from her?'

'She must close her bank accounts right away. Then open new ones under your direction.'

'How do you want paying?'

'Electronic transfer. In advance. I recommend that you use the services of a reputable currency dealer.'

'And when do you think you can secure the end of investigations into Vratsides?' Slaemann asked.

'Say by Friday 28 July.'

'Friday the 28th. No sooner?'

'No. Simply arrange for the currency transfer through your bank in the usual way to my bank in Zurich. You have the relevant details. I guarantee you completion by Friday 28 July. Then I'll be in a position to go ahead.'

'If not?'

'Then we've been wasting each other's time,' said Angell.

'Which reminds me,' Slaemann said. 'My charging rate to

you will be the usual. Fifteen per cent.'

'Then I'm sure you'll want her to agree,' Angell said. He slowly uncrossed his legs and got up from his chair. 'Don't get up. I'll see myself out.'

Watching Angell walk towards the door, Slaemann was once again reminded of something almost feral about the man. He waited until Angell was safely outside his office before turning to the bottom right-hand drawer of his desk. He pressed a button marked STOP and the tape recording of their meeting ended.

14.30

In the Porchester Spa in Bayswater, an architectural relic of the 1920s, Angell sat with his lover and disciple Kim Sang Park on the damp wooden boards.

Alone together, drenched in sweat, they were in the smallest of the heated steam rooms at the far end of the basement.

'How did it go with Slaemann?' Kim asked.

Angell adjusted the crucifix of cut steel on the silver chain around Kim's neck. 'It went well,' he said. 'Slaemann reckons she'll play along. They don't want it getting out. The public will stand for a lot. But they'll draw the line at mucking about with kids. And if Vratsides goes down, a lot of other people will go down with him. When I was with Lady Vratsides you should have seen the photos. The fucking guy's a friend of the US President, the Prime Minister and the Royal Family.'

Kim moved closer to him. 'You know,' he said, 'I'm worried about Straub or Damm or whatever his name is. What he's been telling you had better be true. Otherwise you'll be right in it. It's all right for you to say that you're going for the big one with this, but it can work both ways.'

'What do you mean?' said Angell.

'What I mean is that if Damm has been lying to you, or forgotten to tell you something that he should've done, then things could get very nasty.'

'It can't be wrong, can it?' Angell said. 'You're forgetting something. When Customs lifted that stuff in Felixstowe, where did it come from? Look, Kim, I have to tell you. It was Damm a.k.a. Straub who set the whole Felixstowe thing up. You acted as a willing channel.'

'Well, thanks very much. I've got this scar on my face, nothing but trouble from Customs and the law, and now you're doing business with Damm. If he could stitch me up over the Felixstowe business, how do you know that he won't do the same to you?'

'I can handle him, Kim. He can't go running back to Customs after he's told me what the set-up is with Vratsides.'

Kim waved his hand dismissively. 'Unless Damm's still working with Customs. You don't know that this whole deal hasn't been arranged to get you. For all you know, he's playing both sides against the middle. How can you guarantee he isn't?'

'There aren't any guarantees, Kim. But if I find he's pulling a stroke then he's a dead man. That's a racing certainty. I've told Slaemann to have the money paid in Zurich. Okay, if Damm decides to do a runner then he's not going to get very far, I can assure you. I don't know what Customs may have paid him for the Felixstowe thing. But it can't have been that much. Remember, they only got some two-bit Libyan diplomat declared *persona non grata*. They didn't get the big name or names they want. You're not the only one who can use the grey matter, Kim.' He tapped the side of his head. 'I've thought it through.'

'But why haven't you told me? You owe it to me. You know I pray for you.'

'I know. I wasn't going to jump the gun. What I had to do was to check out as best I could whether what Damm was telling me was true. If Vratsides's wife had thought it wasn't true she wouldn't be coming up with the money, would she? Her sort doesn't become rich by parting with their money when there's no need.'

'What happened when you saw her?'

'I'll come to that in a minute. I made my move before I went to her place.'

'What move?'

'I made sure she got some letters telling her that her husband's a paedophile. And that's what sent her running for help to Slaemann. The way I've set this up I'm creaming it off all ways. Taking the fee for dealing with a blackmailer who happens to be yours truly.'

'When are you going to get Rosslyn for me?'

'Look,' said Angell. 'First things first. You're the one who's worried about Damm a.k.a. Straub. I'll deal with him first.'

'You promised me you'd pay Rosslyn back for what happened to my face.'

'That'll be the easy bit,' said Angell. 'Time for work.'

'Wait. He marked my purity.'

'Should we turn the other cheek?' said Angell, who liked to mock Kim's taste for Biblical quotations.

'An eye for an eye,' said Kim, who in his confused half-and-half state had not entirely abandoned hope of his lover's redemption and a peaceful life. This Angell, his protector, whose chosen name seemed so appropriate, had in adolescence seriously considered the priesthood as a vocation. He would quote Larkin on the subject of parenthood with approval. A lover he reckoned to be a man of style and intellect, who each week explained to Kim the cartoons in *The Spectator*. This man of passion and patience, with a tidy mind and a cleanliness of body, was the focus for his adoration. The Love of My Life. He might be rather British when it came to showing his affection. But his lustful appetites and lover's expertise made up for the discipline of his emotions. No matter that his lover might vanish for days on end without so much as a by your leave. He trusted Angell and loved him. He cherished Angell's declaration that he, Kim, was the first person he had loved and the one person, come hell or high water, he would never abandon.

I'll be with you until hell freezes, Angell would say.

He turned to Angell and kissed his ear. 'We have our love to keep us warm,' he sang softly. He loved to sing the first lines of sentimental songs to his lover, and the steam heat seemed to bring a boyish and pretty timbre to his voice.

When they left the Spa they read together the notice that said the building would shortly be closed for major renovation. The heating system was to be completely overhauled.

'Like me,' said Kim to Angell. 'For you. When you're in Copenhagen I want you to "Say a Little Prayer for Me".'

The imitation of Aretha Franklin was convincing.

'Promise me?'

Angell made no reply.

He was reading the small print of the notice closely. It explained how a computer would monitor the heat for the comfort of future visitors.

'And their pain,' he said.

Kim looked at his lover and wondered what was on his mind.

'An interesting way to die,' Angell added. 'Boiled alive.'

Sometimes, Kim thought, *there is a terrifying look in those eyes. It makes you shiver. As if you are staring into the eyes of someone long since lost to hate and madness. Whose delight lies in thinking up new ways to commit the perfect murder.*

Angell sometimes referred to it as 'post-Modernist murder'. He would say, 'I am an artist.'

And Kim, like now, hadn't a clue who or what his lover was banging on about.

15.35

Back home in the kitchen of their Porchester Road flat near the Spa, Angell practised with his knives.

Watched by Kim, he prepared bream for sashimi. His knives had been made by the great Japanese makers of sword blades: Aritugu, Shoudai Masayoshi and Masamoto. The steel of the blades had been beaten and folded into layers.

Angell's knives, beloved of the Japanese, were the *sashimi bocho*, the *banno* and the *deba*. The single cutting edges were as sharp as the most lethal razor.

With his wrist locked and firm, like his elbow, he decapitated the fish with the *deba*, a knife heavier than a chef's usual cutting knife. Then, to remove the pectoral fin, he made a swift lateral cut from the back of the head to the fish's stomach, turned the fish over, and cut through the spine.

'I love its eyes,' said Kim. 'So round.'

'Unlike yours,' Angell said, splitting the head in half with the point of the knife before he opened up the body. Then he lifted the belly flap and cut out the cartilage between the ribs and spine.

'Watch this,' he told Kim. 'The single cut to remove the fillet.'

He wielded the knife with a surgeon's skill, with the power and movement in the shoulder, and left not a single centimetre of the flesh bruised or ragged. 'Now we remove the second fillet.' With another single cut he removed the membrane covering the stomach.

'Pass me the *sashimi bocho*,' he told Kim.

He sighed with pleasure, slipping the long, straight blade between the skin and flesh, drawing the skin away like peel. Now, holding each fillet by the tip, he sliced them towards his fingers stained with the fish's blood. Each slice was made with a single stroke. He removed the remaining pin bones.

'Like you,' said Angell, 'each slice is silver, smooth, transparent. Here, stick your tongue out.' He placed a sliver of fish on Kim's long, narrow tongue. 'Is it smooth?'

'Very.'

'I love to cut,' said Angell. His admission was interrupted by the telephone ringing above the refrigerator. He wiped his hands on a paper towel.

Slaemann was on the line.

'Has she come to a decision?' Angell asked.

'Yes,' said Slaemann. 'It's a green light.'

'Good. I'll get back to you in three or four days from now.'
He turned to Kim. 'I knew I had persuaded her,' he said.
'I knew you would,' said Kim.
'After the sashimi,' Angell said, 'you're going shopping for clothes. Open the *sake*.'
'I want to go with you,' Kim protested.
'You can't.'
'Why not?'
'Because I want to collect the security wallets.'
'What security wallets?'
'Chemically treated. I don't want the knives to show.'
'Show when?'
'When I go through the Heathrow scanners.'

17.55

Angell and Kim, in matching white Thai silk kimonos, spread out the results of their earlier clothes shopping for Angell's travel to Copenhagen.

Holding a black wool-mix jacket and matching trousers against Angell's front, Kim whispered, 'Comme des Garçons. One thousand and five pounds only. Buttons on the man's side. And from Donna Karen Essentials at Browns, for three hundred and thirty pounds I'm dressing you in a beige satin bias-cut slip with lace trim.'

He spread out more clothes across the thick comforter covering their futon.

'A black satin knee-length dress from Whistles at one hundred and thirty-six pounds. Fine-knit cardie from Jigsaw at fifty-six pounds and a sweet little shell rosary from Portobello Market costing the outrageous sum of five pounds. All your knickers are M and S. Sandals from Dolce and Gabbana.'

'Let's get the hair done,' Angell said. 'Black and boyish. The Audrey Hepburn elfin look is back.'

'Look at these,' said Kim. 'Feel the satin. Oyster-pink jacket and trousers for one thousand seven hundred and forty pounds by John Galliano from Liberty. I want to wear them too.'

'You're too squat, Kim.'

'Oh?'

'Don't stamp your foot. *Cut my hair.*'

'Say *please,*' said Kim. 'Kiss me. Please. I love you. Make love to me. Please.'

Afterwards, in their bathroom decorated with black and white tiles of different sizes, Kim washed Angell's hair.

'Have you done everything?' Kim asked, massaging the muscles of Angell's neck.

'All ready. Early morning car to Heathrow. Tickets for the flight to Copenhagen in the morning.'

Kim touched the livid scar to the side of his upper lip. 'Look at my face, darling.'

'It's very beautiful.'

'It isn't any more. Not since Rosslyn scarred me.'

'It is beautiful.' Angell said. 'It's nothing the plastic surgeons can't fix for us. I love you. You know that. Just let me sort out Damm. And then I'll deal with Rosslyn, I promise you.'

Kim began to cut. 'Are you going to knife him in the throat?'

'Depends.'

'You know what I want you to do for me?'

'Make love again?'

'Most of all,' said Kim. 'And we must pray together for good luck.'

Saturday 22 July

79°F/26°C. Dry and bright with sunny spells. Wind north-westerly, gentle to moderate.

14.00

Dead time in the heat.

Rosslyn reminded Celeste of the phrase culled from Irish terrorist jargon.

Dead time. A lost day of waiting while Straub did his business in the suburbs.

The hours of waiting. When you tried to think of everything and anything except the approach of the danger hour. You thought ahead to the same time tomorrow. The time when you'd look back on it once it all was over. What happened = what you'd never expect. Always worse. It seemed beyond the power of human imagination to predict the outcome.

The accidental death.

The advantageous delay.

The unrequested hand of help.

The gun that jammed.

The impotent explosive.

They had whiled away the morning listening to CDs in a record store.

Rosslyn: Jule Nagel Band. *Butch Jule*. A hit in Germany.

Celeste: *Selena Live*. The murdered Selena Quintanilla's concert at the Colisea Memorial, Corpus Christi.

They ate at Café Sonja.

Rosslyn: a barely touched seafood salad.

Celeste: octopus and garlic.

Rosslyn: his jacket slung over one shoulder.

Celeste: in a cream-coloured Nicole Farhi dress.

They walked in silence near the harbour.

In the heat a ship's horn sounded.

At St Annac Plads the DFDS ferry was taking supplies on board for Oslo.

Ask for Phan, Straub had said.

He told Celeste to wait as long as necessary. In a cab booked for Kastrup.

Outside Sjaellandsgade 12.

16.59

Rosslyn found that there was no sign of Phan Van Quan at the Sjaellandsgade public sauna pay desk.

Van Quan must have gone off duty and been replaced by the African in a collarless white jacket who took his kroner, handed him a small white towel and told him where to change and shower.

Rosslyn, with a white towel round his waist, found his way barefoot down to the second level and the dimly lit corridor leading to the last cubicle on the left.

He peered through the observation slits in the wooden doors of the other cubicles.

All were empty.

Wet heat.

Stench of disinfectant from the john.

The male preserved in old sweat.

Steam.

Dead air.

A quick glance through the observation slit of the last cubicle showed him the feet and white flesh of a reclining naked male on the lower wooden bench. He pressed down the wooden door-handle only to find the door was jammed. A second, firmer push felt as if someone was leaning against the door. With the door an inch or so open, he muttered, 'Let me in, please.'

Getting no reply, he repeated his request. Now, leaning his weight against the door, he felt the soles of his bare feet stick to the hot and damp boards. He looked down.

He thought: *I'm bleeding*.

Must have cut my feet. There was a powerful stench of sweet vinegar. Sweet and sour.

He looked again: *Bleeding badly. But I feel no pain.*

With his full weight against the door he succeeded in getting it open wide enough to see inside.

The artificial coals gleamed dull red in the feeble light. The light was barely strong enough to show him the bloodbath.

Two naked male corpses. Lacerated and hacked, they sprawled across the wooden boards. The nearer, on its front, had been strangled, apparently with a white towel.

For a moment, he thought that one of the bodies, curled up in a foetal position, was a child's. He squinted at the blurred and distorted features and matted hair. Presumably this was Phan, the Vietnamese.

Shivering despite the heat, Rosslyn stepped a very short distance closer to the bodies.

His eyes, stinging with his own sweat in the clammy heat, were growing accustomed to the near-darkness, so he could now make out something of the other features of the carnage. His head spun. His mind yelled at him to identify the other body. Hard at first:

Because he stepped on an amputated hand.

Because the head of the other corpse was dangling upside-down, dripping pulp. Only when he tilted his neck at a painful angle did he know for sure he was staring into the remnants of Jack Straub's brutalized face.

20.30

The British Airways Boeing 737 bumped up through the clouds.

'Like a hot meal at all, sir?' asked the stewardess, weaving her precarious way among the six passengers in Club Class.

'Thank you, no,' Rosslyn told her. 'Just black coffee and a brandy.'

'Same here,' said Celeste.

The name tag said SAMANTHA. She seemed to sense their need to be left alone.

She gave them a smile and moved away towards another passenger.

Rosslyn's nausea returned, together with the memory of his retreat from the Sjaellandesgade public sauna in the heat. An hour after, he had telephoned Drew in London to tell her Straub was dead. Butchered.

'What happened?' she asked.

'I can't talk now. I'll tell you when I see you.'

'Are you okay, Alan?'

'Just about. See you at Heathrow.'

He and Celeste had been the last to board the London flight.

Now, thirty-five thousand feet up, bound for home, he felt contaminated by Straub's sickening end, the lumps of flesh in the steam, the fetid cubicle like a tank of blood. He had no doubt it was intended as a warning to others engaged in Straub's anonymous trade and their paymasters, like himself. He was already familiar with violent death. He had lost several paid informants. Their deaths, usually at the wrong end of a gun, were sudden and remained unexplained. They didn't show at arranged RVs. Often, much later, a new informant would ask:

'Was Aaron, or Johnnie, Ludo Bruce Hyman, or Big Boy Leung, or Anna-Marie one of yours?'

'No,' he'd say. 'But I did come across him or her in Turin. Nice. Chicago. Hamburg. Or Macao. What happened?'

But there was dead and there was really dead.

There would follow another whispered story of a violent death. Revenge killing. The result of the criminal's traditional hatred of the informer, for whom no final solution was foul enough. And he had lost intimate friends from the police and

Customs to both bomb and bullet. Whether law-enforcers or
law-breaking informants, all the dead shared, in different
measure, commitment and a certain courage.

But the carnage in Copenhagen was by far the worst he
had ever seen.

He imagined a run of lurid newspaper articles would
appear in the Danish press about some dead tourists. And
the stories would most probably hint at gay killings; perhaps
a Danish minister's sound-bite warning that Copenhagen
was dangerously close to becoming the sleaze capital of
Europe, worse than Amsterdam or Hamburg.

The police would investigate the identities of the victims,
follow a string of leads to Oslo, Hamburg, Geneva and
beyond, perhaps as far as the East, to Bangkok and Tokyo,
where the trail would peter out. One place Rosslyn hoped
they would not reach was his office at Custom House, the
heart of Team E.

Straub's payoff, in exchange for the name of the main
player in the paedophile industry, was to have been the
climax of *Operation Celeste*. It was to have been a main feature
in HM Customs & Excise Annual Report. The Results for the
Year triumph that would persuade the Financial Management and Accounting Services Committee to overcome their
natural reluctance to make payment to foreign nationals for
intelligence. To make them see the sense of paying out large
and secret fees to key informants like Straub.

The loss of Straub meant damage of another and more
personal kind. There was a limit, after all, to the budget for
the continuation of *Celeste*. All right, under Rosslyn's
personal direction Team E officers, assisted by the police,
had secured the conviction of one vicious paedophile. But
there were plenty more, Rosslyn knew, who were operating
out there. The one conviction had been a single swallow
which certainly didn't make a summer, someone had said.
Now, after the years of cut-backs, financial rationalization
and economic squeeze, Rosslyn had no illusions about the

future of *Celeste*; he knew there would be no shortage of
voices urging that it be shelved. No matter how hard he
fought the desk men in committee, *Celeste* would be
scrapped. Thornley-Miller from Computer Micro Team
Supplies and Data Retrieval, who spoke like a computer
spell-check, would rail against 'reliance upon human intelligence'. John Thornley-Miller, never at a loss for a synonym,
the wordy cyberspaceman, committee man and scourge of
Customs computer illiterates, held the same rank as Rosslyn.
Thornley-Miller's ambition, like his vocabulary, seemed to be
without limit. He believed himself to be a favourite against
Rosslyn for promotion to Chief Investigation Officer. He was
Rosslyn's only serious rival in the promotion stakes, and now
he would press for an inquiry to nail Rosslyn as the
scapegoat.

Straub's death was Team E's loss. And what with his
immediate boss about to retire, the mess would look pretty
bad for Rosslyn's application to step into the top job. Officers
like Thornley-Miller would say Straub had been a reckless
gamble, a secret and expensive punt.

'Who the hell could've rumbled him?' he asked Celeste
again.

'Well, we don't know, do we?' she said. 'He could've
telephoned or met up with any number of people between
the time we left him until you found him in that sauna. Look,
unless they'd sent us over three-handed with someone to
watch him twenty-four hours a day, there was always bound
to be the chance of a slip-up.'

'I told them we needed another pair of eyes,' he said.
'They're living on another planet. I said to Ms Franklin that
the two of us weren't enough, but you know what she's like.
She started reading the Riot Act about budgetary restraint.
What gets to me is that we're the ones who'll carry the can.'

'I don't know why I didn't see anyone suss outside the
sauna,' she said.

'You mustn't blame yourself,' Rosslyn said. 'How would

you know who you were looking for, anyway? Whoever we're up against is some operator. Believe me. I didn't get a chance to check it out, but Straub must have had that gun with him in there somewhere. And it didn't do him any good. I suppose he could just possibly have left it at the hotel. But I wasn't about to hang around that sauna to see if it was there or not.'

'Good thing in one way,' Celeste said, 'that you didn't get the chance. You wouldn't be here now. At least you're still in one piece.'

'For the time being,' he said. 'Drew told me she'd meet me at the airport. You're more than welcome to have a lift.'

'Maybe as far as you're concerned I am,' she said. 'But not in Drew's book. Two's company. Three's none. Are you going to be okay, Alan?'

'It can't get any worse.'

'We'll be beginning our descent to Heathrow soon,' SAMANTHA said. 'Want a top-up from the bar before we close?'

'No thanks,' said Rosslyn.

'Been on holiday have we then?' SAMANTHA asked.

'Sort of,' said Celeste.

'Business with pleasure,' said SAMANTHA. 'That's the best, I always say. Would you mind fixing your seat belts?'

About the only thing I can fix right now, thought Rosslyn.

LONDON

66°F/19°C. Becoming cloudy later with rain in places.
Wind light and variable.

22.15

Disembarking, Rosslyn noticed ahead of him the woman who had been seated behind him in the Club Class cabin. It was the waft of her scent that attracted him.

'What's the scent?' Rosslyn asked Celeste.

'Issey Miyake for Men,' she said.

The woman was tall, rather beautifully dressed in black silk, somehow like a spider. One of those senior career women who travel light.

'Have you seen her somewhere before?' he asked Celeste.

'No.'

'Seems familiar to me.'

'Not to me.'

Somewhere on the march along the Heathrow corridors to Passport Control and Baggage Collection and Customs they lost sight of her.

But Rosslyn saw her once more in the terminal concourse. She was not far beyond a group of chauffeurs and bored cab drivers holding up makeshift cardboard name boards. She kissed both cheeks of a man in a pin-stripe suit. The man had his back to Rosslyn, and he was sure, just for a second, that as the woman kissed her manfriend's cheeks she gave him, or perhaps Celeste, the hint of a knowing smile. The woman had very white teeth.

Rosslyn watched her a fraction longer until he heard his boss's voice call his name, and when he looked into the thinning crowd the career woman and her manfriend had disappeared.

'I'm sorry,' said Drew.

'So are we.'

She gave Celeste a look which said, *Don't say yes to what I'm about to offer*. 'Can I give you a lift into town, Ms Quinceau?'

Celeste smiled at Rosslyn and said, 'No thanks. I'm going to call my boyfriend.'

That was the first time Rosslyn had heard her mention the existence of a boyfriend and he was surprised at the sudden pang of disappointment he felt.

'Thanks for everything, Celeste. See you at Custom House on Monday.'

He noticed she touched the crucifix on the necklace around her neck. Her good luck sign.

22.45

Drew drove him away from Heathrow at speed through the rain.

She was in her early forties, and her straight fair hair framed an oval face with quizzical blue eyes and a wide mouth.

'How are you feeling?' she asked him.

'A bit rough still,' he told her. 'It's good of you to meet me.'

'This time it's okay,' she said. 'But I'm not about to make a habit of meeting my junior officers.'

'Not even this one?'

'Not even you.' She leaned sideways and lightly kissed his cheek. 'I'm taking you home.'

He shivered slightly. He felt the reaction of the shock he had experienced.

Drew glanced anxiously at him from the corner of her eye. 'Soon be there.'

23.30

The rain beat against the skylights of the top-floor Holland Park flat she had converted at the time of her appointment as Chairman and Chief Executive of HM Customs & Excise.

In the kitchen she brought a bottle of Cointreau from her fridge and poured him a large glass, with a smaller one for herself. 'The only positive thing,' she said, 'is that when your informant dies in circumstances like that, it means he probably won't have had time to talk.'

Rosslyn peered at the rain churning across the windows. 'That we'll never know. I don't know who he saw in the last few days apart from me and Celeste. Who he telephoned. I don't know anything. Except he's dead. And had he lived he'd have given me the name I want. Maybe even told me this minute, somewhere out there, who is poring over porno videos and CD-ROMs. Who's looking at that filth involving kids, feeling good to be alive, and thanking God for the safety of their dirty millions. And we're none the wiser.'

'Perhaps, Alan, you should've shown up at that sauna a bit earlier?'

'I'm glad I didn't,' Rosslyn said. 'Otherwise, do you think I'd be here now? I've never seen anything like it. And I promise you, I never want to see anything like it again. Straub told me he'd be carrying a Smith & Wesson. He showed it to me in his hotel room. There was no sign of it in the sauna. What do I know? Why was the Vietnamese there as well? All I know is that Straub knew the one name I'll never get now. How many months have we been set back?'

His voice had taken on a bitter edge. 'If you ask me to do a job, Drew, it does help if you give me adequate resources.'

'You're overwrought,' she said. 'Why don't we talk about it in the morning?'

'No, Drew, I want to talk about it now.'

'You're being a little tiresome, Alan,' she said as if she were dealing with an over-tired child at bedtime.

'You think so?' he said. 'You don't know how tiresome I can be. Particularly when, thanks to you, me and my partner could have got killed. Because you didn't see fit to give us another officer.'

'I don't set the budgets, Alan, I operate within their contraints.'

'In that case,' he said, 'you won't mind if I put in my report that the main reason this operation turned out to be a shambles is because of undermanning.'

'Understaffing.'

'Call it what you bloody like. But if someone ever tells me again they've got the kind of gilt-edged intelligence Straub was offering, and it means me meeting whomsoever again in Copenhagen, well, some other prick can go over and buy a ticket to a sauna.'

'I understand what you're saying. Now it's damage limitation time. Do you think our embassy friend will have put two and two together?'

'Probably not,' Rosslyn said. 'But you can bet your sweet

life they will have done by the morning.'

'You think they'll tie you in to this? After all, you were the first witness on the scene and decided not to report it.'

'Thanks for rubbing it in. You think I should've stayed in there to wait for a whole bunch of Danish plods to show up? Like hell. No thanks. They might just connect Straub to *us*. It depends on what passport Straub was using. He won't have used a UK passport.'

'What sort *was* he using?'

'Don't know. Didn't see it. Didn't ask him. Didn't get a chance, did I? He always had a whole basket of them. Tools of the trade. And I don't know how many bloody aliases. He said there were around four. Straub and Morton Damm were the only ones I knew him by. You know that. Most likely he was using a US passport. The Americans will cause trouble once they've found out.'

'Let's cross our bridges when we come to them.'

'I've had enough for now,' Rosslyn said. 'And I feel bad about Straub.'

'Alan, you win some, you lose some. We've been around long enough to know that. Only thank Christ they didn't get you too.'

'You don't need to tell me.'

'Which still leaves us with the difficulty of finding out who *they* are,' she said. 'And with needing to answer the question of who's prepared to go to such lengths to stop you. Let's go to bed. By the way, I forgot to tell you: your ex-girlfriend left a message for you to call her.'

'What does she want?'

'She didn't say. Our Verity is certainly persistent if nothing else. How did she know you were in Copenhagen? You didn't tell her you were going there, did you?'

'Of course not. She knows the Visa Officer in the Embassy. He'll have told her.'

'I sometimes think you two have unfinished business.'

'She may have,' said Rosslyn. 'Not me.'

'Or Celeste Quinceau, Alan?'

'What about her?'

'You seemed rather hurt when she said her boyfriend was collecting her.'

'You're imagining things.'

'Am I?' she said. 'Come on.' She kissed him on the mouth. Let's go to bed. New white sheets. Egyptian cotton. Especially for you.'

Sunday 23 July

04.05

The woman who broke into Rosslyn's top-floor flat in Eccleston Square had changed into dark jeans, a plain blue sweater, hood anorak and trainers.

She crossed Hugh Street into Hugh Mews, which was filled with overflowing dustbins at the rear of the Animal Welfare Hospital.

A narrow passage led to the back of the row of high houses, where a yard was floodlit. The pool of light enabled her to make sure there was no sign of a burglar alarm system. It also helped her in working on the lock to the outer door. Her transparent rubber gloves squeaked on metal; the fine plastic strip she inserted bent, twisted and released the mechanism without difficulty.

Once she was inside, she locked the door behind her. She climbed the stairs to the top floor.

Here she repeated the procedure with the fine plastic strip.

Inside Rosslyn's flat she stood still, listening. The air was chill and dead. She closed the curtains before turning on the lights. Even in the darkness she could see that the place, unlike her own, was unloved. She made her way through the flat to the front room. Again she went through the same routine of looking, waiting.

Below, she heard dogs barking in the Animal Welfare Hospital.

Finally, she turned on the lights and they showed her what she wanted. Rosslyn's personal computer. The Apple Macintosh LC475.

04.10

It took the woman less than five minutes to make a copy of
Rosslyn's notes for the *Celeste* report, then to insert and bury
a series of pornographic images deep into the computer's
hard-disk memory. They showed Rosslyn committing
obscene acts with a child.

12.30

The heavy curtains in Drew's bedroom shut out the light of
early afternoon.

Rosslyn woke in her bed to the sounds of her washing
machine from the kitchen and the chink of glass and cutlery.

He saw her standing in the bedroom doorway holding a
tray.

'Breakfast for two in bed,' she announced. 'And all the
Sunday papers.'

'Have you been out already?'

'Papers. A jog in the park. All the way to Ken High Street
and back. A swim at Kensington Close. And you slept
through it all. You didn't want to come to?'

'No.'

'I didn't think so. I let you get your beauty sleep.'

She slipped off her white towelling bathrobe. 'Make room
for the Chair.'

He shifted the pillows for her to get into bed.

'I'm washing your clothes. There were bloodstains on your
shirt. One of your socks has got a hole in it.'

'I didn't know.'

'I thought as much. You're staying here with me today.
Anyway, you can't escape until I've dried and pressed your
gear. And later, Alan, after brunch, we'll go to a movie. And
you can have your reward in advance.'

'What reward?'

'Me.'

He tried not to show his lack of enthusiasm.

'Oh yes, and I found this.' She reached for a card on her

bedside table and handed it to Rosslyn.

He read:

> *Aiko Holland*
> *US Customs Senior Special Agent*
> *United States Embassy*
> *24 Grosvenor Square*
> *London W1A 1AE*
> *tel. 0171.499.9000*
> *ext. 7899*

'I think I ought to call Celeste.'

'What, now?'

'Make sure she's all right,' he said. 'She's one of my officers, isn't she? And someone has to call Straub's womanfriend.'

'She can wait,' said Drew. 'She's small fry.'

'I got the feeling she was important to him.'

'Leave it to the Americans.'

'Who's going to tell her about Straub?'

'Why not ask Quinceau?' Drew said. 'If you think so much of her. Call her *later*. And don't forget, she's one of *my* officers too, Alan. And so are *you*. And we are spending today together. This evening we'll finalize your *Celeste* report. Meanwhile, don't spill the muesli on my sheets.'

Monday 24 July

82°F/28°C. Generally hot and sunny, blue skies with a
chance of thunder by the evening.

09.00

The presence of Drew's flow-chart, known as the Egg Timer,
leaning against his office wall would have infuriated Chief
Investigation Officer Richard Gaynor, the Sea Captain, who
was far away from Custom House that morning on pre-
retirement leave at his house in Suffolk. It was a symbol of
the new management style, driven by a hybrid mixture of
theorizing, marketing and half-baked psychology, that was
favoured by the new intake of men and women graduates
who had brought their intellectual baggage to British
institutions in the last decade. Gaynor reckoned none of
them had done a real day's work since birth.

THE ONE-MINUTE EGG TIMER HATCHES PRIORITIES
CELESTE IS THE MODEL OPERATION
OUR ORGANIZATIONAL INITIATIVE
JOB EVALUATION SYSTEMS
TEAM WORKING
APPRAISAL
PRAISE
RECOGNITION
TRAINING & DEVELOPMENT
FEEDBACK FROM STAFF AND MANAGERS
FROM VOICE THE SURVEY OF VIEWS & OPINIONS

And when Rosslyn glanced at Drew's flow-chart he thought: *Gaynor's right*. He asked himself, Why does anyone in his right mind go along with this?

Prayers was the name given to the meetings of the Board that Drew, as Chairman of Customs & Excise, called in emergencies.

She convened them today in Gaynor's unoccupied fourth-floor office at Custom House, headquarters of the Investigation Division, as if she were dropping the bad news on the Division's doorstep.

The windows were open to the blue sky and Tower Bridge and HMS *Belfast* at anchor in the Thames in the sun. A framed picture on Gaynor's desk suggested that the officers of the Investigation Division had for many years been in safe hands. The colour photograph showed the Sea Captain in a morning suit, with top hat at a rakish angle, standing with his former wife in the Mall one summer afternoon bound for one of Her Majesty's garden parties at the palace. The image of the Gaynors, wreathed in smiles, belonged to a happier era.

Coffee was sent up from Waxers, the Custom House staff restaurant. The bigwigs would gather together, as they did now, to discuss in secret what action was to be taken to resolve a major crisis. At these councils of war the full complement consisted of Drew, her two Deputy Chairmen, the service Solicitor, the eight Directors, and two Principal Assistant Solicitors, and John Thornley-Miller from Computer Micro Team: Supplies and Data Retrieval. With the exceptions of Drew and DVATC – the Director VAT Control – all were men.

Never before during his career with Customs had Rosslyn been summoned to Prayers. He'd heard the mood at these meetings was usually grim, sometimes bitter, because failure was usually number one on the agenda. Recognized as some of the ablest of government employees, they were as dedicated to the collection of central government taxation, in the form of VAT and excise duties, as they were to the enforcement of UN sanctions against Iraq, Libya and Serbia/Montenegro. Their remit also covered the prohibition and restriction of illicit dealings in arms and paedophile material. With equal dedication, under her leadership, they were planning to restructure HM Customs & Excise's Investigation Division, to absorb the old-fashioned Collection Investigation Units to form HM Customs Investigation Service. Change was in the air.

'The future of *Celeste* is the only item on the agenda,' Drew began. 'This is a secret operation. Because of its security rating the details of it have not been made available to you previously. I'd ask you to read it carefully. Afterwards, Mr Rosslyn here will talk us through the background and the most recent developments, which may jeopardize the future of the operation. Then, as a matter of urgency, we have to reach a decision as to how far the loss of our key informant affects its future.'

Rosslyn circulated the copies of his report.

SECRET
DRAFT REPORT
OPERATION CELESTE
SIO ALAN H. ROSSLYN
CUSTOMS TEAM E
INVESTIGATION DIVISION
HM CUSTOMS & EXCISE

'I'll take questions at the end,' he said.

While they read, he scribbled a note to Celeste on the back of Aiko Holland's card: CALL HER FOR ME, PLEASE. SOMEONE HAS TO TELL HER ABOUT STRAUB.

He passed it to Celeste and she nodded agreement.

09.25

When they had finished reading, Drew said, 'I understand

you have something further you want to tell the meeting.'

He was impressed by the ease with which she dissembled. She was acting as if she was as eager for new information as the others round the table, whereas she was already in full possession of the known facts surrounding Straub's death. He moved his copy of the report to one side. 'I regret to have to tell you that our main informant, Straub, whose role is described in my report, was found dead on Saturday, 22 July, together with one other person, in very unpleasant circumstances in Copenhagen. The Danish police are treating his death as murder. I have no other information to give the meeting at present.'

'May I ask through you, Chairman,' said Thornley-Miller, 'whether the demise of Straub terminates *Celeste*?'

Drew looked Thornley-Miller in the eye. He had recently given up smoking and put on a considerable amount of weight. 'We won't engage in speculation until we have a full report from the Danes. However, I've asked to be kept informed of the progress of their investigation.'

'I'm sure you're right,' Thornley-Miller said.

You mean you're sure she's wrong, thought Rosslyn. He was grateful to Drew for neutralizing Thornley-Miller, who began to flick through the pages of the report.

'I see CIO Gaynor played a key role in the operation,' he said. 'Shouldn't he be here, Chairman?'

You never give up, thought Rosslyn. *Full marks for effort. D minus for intelligence.*

'Mr Gaynor is on pre-retirement leave,' Drew said. 'I know he won't take kindly to his leave being interrupted, but perhaps you should visit him at home, Alan, and bring him up to date.'

Rosslyn looked down the table at her. 'I think that might be best.'

'I know the development that Mr Rosslyn has told you about leaves a number of questions unanswered,' Drew said. 'But I would ask you to bear with us until we have a fuller picture from Copenhagen, as well as the local embassy.'

Rosslyn was grateful to her for preventing further discussion. His sleep the night before had been continually disturbed by nightmares. At dawn he had woken groaning, covered in sweat. He looked around the table and wondered if any of the others had noticed how rough he was feeling.

'Right,' she said. 'The meeting's closed. But before we leave, may I remind you that both the contents of the report and our discussion are strictly privileged.'

Chairs were pushed back.

Out of the others' hearing, Alan said to Drew, 'Thank you, Chairman, for your help.'

'Don't expect me to bail you out too often, Mr Rosslyn,' she said quietly. 'Let me know what Gaynor has to say.'

'I should have something to report by this evening.'

Leaving the committee room, Rosslyn noticed Thornley-Miller hanging back. 'Chairman,' he heard him say, 'may I have a brief word with you in private?'

Now what's the stupid bugger up to? thought Rosslyn.

EAST ANGLIA

77°F/25°C. Dry with sunny spells. Wind south-easterly, light.

16.10

Lapwing End, on the east coast outside Aldeburgh, was Gaynor's pride and joy.

Here was the benign figure with the broad sailor's hands. The grower of prize-winning vegetables in his Suffolk garden. The week-end golfer with the handicap of twelve. He brought tea, sandwiches and scones with thick cream and strawberry jam to the table on the patio overlooking the river at Blackthorn Reach. The Sea Captain, large and overweight, epitomized reliability and contentment.

The scorched grass of the lawn led downwards through beds of lavender and heather to the flood-bank and the single wooden gate to the River Alde beyond. The wide river was at low tide in the heat of late afternoon.

Rosslyn watched a solitary heron on the glistening mud-banks. Two yachts strained at their moorings. He could hear the clank of the lanyards against their metal masts, the cries of gulls, the distant chug of a motor boat upriver. *Celeste* in all its aspects, the memory of the horror in Copenhagen, his affair with Drew, all seemed a thousand miles away.

'The good thing,' Gaynor said with a scratch at his beard, 'is that when your informant dies in shit like that it most likely means he won't have blabbed.'

'I seem to have heard that before,' Rosslyn said. 'You must have spoken to Sister. That's what she said to me.'

The Sea Captain filled a scone with strawberry jam and cream in silence, lost in thought. 'This is for you,' he said, handing the scone to Rosslyn on a willow-pattern plate. 'My Pauline makes these in Leiston. She makes the best scones in the whole world.'

Called to Duty in the good old days – before the expansion of the paedophile pornography, heroin, cocaine and international arms trade – Gaynor the veteran Duty Man knew no other way of life. Rosslyn had warmed to him at once. He considered he was in the same mould. An operations and outfield Duty Man. In the front line of the war against drugs and arms dealers, international fraudsters, money launderers and now the importers of child pornography. The Sea Captain was approaching sixty and Rosslyn envied the widower his sanctuary, sympathizing with his decision to take early retirement far away from London and the politics of Custom House. Yet his sunburned face was lined with what seemed to be regret and sadness.

Must be asking himself what it's all been for, he thought. *When I finally go they'll say, 'Come back at any time.' But they won't want to see me, and, I don't care.*

Gaynor was old enough to be his father. And Rosslyn wondered again if perhaps he had been a substitute for the son killed in the car crash. Gaynor Junior. His only offspring. Eighteen years old. Coming home from Glasgow University at the end of a summer term, the student had been driving whilst pissed and collided with an articulated wagon loaded with Polish foodstuffs on the M1. It was one death too many. Too close to home. And ever since, whenever Gaynor wore a tie it was always black. Perhaps that'd been the trouble. There had been too many deaths. Like the list of informants. Aaron. Johnnie. Gustavsen. Ludo Bruce Hyman. Big Boy Leung. Anna-Marie in Turin. In Nice. Chicago. Berlin. Hamburg. Macao. Now Copenhagen and Straub too.

Or were there other, more hidden reasons for the pain behind Gaynor's features and the eyes narrowed against the sun?

Since the end of last winter, when the Sea Captain had first announced his decision to retire, there had been something desperate in the way he'd meddled in everyone else's operations. A previous reluctance to engage in internal politics had been transformed into an apparent relish. With a carefree lack of tact, he had invited trouble from his superiors and offence from within the ranks.

Worse, he began to hector superiors and subordinates alike. His bad tempers on Mondays were said to be associated with heavy weekend drinking bouts here in Suffolk by the estuary. His skin turned blotched, then greyish. There were bruises of sleeplessness beneath the bloodshot drooping eyes. Word had it that he was burning the candle at both ends. The signs of stress and fatigue were plain. Was it a reluctance to release the reins of his command; or, as some thought, the apparent lack of any subordinate officer bright enough to step into his shoes as Chief Investigation Officer? There was a lack of obvious talent and wide experience among the candidates for CIO. Unless you considered Rosslyn. Except here there was a problem of rank and hierarchy. Rosslyn would have to be promoted three clear ranks up the ladder. It would be a formidable jump.

And Rosslyn knew that Gaynor's support of his candidacy for the job he wanted was something of a poisoned chalice. Gaynor's backing identified him with the old school, the values of the street investigator who prized human contact, skill and patience. The new school valued computer technology and electronics. Those skills and resources were epitomized by Thornley-Miller, who waffled on about the New Age of green-screen solutions and the cyber-processing of criminal intelligence, phrases he culled from his stack of monthly computer journals and repeated *ad nauseam* to anyone who could tolerate his obsession.

Apart from Gaynor, Commander of the British Empire – even that title sounded like an encumbrance from another era – there was another card in Rosslyn's hand, a card he couldn't place face-up on the table: his relationship with Drew. Both she and Gaynor, for obviously different personal and professional reasons, supported his candidacy. Rosslyn assumed that Gaynor had no idea he was sleeping with the Chairman. One day, perhaps when the Sea Captain's retirement was final, if it ever seemed appropriate, he might confide in him. Man to man. Hadn't the old boy told him it was a good day when he ditched Verity? 'Sleeping with SIS,' he'd said, laughing. 'That's something even I've not done. Not that the opportunity presented itself. Thank Christ. Tarts.'

Rosslyn watched him toss the few crumbled remains of the scones to sparrows fluttering around the marble bird bath.

'I think I'd better let you know,' said Gaynor. 'I wasn't going to tell you this. But I've changed my mind. You're not the only visitor I've had here today about *Celeste*. SIS showed up unannounced. A man called McEvoy, one of their legal people, with a woman, his junior. Legal advisers is what their IDs said they were.'

'What did they want?'

'General background. Ideas. Names. Speculation. Didn't the Chairman mention to you that they're showing a sudden interest?'

'If she knows, she never said.'

'I had the impression they want to bypass her. And you too, Alan. That's why they came to see me.'

'What did you tell them?'

'Tell them? I didn't tell them anything. They already knew the contents of your report. In fact, they even had a copy of it. They knew about Straub too.'

'It isn't any of their business.'

'That's not what they think. Now they think it's theirs too.'

'Why?'

'Maybe they'll tell you,' Gaynor said. 'All in good time. But for what it's worth, I advise you to say nothing. That's if you want to keep *Celeste* red active. I have the impression that they want it aborted. And that's not what you want, Alan, is it?'

'Level with me, Chief. You must have an idea what it is they want.'

'If I was a betting man I'd put my money on them having a name they don't want brought into it. It's not a racing certainty. Only a guess that some wire somewhere has been crossed. Some connection made that's sort of given them a shock.'

'Like what?'

'I don't know, Alan.'

'What else did they ask you?'

'A lot about you.'

'Me?'

'Your prospects. The future. Ambitions. Reliability. A lot of personal stuff about Verity.'

Gaynor looked at Rosslyn in silence until the tension was broken from the estuary, where a motor boat had come into view. It had slowed, its engine idling in neutral. The helmsman seemed to be assembling fishing gear.

'It'd help your prospects,' Gaynor said at last, 'if you had a steady relationship with a woman, Alan. You see, I think they only showed up here to look at your background in general as a suitable candidate to take over from me.'

'It wouldn't be MI6 who'd do that,' Rosslyn said. 'You know as well as I do it'd be MI5 who'd do the vetting.'

'I know. I made the point to them.'

'What did they say to that?'

'That *Celeste* was, as they put it, "in the frame of their inquiries".'

'Didn't you press them for an explanation?'

'Indirectly,' said Gaynor, lifting a pair of binoculars from the table.

'What did they say?'

'What you'd expect. "We can't disclose the background to our visit. You'll appreciate that, Mr Gaynor," they said. "May we call you Richard?" they said. "If you wish," I said. And then they said something like, "It touches upon issues of national security, Richard. And an operation or network of operations of our own." Pompous buggers.' He paused to focus closely on the motor boat and the solitary fisherman. 'I don't know what that arsehole thinks he's doing. I happen to know the only fish out there at present are bass or some sole with ragworm or something in the buggers. You look.'

He handed the binoculars to Rosslyn.

'Your eyesight's not what it was, Chief,' said Rosslyn. He focused the binoculars on the boat and then on the person fiddling with what might, or equally might not, have been fishing equipment. He noticed bright yellow waterproofs. A black and white chequered neckscarf. 'It's a woman out there.' She had long dark hair.

'Isn't she fishing?'

'She's got a gun,' said Rosslyn.

'Are you sure?' Gaynor said. 'Here, let me see.'

'Hang on. Hard to see her face,' said Rosslyn. 'Christ, I don't know what the fuck she thinks she's going to shoot.'

'The only people who shoot out there are members of the Leiston Wildfowlers. I didn't know they had women members.'

'What do they shoot?'

'Canada geese. Duck. Pheasant. Partridge. Anyway, they use a kind of flat boat. Not what she's in. What sort of gun is it?' said Gaynor.

'A rifle. I can't quite make it out.'

He passed the binoculars to Gaynor, who watched the boat for a short time. 'She's put the gun down. She's looking at us, Alan, with binoculars too. She's making ready to go.' He set the binoculars on the table and as he did so the engine started and the boat headed off downriver on the tide. 'Sod her.'

Rosslyn watched the Sea Captain clear the table. 'I suppose you don't want to stay for a bite to eat?'

'I have to get back to London,' Rosslyn said. 'Thanks anyway.'

Loading the dishwasher in his kitchen, Gaynor said, 'Watch your back, Alan. I'm sorry I can't be around to do it for you. Remember, there's one thing I do want to see. The job meant a lot to me. I'd like to feel that whoever takes over isn't going to undo any good work I may have done in thirty years.'

20.05

said the clock on Rosslyn's dashboard when he pulled into the car-park of the Little Chef beyond Colchester.

He ate bacon, egg and chips at a table with a view of the forecourt and the motorway beyond.

He had almost finished a second cup of coffee when he noticed a woman in the forecourt filling her Peugeot at the pumps. The hair, long and dark, seemed familiar. And so were her clothes. She was wearing a black jacket and matching trousers similar to a suit Verity wore. And then he noticed the black and white chequered scarf.

Where have I seen that scarf before?

This was the woman improbably fishing in the distance at

low tide. The woman with the rifle in the motor boat.

Now she was hiding behind dark glasses. He watched her paying at the cash desk. It was hard to tell her age. Over forty, maybe more. The arrival of a VW camper van temporarily blocked his view of her.

He left his coffee unfinished on the table and moved towards the door.

'I think you've forgotten to pay, sir,' said the woman at the till.

He was trying to get a better view of her and pay his bill at the same time.

'Forget the change,' he told the woman at the till. He handed her a ten-pound note.

From the doorway he was just in time to see the Peugeot leaving by the slip road for the motorway heading south.

He drove his car to the petrol pumps, filled it, and walked to the cash desk to pay.

'Twenty pounds exactly,' said the man at the window.

'Didn't my friend pay for my petrol?'

'What?'

'I told her,' he bluffed. 'Your last customer. I told her to pay for me.'

The man said, 'What was her name?'

'It's on her credit card slip.'

'The last one,' said the man, retrieving the credit card slip, 'is a woman called Angell. Initials G. R. D. She paid fifteen pounds fifty. Anything else you want to know? She hasn't paid for you. Sorry.'

'She's got a memory like a sieve,' said Rosslyn. 'What's the damage?'

'I told you. Twenty quid exactly.'

'Amnesia runs in the family,' said Rosslyn.

He walked back to his car.

Opening the car door, he wondered where this woman Angell fitted in. Perhaps it was a coincidence. Perhaps it was more than that.

Back on the motorway, he put through a call on his car phone to Drew at home in London.

'I briefed the Sea Captain,' he told her. 'He had nothing more to add. Only he's had a visit from Vauxhall Cross.'

She sounded apprehensive. 'Did he tell you what they said to him?'

'Nothing specific. Except they've got a copy of the *Celeste* report. It sounds as if they're showing more than a little interest. You sound worried. I want to ask you a favour.'

'Hang on,' she said, 'while I go into another room.'

He heard her make her apologies to someone. Then a woman's muffled voice in reply.

A moment later she was back on the line.

'Can you run a check for me, please? Get this down, Drew. A women called Angell. Initials G. R. D. In her late forties, maybe early or even late fifties. White. Slim build. Dark hair, almost shoulder length. Driving a black Peugeot saloon. SG 129K. Presently heading south on the A12 in the Chelmsford area.'

'Who is she?'

'That's why I'm asking you to have her checked. I saw her when I was at Gaynor's place. She was making out that she was fishing in the Alde. The Sea Captain says there aren't any fish where she was pretending to fish. Then I see her again, would you believe it, a few minutes ago. Here. Outside a Little Chef. It may be coincidence. Or it may not. And she has a rifle. Gaynor and I both saw it.' He paused. 'Is there someone there with you?'

'No.' She sounded evasive. 'No. I'm on my own.'

'There's a problem?' he asked.

'Maybe, Alan.'

He had never heard her quite so defensive.

'What is it?' he asked her.

'I had a phone call. Some people from MI6. Let me deal with them. I'll run your check and call you back.'

He continued driving south at high speed on the motorway.

20.45

The Peugeot was parked close to the parapet of the deserted bridge above the motorway. It offered a perfect view of the oncoming southbound traffic, which had thinned out after the interchanges at Handley Green and Margaretting, the sun edging windscreens with crimson.

A light wind had risen. It tossed the wild grasses and roadside flowers growing among the litter by the parapet.

The window of the Peugeot was open. The driver had already positioned the loaded rifle and covered it with yellow waterproofs. The weapon was aimed towards the three lanes of oncoming traffic below. This way it could be manoeuvred at the last moment to be precisely on target.

The range was about seventy yards. From the bridge, it had proved impossible to calculate the exact speed of the oncoming cars. It might be seventy, it might be more.

20.50

The fading light.

Dust in the air.

The stench of exhaust fumes.

A police patrol car speeding in the other direction.

No one remembers a car parked for five minutes.

But a car parked for half an hour or longer is more likely to be noticed in an isolated place.

You didn't want to be seen hanging around for too long.

The idea mustn't take your mind off the job in hand. You had to steel your nerves.

Calm yourself.

Breathe slowly.

Treat killing as a routine to be followed with mechanical precision.

20.55

Rosslyn's car came into view, overtaking a German tourist bus.

The yellow waterproofs were drawn aside.

The gun held steady.

The windscreen was in the sights.

The index finger squeezed the trigger.

The first shot, low, struck and exploded the left tyre.

Two more shots hit the bodywork.

Rosslyn's car slewed, leaving a trail of metallic sparks.

Somewhere below there was a deafening scream of metal against concrete.

A screech of rubber.

A single thud which reverberated along the structure of the bridge.

20.56

No trace remained of the Peugeot's presence on the bridge.

No cartridges were found, no spent bullets.

No trace was found at the scene of the gunshots which would have pointed to the deliberate and planned attack on the Customs officer returning to London that night.

23.45

No immediate connection was made between the accident and the unlocked Peugeot found apparently abandoned in a hurry within sight of Hackney Marshes.

Some yellow waterproofs were found on the floor behind the driver's seat.

Nothing else.

Tuesday 25 July

01.00

The police had found Rosslyn's ID at the scene of the accident. Drew had been informed and had driven to Broomfield Hospital, five miles outside Chelmsford's city centre.

She found him sleeping in a private room off B12 ward.

The duty sister described the massive bruising to his shoulders, chest and legs. She told Drew not to wake him. She muttered something about his being 'lucky to have survived'.

Without telling the sister who she was, just saying she was his 'partner', Drew asked what had happened.

'They brought him into Casualty at about quarter to ten,' the sister explained. 'He was conscious. Badly shocked though. The police insisted on a blood test. They couldn't believe that anyone could drive like that without being under the influence.'

'Was he able to say anything about the accident?' Drew asked.

'No. We wanted him up in the ward as soon as possible in peace and quiet. We told the police his statement would have to wait. They didn't like it much. But then they never do.'

'Was he able to say what he thought caused it?'

'Well, he rambled on about some woman in a chequered scarf with a gun. Didn't make any sense. When he started talking about an angel the doctor gave him a shot of something to knock him out.'

'Do you get a lot of accidents like this?' Drew asked.

'We have done lately,' said the sister. 'Summer weather. The kids get bored. Not enough to do. A couple of months ago one of them threw a brick from the bridge across the motorway into the oncoming traffic at the same spot where your partner crashed. A woman was killed.'

'Did they get anybody?'

'No,' said the sister. 'But in your partner's case it seems no one was to blame. Just a blown tyre. He obviously kept a cool head when it burst. If it hadn't been for the lightness of the traffic as well as the judgement of the German coach driver, there might have been serious loss of life. Look, why not get a good night's sleep and see your partner in the morning?'

'Will I be able to take him home tomorrow?'

'It depends on what the doctor says. But if you're going to be looking after him, I imagine they'll discharge him.'

I'm not the only one who wants him out of hospital, she thought. There had been a telephone call from SIS head-quarters at Vauxhall Cross, from a man called McEvoy, who said that he and a colleague had spoken to Richard Gaynor at his home in Aldeburgh earlier in the day. 'I believe we should see Mr Rosslyn in person,' McEvoy had said curtly. 'As soon as possible, if that's in order. We feel it's a matter of courtesy that we let you know we want to question him.'

She had asked him for more details.

'It's an operational matter,' McEvoy had said. 'I'm sure you'll appreciate it isn't in Mr Rosslyn's interests that you and I discuss it at this stage.' She hadn't appreciated it. She was left with no other choice than to agree to her subordinate being interviewed by SIS. She was concerned that McEvoy had used the word 'question'. It sounded more of a threat than an invitation to co-operate.

The sister said, 'Look, this must have been a shock for you. Why don't you stay the night?'

'I think I should get back.'

'I don't think you should drive home now,' the sister said. 'Why not get a good night's sleep? There's a room you can use off the ward here.'

Drew felt drained. She was grateful for the sister's offer of tea, a sandwich, and a sleeping pill.

Without the pill, sleep in the small private room at Broomfield Hospital would have been impossible.

LONDON

75°F/24°C. Hot and sunny. Wind south-easterly, moderate.

01.58

on WPC Helen Cliff's wrist-watch meant she was nearly at the end of her duty shift in Porchester Road in the heatwave.

Her fellow officer had already headed for the station, leaving WPC Cliff to buy cigarettes and new batteries for her tape recorder from the late-night store near the traffic lights. Except her purchase was delayed by a shrieking woman telling her what any fool could hear for herself.

A burglar alarm was howling.

The woman was insisting the noise be stopped. 'Fucking noise pollution.' She waved at the clanging alarm bell above the top-floor balcony. 'My kids can't sleep.' Above the bell-box a red light was flashing. 'You're a woman. You should understand.' She pointed at WPC Cliff's new-style baton and the quick-cuff pouch attached to her trouser belt. 'Can't you do something?'

WPC Cliff might have told her she had more urgent tasks to finish in the early hours, might have left the alarm to be investigated by another officer. She knew what it felt like to be short of sleep.

The incident in the upstairs flat might not have been discovered till daybreak or even later had not the woman been quite so distressed.

02.09

Entering the block of flats by the front door, WPC Cliff made a mental note of the time. The door was wedged open with a carton of semi-skimmed milk that reminded her she had no milk at home for breakfast.

She walked up the several flights of stone stairs to find the top-floor flat. Its door was at the end of a narrow and dimly lit passage. This was yet another scruffy residential block. The flat's only door, painted battleship grey, was shut.

She rang the bell. There was no answer. She waited before she tried a second time, then a third. Still no answer. She was about to call in to the station to report the location of the deafening alarm when she noticed the stains between the edge of the rubber doormat and the gap, only a fraction of an inch, at the bottom of the door. With her left shoe she edged the doormat to one side. She looked more closely at the stains. Dark sticky liquid.

She realized that the liquid seeping across the floor was blood. She hesitated, looking at the glistening pool near her shoes, listening to the alarm; one hand on her Storno personal radio, the other on the door-handle. To see if she could confirm her growing suspicions, she tried the handle. To her surprise it turned. The door was unlocked. But something inside was preventing her from opening it fully.

She pushed against it firmly.

Still it held; but then she managed to open it wide enough. She looked inside.

She saw a light on in the hallway. With another push, she succeeded in opening the door wider. The carpet was thick with blood.

Now she called the station on her radio. 'Bravo Hotel. Two One Four. Bravo Hotel. Two One Four.'

She could just make out the CAD officer's reply, 'Go ahead, Two One Four.'

Assistance required at top flat. Figures three eight. 38 Porchester Road, W2.'

But there was no reply. Trying a second time, she found the transmission still failing. The detachable battery at the base of her Storno radio must have run low.

She prayed there was still enough power in her tape recorder's batteries to record her first impressions of the scene. She began to talk into the recorder:

WPC Helen Cliff. 02.16 hours. Tuesday 25 July. Top Flat, 38 Porchester Road, W2.

Bloodstains to the exterior of the flat by the front door, which is unlocked. I have pushed this open by using my fingertips, only one inch to the left of the brass and china door-handle.

The door is partially blocked by the corpse of a woman in her late twenties, maybe early thirties, slight build, long hair, probably Asian, Chinese, oriental in appearance wearing a heavily bloodstained peach silk nightie with lace trim.

Her eyes are open. There is no sign of corneal reflex.

In the hallway of the flat the walls are extensively spattered with blood. Some is present on the ceiling. Evidence that a violent struggle has taken place. Broken glass. Smashed mirror. Lamp broken on the carpet.

In main living area, further signs of violence. A broken glass-topped table. A television on its side. The curtains are drawn across the windows. Electric lights are on. There are several strong odours, mostly of a woman's scent. I have moved no objects.

For a third time, I have tried to call in to the station to report the incident and failed. I will try a fourth time and if I then fail I will use the telephone in the living area.

In the bedroom there is another corpse.

A naked white male in his thirties on the bed, lying sideways awkwardly, back and rear upwards. It is not immediately possible to see if rigor mortis has set in. I doubt it has.

The body is lying in a great quantity of blood. There are no signs of a murder weapon. But burn marks and perforations to the skin, contusion rings and black rings, indicate the man died from gunshots. There is fresh blood froth around the mouth. There is definitely no sign of a corneal reflex in the eyes. There is a pile of clothing, male and female, beside the bed, also covered in blood.

Face-up, next to a grey pin-striped jacket, is a company Visa card bearing the name L. W. J. Slaemann. Slaemann & Co., Solicitors.

Returning through the flat, in the kitchen, there is a quantity of mail on the window-sill bearing the names Kim Sang Park and Jeong-Kyu Hang.

A quantity of red and white wine has been spilled across the light green carpet.

Several ashtrays are filled with filter cigarette butts, some marked with a coral-red shade of lipstick.

On a second examination of the body I take to be Kim Park Sang or Jeong-Kyu Hang, and viewing the corpse at floor level, it is clear that although dressed in a woman's nightie, the corpse is male.

I have made a fourth attempt (02.25 hours) to report the incident on my mobile and will now use the phone in the living room.

I intend to remain at the crime scene until officers arrive.

WPC Helen Cliff. 02.35 hours, Tuesday 25 July.

Top Flat, 38 Porchester Road, W2.

02.42

The Duty Officer answered her call.

He agreed to send for the CID, the Scene of Crime Officer, and spelled out the address.

02.51

As the police officers arrived, a woman stepped out of the darkened doorway across the street. She was looking towards the main entrance of the block of flats.

The young woman police officer now standing on the pavement had obviously been posted there to prevent unauthorized persons from entering the building.

The woman in the darkened doorway seemed anxious to be gone. She walked some distance up Queensway.

Further up Queensway, the Royal Park Casino doorman was hailing cabs for Arab and Chinese clients.

'Can I get you one, ma'am?' he asked the woman.

'Thank you,' the woman said, and handed him a two-pound tip.

12.30

Nearing London, with Drew driving, Rosslyn asked, 'Did you come up with anything on the Angell woman?'

'Yes. But she must have been using her husband's credit card. The only Angell we located is Chairman and Managing Director of a firm of inquiry agents in Savile Row. I had someone ring their offices. No reply. We ran a 609. Criminal Records have no record of any previous. Nothing.'

'What about the car?'

'It belongs to a solicitor in Mayfair,' she said. 'Judging by his address I doubt he has many legal aid clients.'

Rosslyn's shoulders ached. The painkillers, co-praxamol, had the effect of making him feel light-headed. He found it difficult to concentrate. 'Did I tell you,' he asked, 'about Gaynor?'

'What about him?'

'He told me two SIS people had been to see him.'

'About what?' Drew said, as if she knew the answer.

'About *Celeste*.'

'That doesn't surprise me. It doesn't take a great mind to fathom out what *they* want. What's mine is thine. What's thine is mine.'

'They've been busy.'

'Oh, and they want to see you too, Alan.'

'What are their names?' he asked.

'The man's called McEvoy.'

'That the same one who went to see Gaynor,' he said. 'Who's the other one?'

'A woman called Hughes,' Drew said. 'And they want to see you as soon as possible.'

'Can't they put their chat on hold?' he said.

'I could always ask,' she said. 'Once we've got home.'

'Can't you tell them I'm not in a fit state to answer questions?'

'Look.' She was becoming irritated. 'You can't always expect me to bend the rules just because it suits you.'

'You look. I'm not asking you or anyone else to hold my hand.'

'That's good,' she said, 'because I'm not volunteering. I can tell you, Alan, that they're not pleased. They don't like dead bodies lying around in saunas. Least of all ones they haven't left there themselves. You and I know there are a lot of questions that need answering. And they just happen to be in there first.'

13.15

Their arrival outside Drew's flat at Holland Park was watched by a man and a woman in a Rover parked outside the Greek Embassy.

Some five minutes later, the door-bell to Drew's top-floor flat sounded.

A man's voice came over the entryphone. 'Mrs Franklin?'

'Yes.'

'We called yesterday,' the man said. 'McEvoy and Ms Hughes. May we come up again?'

'This isn't really a very convenient moment,' she said.

'I appreciate that. This need only take five minutes.'

'You'd better come in.'

From behind her, Alan said, 'For Christ's sake, you're not inviting them in, are you?'

'Don't you worry,' she said. 'I can handle them.'

She opened the door to McEvoy. He was a round-shouldered man of medium height with sandy hair greying slightly at the edges, wearing a blazer and the bright tie of a minor public school. His companion, Hughes, an unmemorable woman with a pinched face, smelled strongly of medicated mouthwash. She was carrying a brown envelope marked PLEASE DO NOT BEND.

Rosslyn was on the sofa in the sitting room, and when they came through the door he made to stand up. The effort pained him.

'Please,' said McEvoy, 'don't get up.' He gave Rosslyn a smile of insincerity. 'In the circumstances,' he said, placing his briefcase on the dining-room table, 'I very much appreciate your presence. Rather bad luck. In a lot of pain, are you?'

'It's not too bad,' said Rosslyn. 'Could be worse.'

'Must have been quite a shock,' McEvoy said. 'I should think you're feeling a bit below par, but this won't take too long.'

Hughes passed the brown envelope to McEvoy, who slit it open with a dirty fingernail. 'I'd like you to look at these photographs,' he said. 'Scene-of-crime officers took these last Saturday in Copenhagen. Our friend at the embassy got them from our American colleagues.'

'Are the Americans involved?' Rosslyn asked.

'Are you serious?' said McEvoy. 'Straub may have been an American citizen. But the last thing they want is to be seen to be involved in one of our operations. Correction – *your* operation. Particularly one that's turned out like this. Look at the photographs. See for yourself.'

The photographs, five in all, showed the two corpses in the sauna at Sjaellandsgade 12. Rosslyn set them aside and felt sick.

'I'm sorry we had to do it this way,' McEvoy said. 'But it saves time, doesn't it? You and I both know that you were there. We just wanted to refresh your memory, that's all.'

Rosslyn thought: *I wonder where they dragged you up from.*

McEvoy was doubtless one of C's latest protégés. The new and unattractive face of SIS. The old guard had enjoyed a good innings. Theirs was about the only British institution to have avoided public censure in recent times. Mainly, Rosslyn felt, because no one knew what went on in their secret post-Modernist temple at Vauxhall Cross. McEvoy, like C, was one more hatchet man from the club of the arch, amoral and manipulative. An uneasy truce had been agreed with MI5. SIS mistrusted the route the good old country was taking into the new century. 'Seems appropriate, you know, that Her Majesty's Secret Intelligence Service is housed,' the new C was apt to say to anyone who would listen, 'in *New Century House.*'

McEvoy continued, 'Mr Gaynor's given us something of the background to this operation of yours. But we thought it best to talk to you alone. Although the matter doesn't entirely fall within our operational purview, there are what I believe are nowadays called *areas of interface*. Or, to put it more succinctly, your business is sometimes our business.'

What's mine is thine et cetera, Rosslyn thought. 'I appreciate that,' he said.

'I wonder,' said McEvoy, 'if you really do. Clearing up other people's mess isn't something we take great pleasure in. It costs us time and money and tends to lose us what few real friends we still have abroad.'

'I hear what you say,' said Rosslyn. He held up one of the photographs. 'But this couldn't have been foreseen by anyone.'

'Foresight doesn't seem to be your strongest suit, Mr Rosslyn, does it? Our information is that Straub is by no means the only informant of yours to have left this world in rather unfortunate circumstances.'

This is all I need, thought Rosslyn. *Another public school prat.* 'I suppose even you,' he said, 'lose some people some of the time.'

'Surely,' said McEvoy. 'All of them, all of the time. However, we're here not to discuss *our* operations but yours.'

Rosslyn noticed that Drew was staying silent. He looked across at her. She looked back at him, slightly embarrassed. She said rather too hurriedly, 'Why don't I make some tea?'

'Why don't I help you?' Ms Hughes offered. It was the first time she had spoken. The nasal twang was pure Estuary English. She followed Drew into the kitchen.

'I don't know, Rosslyn, what sort of standards you apply to your work,' said McEvoy, 'exactly what sort of outfit you're really running. Whatever it is, your current investigation, *Celeste*, is causing a large measure of inconvenience. Upsetting the police in Copenhagen may be par for the course in your line of country. But I'm bound to say it isn't in ours.'

'I wouldn't know about your line of country,' said Rosslyn. 'But even we've had our successes. It's a matter of public record. Whereas of course yours isn't, is it?'

'Oh, let me disabuse you,' said McEvoy. 'Where it matters, our record is most certainly seen to be a very successful one indeed. If I were you, I'd cherish yours as a fond memory. Because *Celeste* isn't an operation anyone else is going to remember with much affection, or indeed admiration.'

'It will be very different,' said Rosslyn, 'when I find out who's responsible for what happened in Copenhagen. When I discover who did it. *Who's done what.*'

'Quite honestly, Rosslyn, we don't know *who's done what.* Let's not cry over spilt milk – or should one say blood? Rather a lot of blood, in fact. Let's just leave it with the Danes. We've had to smooth their very ruffled feathers and we're getting sick and tired of running around after you clearing up your mess. I've been sent here by my superiors after a very great deal of discussion. Your name appears with embarrassing frequency on our agendas at Vauxhall Cross. I'll be brutally frank. Our friend at the Copenhagen embassy was considerably underwhelmed by your deeply casual attitude. Insolence is one thing. He put that down to too much alcohol. You and your black woman were knocking it back in front of him. But what really struck him, and by God he's a bloody fine judge of such matters, was your conspicuous lack of gut professionalism. D'you follow? I have to tell you in words of one syllable. Enough's enough.'

'What do you want me to do about it then?' Rosslyn asked.

'I was beginning to wonder when we'd get round to that,' said McEvoy. 'Let me put it in terms that even you can understand.' He drew a finger across his throat. '*Operation Celeste* is dead. Finito. End of story.'

'Who says?'

'My director,' said McEvoy. 'And yours.'

'My boss?' Rosslyn asked. 'She's here. Let's ask her.'

The two women returned from the kitchen with the tea.

'Its kind of you,' McEvoy said. 'But now that Mr Rosslyn understands the position we can call it a day. There's nothing more to add.' He turned to Rosslyn. 'I'll leave the photographs with you as a souvenir. Thank you, Mrs Franklin, we'll see ourselves out. I'm most grateful for your help.'

Which is more than I am, thought Rosslyn.

McEvoy walked to the door and opened it. 'All fit?' he said to Ms Hughes.

She followed him out, closing the door quietly behind her.

Rosslyn turned to Drew. 'You could at least have told me.'

'Told you what?' she said.

'You know what I'm talking about.'

'What?'

'That you'd agreed to abort *Celeste*.'

'I'm sorry,' she said. 'I meant to. But I didn't have the time.'

'You should've made time,' he said. 'You seem to have found time to stitch me up with those creeps.'

His body ached. 'I think I ought to go back to my place,' he said.

'Why not stay here?' she asked.

'No, I need to check my mail and fax.'

'You're not saying I've let you down, Alan, are you?'

'Let's just say I don't think you were a very great help.'

The pain showed in her face.

'Why don't we talk about it later?' she said. 'Oh, and one more thing, Alan. While I remember, your friend Quinceau wants to see you at your flat. Something about a personal matter. I'm sorry I didn't get round to telling you before. She left a message. Said she was calling from a payphone. How did she know you'd be here anyway?'

'I've no idea. Someone must've told her.'

'You're not lying to me?'

'I don't know who told her. What's more, I'm too bloody tired to really care.'

'Well, you'd better get a move on. She's calling at your place at half-past four. So you'd better go to your little bimbo.'

She went to her bedroom and slammed the door.

16.10

Afternoon sun slanted across the front room of Rosslyn's top-floor flat in Eccleston Square.

He fetched a pile of mail from his doormat to the kitchen table. Circulars from estate agents telling him they had received numerous inquiries from clients keen to rent his flat.

A request from the council asking the previous occupant to check his name on the electoral roll. Was he over seventy years of age?

He felt tempted to answer, 'Yes, I feel it.'

There was a letter from Personnel at Customs Head-quarters confirming the time of his personal assessment appointment.

Headed SUBJECT: PROMOTION BOARD, it confirmed the time and date of his Personal Appraisal interview with Dr Claudine Hecht. The psychiatrist's address was in Harley Street.

Copies had been circulated, he noticed. He saw Mr J. Thornley-Miller's name was on the list.

So that was why Thornley-Miller had asked Drew for a private word after the meeting at Custom House. He was competing for Gaynor's job. Yet Drew had said nothing about it.

The light on his answerphone was flashing. There was a message for him from Verity: 'I hope all went well in Copenhagen. Want to see you. So does Daisy. If you want to come over for a bite here, call me. Miss you. Love.'

He was tired; his eyes ached, the lids twitching. When he closed them, tiny yellow flashes appeared. His mind was filled with images from the sauna. Those dead faces. Images of flowing blood merged with Drew's troubled eyes. Verity's voice. The Straub fiasco. The end of *Celeste*. They couldn't have happened at a worse time.

It was the memory of McEvoy that troubled him the most. He had been around the security services long enough to recognize the boot was going in. He'd heard how their officers like McEvoy put the frighteners on you by saying, 'If you don't follow our advice, you really will have to face the consequences to your career. We can't pretend your future will be other than bleak and extremely short.'

Or they adopted a spurious tone of confidentiality and said they trusted you.

'At the end of the day, we're all on the same side. When push comes to shove, we're all in the same boat together.'

Or they confided, 'There are only three sorts of people in the world we inhabit. Number one, us. Number two, them. Number three, fuckers. Best, don't you feel, to dump the rest and stay with Number one, us?'

Then, as a seal of brotherhood, they told you a whole heap of bullshit.

He suspected McEvoy and his superiors at Vauxhall Cross had some personal version of the game and rules of misinformation.

He looked again at the photographs. One thing you could be sure of was that you never got to the whole truth.

He was tired of their games. He had enough to worry about just dealing with the paedophile pornography. Sometimes, as if the brain circuits were overloaded, the memory turned off. Blanked out. It was strange. Maybe, burning out, he had stared at too much horror.

16.30

His doorbell was ringing and went on ringing until he answered the door.

Celeste was standing under a broken umbrella. 'Where have you been, Alan?'

He showed her into his flat.

'You'd better lock and bolt the door,' she said.

'You heard then?'

'About what?' she said.

He told her about the accident.

'I'm sorry,' she said. 'You keep your door locked, Alan. Because I've seen Aiko Holland.'

'How did she take it?'

'She took it badly. She obviously loved him. And she must think a lot of you too. She's been trying to reach you and obviously couldn't. In exchange for giving me this for you, she wants to see you. There's more of the same where this came from.'

'What is it?'

'You read it,' Celeste said. 'Make your own mind up. I have mine. And it looks like shit to me.'

She handed him a slim brown envelope. It was dog-eared from the rain.

'You read it while I make tea,' Celeste said. She breathed in deeply. 'God, this place stinks. I'd no idea you lived in such a pit.'

'What's wrong with it?'

'You need a decent woman in your life.'

'I've reached much the same conclusion.'

'About bloody time.'

'While you're about it,' he said, handing her the envelope containing the photographs of the Copenhagen bloodbath, 'take a took at these.'

He sat at the kitchen table and began to read the contents of the envelope Celeste had brought.

16.40

There was a short covering note to the letter, dated Monday 24 July and bearing the address and telephone number of a Geneva bank.

In Confidence
Dear Ms Holland,
We have been requested by our late client, Mr Morton Damm of Eurotel Guides, 8–9 Shibaura, Minato-ku, Tokyo, in the event of his death, to forward by means of telefax the following letter to you in confidence and are pleased to do so.
Sincerely yours

It was signed in a tidy hand by a Dr Mauro Gagliardini.
   Rosslyn read the letter:

                    Eurotel Guides
                      8–9 Shibaura
                       Minato-ku
                        Tokyo

Aiko,

If you receive this letter it will be the end product of a deal I've been making for Rosslyn of UK Customs. This letter means I have not been able to obtain the information he requested, or if I have, that I have been prevented from passing it to him. I'm sending this via you because I imagine UK Customs are as unreliable as their other outfits. Rosslyn's okay, I think. He's working with a black woman, Celeste Quinceau. I'd say she's good.

I want Rosslyn to know that I believe the name

he should be looking at is that of a man called Angell with whom I have had dealings in recent times. He needs to know the details of his background if he's to understand the extent of the threat Angell poses to him. Depending on how up to date you are, I guess you can vouch for some of it.

Angell's been hired by a person or persons who've acted informally with great effect, from time to time, on behalf of SIS to collect sensitive political intelligence. Both in the Middle East and, to a major and very sensitive extent, at top level in Washington. Friends of SIS too, as well as London lawyers, have used him to considerable benefit. Angell trades on his reputation for being both conservative and discreet. That's what we'd expect, of course, from a former MI5 man. He'd still have been with them except he retired voluntarily to establish his own outfit. He's well known to SIS.

He has a finger in Rosslyn's operation <u>Celeste</u>. He will remember Kim Sang Park a.k.a. Jeong-Kyu Hang. Angell is Park's lover.

<u>But more importantly you have to tell Rosslyn</u> <u>that Angell has received a commission to</u> <u>terminate Operation Celeste.</u>

Rosslyn paused. His hands were shaking.

What game had Straub been playing?

He looked at the end of the letter: 'Love to you. Believe me. Sincerely, Jack.' Straub's style all right.

This, for Rosslyn's record, is the sum total of my intelligence on him. He needs the full psychological profile of Angell. It's based on an FBI file. He checked me out. I had him checked out.

Angell is a professional killer, a man Rosslyn's people would be wiser to avoid. Tell him, if it helps, that his name isn't Angell at all. He was born Howard Barry Batten.

The FBI told me that SIS once briefly considered Angell/Batten on the basis of an Oxford recruiter's recommendation. They turned him down as a potential candidate. They also sacked the recruiter who'd put his name forward.

I want you to have Rosslyn expose him for what he is. Mainly the background you must give him is this:

Angell (Howard Barry Batten) was born in Great Yarmouth, Norfolk, UK, on 20 February 1955. An only child, his parents were lapsed Roman Catholics. His father worked as a packer in a fish wholesalers, his mother as a hotel cleaner. A childhood tragedy was a significant and determining factor in his psychological make-up. He once told me that a school playground incident was the reason for the loss of his left thumb. After his recovery, in revenge he attacked one of his assailants and tormentors, a schoolgirl, and was removed from school and the Great Yarmouth area, and taken into care in Norwich.

You can skip the record of the father's convictions for GBH and the mother's alcoholism, her remarriage to a man who was found guilty of persistent child abuse. The young

Batten (Angell) had been one of Mrs Batten's second husband's victims.

As a result of his grandmother's influence, he had the idea of entering a seminary to train for the priesthood. But he elected not to, because he sought, so he said, to provide financially for his grandmother's old age. Which, according to this version, was about the only good thing Angell ever tried to do.

During his secondary education, either his good looks or his precocious intelligence, or both, found favour with a pair of teachers who taught English and put on amateur dramatics. He won a place at Balliol, Oxford, going up in October 1974 to read English. There he cheated his way to a degree in 1977. With the assistance of a married homosexual tutor, whom he blackmailed, he remained in Oxford, where he read for a B.Litt. in sixteenth-century English literature. His studies were incomplete when his grandmother died. Distressed, he left Oxford in 1979.

Whilst up at Oxford he showed a somewhat unusual, if not morbid, interest in forensic science, in human and animal anatomy. He took a part-time interdisciplinary veterinary and human anatomy course at Oxford Polytechnic, during which he specialized in dissection. He also joined the Officer Training Corps and was commissioned into the General List of the Territorial Army Volunteer Reserve on 7 September 1978.

His references for this commission read favourably enough.

They said he showed no ideological or political interests. A marked degree of mental stability. They said he was trustworthy. Had a conspicuous streak of puritanism about him. Not a reckless man. Highly self-disciplined. He used to spend a lot of time alone testing his capability for endurance and survival in the countryside of Wales and North Yorkshire. Batten was a solitary man who liked to test the limits of his mental and physical prowess. He showed a rather cold mind and a ruthless approach to his work. For a time he was a prison visitor at HM Prison Oxford and befriended a transsexual recidivist.

During his career at Oxford he applied for appointment as an administration trainee in the Home Civil Service and attended the Civil Service Selection Board (CSSB) in 1977, but met with no success. His failure was the result of doubts about his intellectual or academic abilities rather than qualities of character.

His cognitive tests and written work at CSSB were somewhat below average. The Board did not feel he was up to the required standard. Batten apparently considered himself in general terms, in name and in manner, to be socially inferior. At some point he changed his name by deed poll to Gerald Richard Denis ANGELL. A contact at Oxford, Dr F. G. Harvey Lawrence of St Antony's College, suggested him as a possible recruit for the Security Service.

Batten, now ANGELL, was invited to an exploratory meeting at the Oxford and Cambridge Club in Pall Mall in November 1978. A more formal interview followed later in

November, conducted by the director of personnel branch, the head of staff management section, and the recruiting officer. He impressed the board with his charm and personability. He was considered to be prima facie suitable and eight written references were therefore requested.

These references included the headmaster of St Mary's High School, Great Yarmouth, Norfolk, where Angell had attended; the Registrar of Great Yarmouth and District General Hospital, where he had been employed as an assistant in the mortuary between school and university; the Master of Balliol; his supervisor while he worked towards the degree of B. Litt.; and the Librarian and lecturer in English language and literature at Balliol (both deceased); as well as four additional referees, all suggested by Angell himself as individuals who had known him well for more than eight years.

All the references suggested Angell was a suitable candidate for the security service. He was then positively vetted, invited to another interview conducted by two MI5 directors and an assistant director, and told he should attend a final appointments board once he had reached the age of 25. MI5 were aware he had failed a CSSB but this was not held to diminish his potential as a candidate for recruitment.

For about a year unaccompanied he travelled extensively in Scandinavia and later South America, particularly in Brazil. His recruiting officer kept in regular touch with him, as far as was possible, by letter.

While Angell was in Brazil, a recruiter, Dr Ricardo Luis de Moraes, suggested him as a candidate for recruitment to SIS. Accordingly, Angell was introduced to the Visa Officer and Second Secretary at HM Embassy Brasilia, Mrs Anne Davie-Chisholm.

SIS inquiries suggested he was frequenting clubs in Rio, in various degrees of disguise, with a transsexual prostitute with known underworld and vice connections.

Not surprisingly, if you refer back to my remarks about his time as a prison visitor, it was further established that Angell was living with the transsexual prostitute in rented accommodation in a Rio suburb.

When confronted by Mrs Davie-Chisholm, Angell emphatically denied his associations. He also wrote to his security service recruiting officer in London denying them, and he threatened a course of legal action unless he received a written apology.

No such apology was made. And it was agreed that the record of the suggestions about Angell's personal proclivities and choice of friends be filed. No further approach was made to him; no further contact with him was established whilst he was in South America. The services of Dr de Moraes were discontinued.

On return to the United Kingdom he appeared before the final security service appointment board and a conditional offer of appointment was made to him. The PV field inquiries were favourable. He passed a medical examination.

The missing thumb was not held to be a disability that would disqualify him.

After induction training, the first period of his career was spent studying the Communist Party of Great Britain. Then he attended the nineteen-week course for intelligence officers, both MI5 and SIS, in Portsmouth. Again, he performed well.

His appointment was finally confirmed in September 1983. Thereafter he worked variously in sections dealing with counter-terrorism and training. It was during this period that he decided, apparently for financial reasons, to resign from the security service and seek employment on his own account as a security or inquiry agent in the private sector to make much more money.

He undertook confidential inquiries with some success on behalf of Beattie Electronics, Coventry; Kingfisher Percy, Solicitors, Windsor; mainly for Slaemann, Solicitors, Brook Street, Mayfair, London, whom Rosslyn should check out. Santander Financial Investigations, London WC1; Stoll Associates, London W1; and various private commissions made through RFA, Rafael Film Agency, of Los Angeles and New York City. He was known to travel widely in the United States, Eastern and Western Europe, the Middle and Far East, and Australasia.

I first met him in Copenhagen in 1992. He was introduced to me by two separate sources: BfV and DGSE agents. Subsequently we met with an FBI officer from the US Embassy, London.

Between 1992 and 1994, reports were received from:

   MOSSAD: Tel Aviv, Israel (Central Institute for Intelligence and Special Duties)

   DGSE: Paris (Direction Générale de la Sécurité Extérieure)

   BfV: Cologne, Germany (Bundesamt für Verfassungsschutz)

   PSIA: Tokyo, Japan (Public Security Investigation Agency)

that Angell had acted for terrorist organizations and/or support groups including:

   PFLP-SC (Popular Front for the Liberation of Palestine Special Command)

   AD (Action Directe)

   BK (Babbar Khalsa: Sikh)

   C-H (Chukaku-Ha: Nucleus or Middle Core Faction)

Surveillance and counter-surveillance officers in the United States, Europe, the Middle and Far East, reported that his commissions involved:

- the highly successful linked acquisition and sale of secret and major criminal intelligence.
- the blackmail of two international industrialists, three prominent members and contributors to religious movements and established churches.
- compromise of two figures in the world of international film and entertainment.
- murder of key informants, intelligence agents, trial witnesses and US law-enforcement officers.

Rosslyn should know that I let Angell think I was short of funds. That I needed new commissions.

You at US Customs wanted me to find out his agenda.

I wanted to offer him a name. Then the Visa Officer at the British Embassy, Copenhagen, approached me with a deal. He wanted the same intelligence as Angell. Maybe they were working in tandem. You know how it is. All kinds of names show up along the line. Some you believe in, some you don't.

One name showed: VRATSIDES the financier, of AVI London and NYC. The material Rosslyn impounded at Felixstowe originated with Vratsides. It went to WATIYAH, the diplomat who's in Tripoli. I believe Vratsides somehow paid him off.

I offered him some of this. Angell said he wasn't in business for this kind of sleaze. But he said if and when he was, he'd come back to me. I contacted him twice more, made an offer. I told him I was certain Vratsides was as guilty as shit. The man is a personal friend of the UK Prime Minister and the Royal Family. He's even been their weekend guest. He's also a friend of the US President. I told Angell he'd be out of his mind not to sell this on to Rosslyn.

Why didn't I sell it straight to Rosslyn then? Because I wasn't completely sure. I had to know I could nail Vratsides for the Brits. So I went back to the Lund/Copenhagen connection. Contacted Rosslyn.

Tell Rosslyn to keep Celeste red active on his own account. Pursue it. I hinted to him that if he needs to check this out he should contact you.

I don't need to tell him to watch his back. You too, even. Maybe also his assistant, Quinceau.

Something I must add. Rosslyn once asked me for my real name. Tell him it's Holland, that you and I were once married.

I don't have a claim on you, or Rosslyn, I know. But if something unpleasant happens to me, I'd like to feel that you could rely on him for support. I don't have to tell you that I've cut a few corners in my time. I'm sorry, but I'm not sorry. You're straight. I caused you a few headaches as a husband. But you're entitled not to have any more aggravation on my account.

This letter, as you'd say yourself, is just by way of being a precaution.

> Love to you.
> Believe me.
> Sincerely,
> Jack

16.55

'I took the liberty of cleaning up your kitchen,' Celeste was saying. She set two mugs of tea on the table. 'This man Vratsides,' she was asking. 'Who is he?'

Rosslyn's copy of *Who's Who*, junked by archives at Custom House, was a year out of date.

He turned up the Vratsides entry and read it out to Celeste.

VRATSIDES, Sir Achilles Elias Dimitri, Kt 1990; Chairman AVI; V–Two Corporation, Los Angeles. b 14 April 1932; s of Aristotle Vratsides and Katie Politis; m 1st, 1954 Calliope Arvanitis (d 1956); 2nd 1975 Giselle Hammond Cunningham, one s. *Educ.* University of Athens, London School of Economics. *Publications*: London: A New Heart for England, 1993; contributions to learned journals. *Recreations*: cinematography, photography. *Address*: c/o AVI 222 Capodistra Street, Athens 147, Greece. *Clubs*: Athenaeum. Traveller's (Paris).

'That's the name he was going to give me,' said Rosslyn. 'Vratsides. Or so he says in the letter. The trouble was, he tried to be too clever by half. He knew too much. He's got himself killed. He could've got me killed. The net result is that I'm being shat on from a great height. And *Operation Celeste* is being closed down. See, it's here in his letter. He knew this Angell was highly dangerous. But what does he do? Keeps it to himself. And then he tries to play the Lone bloody Ranger.'

'Aren't you being a bit rough on him, Alan? After all, the poor bastard's dead, isn't he?'

'You think I'm being rough on him? All I know is that if I'd been there in that sauna a few minutes earlier we wouldn't be talking here and now. What smartarses like Straub never realize is that the shortest distance between two points is a straight line. Which is quite a good way of putting it, I think.'

'He may not have been much good at geometry. But you ought to try to be fair to him. He was trying to warn you.'

'I'm not interested in being sentimental about this. I've sweated blood over *Celeste*.'

'I know.'

'So have you. And thanks to his convoluted efforts at free enterprise, the operation is as dead as he is, along with Phan Van Quan. Now he's telling me that this Angell has a commission to kill me too.'

'Are you sure it was Angell who killed him?'

'What do I know? Listen, I called Drew about that woman I saw near Gaynor's place. The one with the rifle. Is this Angell's wife, or lover, or what? Who is she? Why would she have that credit card? Angell's sort wouldn't make that mistake in a month of Sundays. They might have your credit card. But they wouldn't be using their own. Then there's this Vratsides. What's his game? Look at the background. Friends in high places. Oh yes, we've heard that before. Royal bloody Family. Prime Minister. US President. Terrific. Straub must have taken leave of his senses. Look at what he says: "I had to

know I could nail Vratsides for the Brits." Well, hooray for
him. Why couldn't he have just done what I asked him to do?
Instead of which he gets himself up to here in shit with
Angell. And these people are on the loose. Either Angell or
Vratsides is looking for us right now. Thank you very much.
What else has he given us? Slaemann. Solicitors. Brook Street.
Bloody Mayfair. Why didn't he sell the info to me in the first
place?'

'Why don't you get Verity to check out those connections
with MOSSAD and the rest?'

'She won't do that.'

'Won't or can't?'

'Both. And now we have Drew in all her imperial majesty
backing SIS's intention to put the brakes on. Am I right or am
I right?'

'You mean wrong.'

'No, I don't. I mean I am *right*. They're covering Vratsides's
arse.'

'You're joking. They can't be. For Christ's sake, the man's a
piece of filth.'

'If what Straub says is true. And that could be one big if. I
mean, if there's a single untruth, one deception, however
minor, one bluff. Then, if we act on any of this, we'll be
crucified. Let me check this thing with the Italian. The one
who sent it. What's his face – Gagliardini? Whoever he is
when he's at home. I want to call Gaynor at his place.'

17.15

'What d'you mean,' said Gaynor on the telephone, ' "*you'd
better keep your doors locked*"? What makes you think this
letter's on the level? You know yourself that Straub was
about as trustworthy as shit. Never mind *his* names. What
names have *you* got?'

'Let's not talk about it on the phone, Chief.'

'What do you want me to do then?'

'Just take my word for it.'

'Why should I, Alan?'

'Because I've just been on the phone to this Italian, Dr Gagliardini.'

'Who is he?'

'The man from the Geneva bank who forwarded the letter. I called him at his office in Geneva.'

'Why should we believe *him*?'

'Because he says he's prepared to sign a statement, if it comes to court. He's prepared to swear that the letter's straight.'

'Sweet Jesus Christ,' said Gaynor. 'You're prepared to believe some Italian banker you've never even met? What, have you gone soft in the head? I worry about you, Alan. An Italian. *Mamma Mia*.'

The Sea Captain, committed Freemason, always on the level and always on the square. He had a profound if irrational dislike for all Catholics and Continentals.

'I believe Jack Straub,' said Rosslyn.

'He's dead.'

'I know.'

'So why not leave it, as we've been told to do?' said Gaynor. 'With SIS. This one's so bloody iffy, why not let those buggers have it on a plate? With a bit of luck, it'll go sour on them. And they'll be the ones with egg all over their revolting faces.'

'Because this one's my baby, Chief. I set it up. I want a result. If Straub's letter's on the up and up, I'm going to nail this man Vratsides. I don't care who his friends are.'

'So you're prepared to proceed on the basis of your dead informant's letter?'

'What else can I do?' said Rosslyn.

'Listen to me, Alan. The only language informants understand is money. If you've got this for free, it's a worry. It could be bogus, or it could be straight.'

'Right then, what do I tell Drew?'

'I don't want to spoil your illusions,' Gaynor said. 'But the fact is she's really double-pleased about Straub's death. It's given her the get-out. Think about it. She didn't fight SIS very hard, did she? What did she say to me? I'll tell you. She said to me, "Enough's enough. If you've no substantial objections, the Straub files should be destroyed in the usual manner along with whatever records of our dealings with him. I see no reason for us to preserve the history of our mistakes." That's what she told me, Alan. I'm just surprised she hasn't got on to you yet.'

'Well, I'm not all that surprised, Chief. The files are your territory. Are you telling me we've been told to back off the fucking paedophiles, the porn business, after everything we've achieved? Listen to me, Chief.'

'I'm listening. And I'm sorry, Alan. You'd better speak to Drew yourself. She's made her position plain to me. She told me, "If the end of *Celeste* means a few paedophiles are allowed to roam out there on the loose a little longer, then so be it. Let's leave it to the police. The Investigation Division has to return to established and traditional procedural basics. Man-hours to be accounted for. Foreign travel restricted. That's what Whitehall wants. That's what Whitehall's going to get." ' He paused. 'I'm not trying to be crass about this, Alan, or insensitive. But have you two had a falling-out or something?'

'I'm talking business.'

'So am I. So's Ms Franklin.' He mimicked her voice. ' "I'm afraid altogether the harder part is that the powers-that-be want success and, I'm sorry, we can't disguise the fact that *Celeste* is an unmitigated disaster." '

'That's balls, Chief,' Rosslyn said.

'That's a perfectly understandable reaction from an emotional, subjective point of view.'

'It's my *objective* view,' Rosslyn said.

'I don't want to argue semantics with you, Alan. What is clear to me is that what you've been through has got to you. It would have got to me too. It must have been pretty traumatic, I should think. In the old days, if I'd have been you and that had happened, I'd have disappeared somewhere with six bottles of Scotch. Nowadays, I suppose it's all Sister's caring and counselling. Anyway, you've still got your Promotion Board, Alan. Have you arranged the preliminaries? Aren't you supposed to see a shrink, or something?'

'Claudine Hecht, that's right. They've given me an appointment.'

'Then forget *Celeste*. Make a success of your Promotion Board. Nothing comes easy.' The same old platitudes from the Sea Captain.

'Chief, just what would persuade you to back me?'

He heard Gaynor laugh. 'Shall I tell you something?'

'I have the feeling you're about to.'

'You'd better believe it. Let's put it this way, all I've got is my pension. With you it's different. You're still young. Compared to me, you've only just begun. You've as much to lose by reopening *Celeste* as I have. We can't afford to be wrong.'

'Who says I'm wrong, Chief? I've never known you chuck your hand in. Why should you expect me to? Just in case you're interested, I don't want a future where I'm licking arses just to survive. I don't believe you're worried about your pension. Now listen to me. I've never asked you to do anything for me before, have I?'

Gaynor was silent.

'Well, I'm asking you now.'

Another silence.

'Are you there, Chief?'

'I am here, Mr Rosslyn. What is it you are asking me?'

'I am asking you to be in your office at eight tomorrow morning. Because I need to fight my enemies on the inside before I deal with those outside. Zero eight hundred hours, tomorrow Wednesday, Chief?'

'Tell me,' Gaynor said, 'how are those bruises, Mr Rosslyn?'

'Never mind my bruises. They're terrible.'

'Sorry I asked,' Gaynor said. 'I always was a soft touch. I'll be there, Mr Rosslyn.'

17.20

Going private is the euphemism for the Customs Investigation Officer's decision to approach intelligence sources in the private sector. These *int. sources*, along with a few investigative newspaper and television journalists, are the men and women executives in the fast-expanding private intelligence and security industry.

Int. sources: the inquiry agents work in an industry which has grown with such rapidity that firms conform to a wide range of definitions, be they detective agencies, security consultancies or credit investigation services. Sometimes they consist of no more than one man or woman operating freelance. Often from a bed-sit equipped with just an answerphone, camera and tape recorder. Old-fashioned gumshoes for hire to suspicious wives tailing husbands dodging in and out of hotels in King's Cross or Bayswater.

The grandest, most reputable and effective do not appear in Yellow Pages. Like Argen Limited of Jubilee Place; Kroll Associates UK Limited of Savile Row; Saladin Security Limited of Abingdon Road; or the Intercontinental Group Limited (IG) of Berkeley Square; their commissions are mainly undertaken as the result of word of mouth. GRDA Associates of Savile Row, also absent from the Yellow Pages, was believed to enjoy a reputation that matched its peers.

Going private or GP (or as the Sea Captain called it, 'SCTTW' – 'Sailing Close To The Wind') is not a process an investigation officer like Rosslyn seeks. In any circumstances, approval has to be obtained from superiors reluctant to jeopardize their own careers. Nevertheless, unwritten law allows that if all else fails, GP may be used as a last resort.

More often GP is used to gain background *int.* on Middle Eastern targets. The embargoed sale of arms to Iraq during the Gulf War is said to have been a case in point. Money does not, of course, change hands between *int. sources* and Customs & Excise investigation officers. Rather, payment is made as a favour; a favour to be banked in exchange for *int. dirt* on the national and international great and good at some future date. Sometimes a *small fee* is paid for various high-risk favours the security services require. *A little dirty work* they don't wish to do themselves.

Like the *small fee* paid for the apparent afternoon suicide in a West London hotel room in the days of arms-to-Iraq (*murder by a hotel cleaner, an illegal Filipino immigrant*), covered by the hurried issue of a Public Interest Immunity certificate double-signed by the Home and Foreign Secretaries. There had been a sunset drowning of the Iraqi agent among tourists on a Spanish beach. Rather too much alcohol had been found in the balding Iraqi's blood (*fellow-bathers held the victim too long beneath the surface in a game of sex*). The M40 motorway cremation of the gay squealer from GCHQ in his early-morning car collision with road repair vehicles. (*The warning cones were being positioned by two sub-agents temporarily employed by the contractors. The charred human remains hauled from the burning wreckage identified from the dental records.*) Another GP case in point was the information Rosslyn had gained on the Libyan, Jadallah A. Watiyah of Neuilly-sur-Seine, which had led to the diplomat's early-morning arrest last 4 March in Sloane Street in the early days of *Operation Celeste*.

Rosslyn had been scrupulous in protecting his source, Douglas Milo of IG. *Int.* had finally led to Watiyah's exposure as a paedophile. He had to be. If word got round that you weren't protecting your sources, inquiry agents became inexplicably busy. He had therefore made no mention of Milo in the *Celeste* report. Milo had a series of photographs taken of Watiyah. Outwardly a devout Muslim, the pictures showed him drinking heavily in a bar in St Martin's Lane with a homeless youth who looked no more than twelve years of age. Milo's contacts in the DGSE, the French secret service, has also come up with the Libyan's CV and the extent of his considerable importance to the Tripoli regime.

In return, Rosslyn had given Milo both the numbers and current bank statements of five Belgian and Italian business-men. Details of their deposits accounts in Geneva and Lugano banks.

Later Milo had taken Rosslyn for dinner at Green's Restaurant & Oyster Bar, owned by his friend Simon Parker Bowles, erstwhile brother-in-law to Camilla. There he had told him that the *'Lugano int.'* helped a Saudi client to bring off the highly advantageous purchase of a chemical plant on the outskirts of Turin. The Saudi had been saved almost $90 million. Milo said, 'I've received my end as well. Any time you need my help, old thing, my time of day is your time of day.'

Milo, thought Rosslyn, had been born with a silver spoon in his mouth. He'd never known quite how dirty Milo's spoon could get. Some questions were better left unasked.

He called IG to ask Milo for his time of day.

17.25

'Got a name?' Milo drawled.

'Two,' said Rosslyn. 'Vratsides and Angell.'

'I see. Can't talk now. If it's either of those shits you've just mentioned, you'd better drop in fast.'

17.50

Sprawled back in his chair, Duggie Milo loosened his frayed Old Etonian tie. In his early thirties, he was unusually tall with very long, slightly bowed legs. A photograph on the wall behind his desk showed him at the Guards Polo Club with the Prince of Wales. As an IG Managing Director, Milo oversaw the major cases in *crisis management* and *malicious product tampering*. He'd once been locked up for a month in Colombia. On a kidnap and ransom case, one of his sub-agents had mistakenly told the Bogotá police to arrest the wrong person. Otherwise, Milo's career had been one of the most successful in the business.

Rosslyn watched Milo biting his nails as he read the letter from Straub at speed, then looked at the photographs of the corpses in the Copenhagen sauna.

'Your friend Straub,' Milo said, 'I don't know him.' He interspersed his comments with short sniffs as if he were checking off an inventory of distasteful junk. 'Or Mrs Holland. Gagliardini I don't know either. But his bank is one of the more respectable ones. Not as watertight as Lombard Odier in Geneva. But it'll do.'

He flicked over the pages.

'Angell frankly gives dishonesty a bad name. I suppose there is a possibility that he might rub you out. I wonder if friend Straub's game was to get you to settle an old score on his behalf. One can't vouch for the American's reliability. Park or Hang, the slit-eyed rice queen, sounds dreadful. Happy to say I've never heard of him either, or should one say *her*?'

He unfastened the staple from the top left corner of the pages, then spread them out on his desk in a row. 'Most, if not all, of what your man says about Angell's life and times is pretty well right. I do know he's proved extremely hard to nail down in the recent past.'

He reread a page.

'What interests me is how very detailed an account of Angell's past is given here. It seems to me that Straub was determined to convince you of Angell's extreme unpleasant- ness. It's rather as though Straub was *desperate* to convince you, don't you feel?'

'He has now,' said Rosslyn.

'So I see,' Milo said. 'It wouldn't surprise me one bit if, in spite of what MI6 or even 5 said, they'd kept Angell dangling. It depends on who's been running the shit. There'll be no mention of him on their books in *this* case. Not in an official way. You'd best follow the smart money. Who's he working for?'

He held up one page of the letter. 'And here we are. Leonard Slaemann. Met him at the Garrick once or twice. Perfectly reputable firm. But Slaemann struck me as a bit of a bore. Rather a High Church sort. Read law at Balliol. Same generation as Angell probably.'

He turned to the list of Angell's commissions reported by the several foreign secret intelligence agencies.

'Some of these I can vouch for,' Milo said. 'But not the final one. "The murder of key informants . . ." and so forth. Here again, I doubt you'll get much joy out of 6 as far as the Copenhagen Visa Officer chappie's concerned. They won't admit to anything. So that deals with Angell. Rather you than me, Alan. I'd watch your step.'

He leaned a long way back in his chair. 'Vratsides is a different kettle of fish.'

'Tell me,' Rosslyn said.

'All I can tell you about Vratsides that's new is that recently he's lost very large sums of money indeed. That's to say, he's nowhere near as loaded as he once was. There was some rumour in Liechtenstein that he might even be on the verge of going down the slot altogether. And I heard it again, only a week or two ago, from a friend in Vienna who'd seen Vratsides in Nassau drinking with some pretty unsavoury characters. There is an argument for saying that he might be trying to recoup his losses by top-level trading in smut. I know as well as you do that there's big money in it. Though whether or not he actually practises sex with children is a matter I wouldn't know about. I'd have thought he might have shown up in Manila, or Bangkok, Chiang-Mai even. There again, there's a crackdown out there on that sort of thing, isn't there?'

'Of a limited kind,' Rosslyn said. 'A few cases pending against foreign tour operators. Nothing much more than that.'

'But of course, that is what you might call, to coin a phrase, the fag end of the trade. Now let's look at his connections.'

'Was Straub right?' Rosslyn asked.

'Yes, absolutely,' Milo said. 'To save you a lecture, I telephoned my brother-in-law at *The Times* to see how their obituary people rate him. Vratsides was taken quite ill a year or two ago. They thought he'd snuff it. So they keep his obit up to date.'

With a slight smile, he handed Rosslyn the draft pages faxed from *The Times* during the last hour.

THE TIMES

OBITUARY

SIR ACHILLES VRATSIDES

Sir Achilles Vratsides, investment adviser, philanthropist and art collector, died in xxxx, on xxxx aged xx. A British citizen, he was born in Parga, Greece, on 14 April 1932.

SIR ACHILLES VRATSIDES amassed one of the greatest Anglo-American private fortunes of modern times. A naturalized Briton since 1958, during the 1970s he built up a privately owned investment management company in New York to which he gave his name, Achilles Vratsides Investments. The success of AVI, as it was known, not only established it as a major force in international finance, but also achieved vast returns for its many private clients on both sides of the Atlantic as well as in the Middle and Far East.

Always an intensely private man, of good looks and persuasive charm, Sir Achilles Vratsides was born in Parga, the son of a fisherman. He left home when he was 19, took a master's degree in political science and economics at Athens

University followed by postgraduate studies at the London School of Economics. In 1959 he joined the Wall Street stockbrokers Pagnall Bruce Toddeson Inc. and in 1976, backed by private investors, he established AVI, the Netherlands Antilles based fund management company that would make his fortune. The company's substantial earnings from management fees were further augmented by shrewd reinvestment. The one blemish to his record occurred in 1987 when, amid a climate of increased Wall Street legislation, he was fined by the Commodity Commission for violations in the trading of financial derivatives.

Slim in stature, vigorous and fit, Sir Achilles, an habitué of spas, was an avowed teetotaller and non-smoker. Always immaculately dressed, he was a committed Anglophile, courteous and somewhat detached in manner. He was fluent in seven languages.

Alongside his considerable business activities, Sir Achilles was also extremely active in charitable work and contributed significantly to many child welfare programmes in developing countries. He was also co-founder, with his wife Lady Giselle, of the aid agency World Child Survival and it was as much for this philanthropic work as for his achievements in commerce that he was knighted in 1990.

As AVI expanded, so its capital growth enabled Sir Achilles to implement a policy of massive diversification. AVI became especially active in developing countries with investment programmes directed at social, medical and engineering projects. These were often achieved in collaboration with the International Finance Corporation, the World Bank's private sector arm, and it was during this period that AVI's assets reached the billion-dollar level. It was also at this time, from his office in Washington, that Sir Achilles consolidated his relationships with the US Treasury and State Department and became a frequent guest at the White House, where he was held in high regard.

Similarly, in his adopted home of the United Kingdom he and his wife Lady Giselle, a long-standing friend of the Prime Minister's wife, were both frequent guests at Downing Street and Chequers. Sir Achilles acted informally as a private adviser on international monetary affairs to both the Prime Minister and the Chancellor. Indeed, his closeness to both

Westminster and Washington gave him a crucial albeit unofficial role in restoring and repairing damage to the 'special relationship' in the early 1990s.

In 1992, he was one of several speculators who exploited the British government's decision to defend the level of the pound in the European Exchange Rate Mechanism. At the time this stratagem was reputed to have earned him profits in the region of £900 million. The decision of the British government to devalue the pound cost the British taxpayer over six billion dollars. Sir Achilles was one of several major offshore investment managers whose identities were not revealed. It is perhaps a measure of the esteem and affection in which he was held by the Prime Minister that this raid on the British pound did little to diminish their close personal friendship.

Although he consistently sought anonymity in both international financial and philanthropic circles, he recently published a series of CD-ROMs in which he outlined his democratic socialist views for the regeneration of inner cities in Europe. In *London: A New Heart for England* he advocated a philosophy of strong self-help, urging politicians 'to put the Great back into Britain'. He expressed the view 'that the British are all too willing to sell themselves short' and attacked what he felt was 'a sinister wave of cancerous cynicism in the British media that persistently assaults the notable strengths of the British character to be found in the Armed Forces, Diplomatic Services, the Arts and the British sense of humour and fair play'. His views were widely applauded by leading figures of all political parties, leading architects and designers, and to Sir Achilles's apparent pride were frequently cited by the Prince of Wales as exemplary.

A lifelong and committed socialist and a generous supporter of the Greek Orthodox Church in London, he was intolerant of those who found contradictions between his beliefs and the complex financial affairs of AVI which dominated his life. In a rare interview, he revealed that the epitaph he would prefer was 'This man's vision served the world's children and mankind.'

He divided his life between his many homes: a mansion in Newport, Rhode Island; a town house in Georgetown, Washington, DC; an estate in Greece near Kardamyli in the

Mani; an eighteenth-century Parisian villa in Neuilly-sur-Seine; a villa at Malibu, California; and a luxurious home overlooking Kensington Palace in London, where he housed arguably one of the finest and most comprehensive collections of documentary films and photographs in the world.

For several years he was variously a Trustee of the British Museum, Victoria and Albert Museum and the National Gallery. He was especially proud to be allowed his own entry pass to these institutions, which he was said frequently to visit at night with a favoured companion. He was also a Governor of the British Film Institute and a Member of Council of the Royal College of Art.

In 1986, he privately commissioned the construction of a digital scanner to develop special effects technology in film production. V-Two, a small company in Los Angeles, offered digital film-scanning services to major television and film production companies.

?? (At the time of his death, Sir Achilles was planning a substantial move into film, television and electronic publishing in the United Kingdom, and his close acquaintance with leading figures in the British film industry and the Chairman and several governors of the BBC had led to proposals for a children's film and television channel, BBC AVTV.)

With his autistic son Elias, he shared a fascination for helicopter design and aerial photography, and he was the holder of a helicopter pilot's licence.

In recent years, Sir Achilles and the Vratsides family were regular weekend guests of the Royal Family.

Lady Giselle, one of the most accomplished cooks in the modern Italian style, held many parties at their Kensington home. At these memorable events leading artists, architects and writers mingled with ministers and politicians of several persuasions and diplomats from many countries; all were invited to bring their children, of whom Lady Giselle, a talented and prolific amateur cinematographer, would make charming family records.

His first wife, Calliope, predeceased him. He married secondly Giselle Hammond Cunningham, the former fashion model, in 1975.

?? (He is survived by his widow, Lady Giselle, and their son, Elias.)

18.25

Rosslyn asked Milo why MI6 was showing so much interest in *Celeste*.

Milo said, 'Could be anything.'

'Could they be behind my boss's intention to abort *Celeste*?'

'More than probable,' said Milo, 'given Vratsides's sphere of influence.'

For a time, the discussion went round in circles. From Straub to Vratsides. From Vratsides to Angell. And then, full circle, back to Rosslyn and Drew and the Copenhagen photographs.

'It may sound over-cautious, Duggie,' Rosslyn said, 'but I'm worried about these photos. I can't fathom out why MI6, who never do anyone any favours, should be so forthcoming. They have to be very keen to protect someone or something to have shown them to me. Are we talking Vratsides or even someone else?'

'Who knows?' said Milo. 'You can't exactly waltz into Vauxhall Cross and ask. But if you could let me hang on to these here, there's an assistant director of ours down the corridor who may be able to get us an opinion.' He lifted a telephone. 'Kasuo? Come in a minute, would you?'

He turned to Rosslyn. 'Write her name down, would you? Kasuo Satomura.' He started to clean his nails with a bent paper clip. 'Then I'd begin on the doorstep, if I were you. It's only a short walk to Slaemann's offices. Get him to talk to you. He might even level with you about Angell.'

'And Vratsides?'

'He's different.'

Kasuo Satomura came into the office silently.

'Kasuo,' said Milo. 'Here.' He handed her the photographs and waited for her to examine them. 'What do you make of those?'

She examined the photographs.

'This is the work of a psychopath,' she said.

'What we want to know,' said Milo, 'is why MI6 went to

the lengths of showing them to Mr Rosslyn from Customs Investigation Division. What's the hidden agenda?'

'You want me to ask my contacts?' she said.

'Find out whatever you can from them,' said Milo.

'How long have I got?' she asked.

Milo looked at Rosslyn.

'I'd like your opinion as soon as possible,' Rosslyn said.

'I have to be in Bahrain tomorrow,' Kasuo Satomura said. 'I can try to get you an opinion by, say, Thursday evening.'

'I'd really appreciate it,' Rosslyn said.

Satomura took the photographs and left.

'Not getting paranoid, are we?' said Milo.

'Not yet,' said Rosslyn.

'You've no other idea as to what may be behind the showing of the photos?' Milo asked.

'I'm not sure what I think at the moment,' said Rosslyn. 'All I know is that the two SIS people who gave them to me said something about me keeping them as souvenirs. I had the feeling they were trying to tell me something. It came over as a fairly heavy warning. Lay off. Or else.'

'Or else what?'

'Or heavy shit.'

'I hope not,' Milo said. 'Kasuo will let you know if you need to worry about the photographs. You can rely on her. She's the best. Completely discreet. There's no one better.'

'Who are her contacts?'

Milo twisted another paper clip until it snapped. 'Better leave that unsaid, if you've no objections. I'll call you if she finds anything you need to know.'

'At home, please,' said Rosslyn.

'Of course. I hope you won't take this amiss, Alan. I'd tread very carefully with Vratsides if I were you. Likewise with the Holland woman.'

'I thought you said you didn't know her?' Rosslyn said.

'I don't personally. Obviously Straub must have told her about you some time ago. I suppose she took the line that a friend of Straub's was a friend of hers. A little love, so I'm told, can sometimes work wonders. But take my word for it, after Ames the NSA and CIA are very hard indeed on miscreants. I very much doubt she had permission to show you that fax. No matter that it came from her husband. She's treading some sort of dangerous path.'

He reached for one of his four telephones. 'Let me try Slaemann for you.' After two attempts he gave up. 'For some reason there's no reply. Must have gone home. There we are. As I told you, tread terribly carefully with Vratsides.'

19.35

Celeste had been waiting outside IG's offices in Berkeley Square.

'How did it go?' she asked.

'Milo seems to know a great deal.'

They walked in the direction of Green Park.

Rosslyn continued, 'Some of it I'd have preferred not to hear. Still, you can't have it all ways, I suppose. Anyway, he filled me in on Vratsides. And Slaemann. It looks from what Milo says as if Straub was on the level with us. And, let me tell you, this Angell's fucking dangerous with a capital fucking D. If only Straub had given it to us straight off instead of trying to play both sides against the middle, I reckon he'd still be alive today. Instead of which he's dead and we're dealing with some very heavy people.'

'Did you show him the photos then?'

'Yes. He's having someone look at them. He certainly runs a pretty professional outfit.'

They were standing on the pavement. 'Say Angell has a contract,' said Rosslyn, 'what sort of fee do you reckon he'd ask?'

She guessed. 'A hundred thousand, say?'

'Maybe more,' said Rosslyn. 'So you're looking at someone with a lot of cash to throw around. Say you're looking to put a bullet in the brain of a Customs officer. You wouldn't do it here. So overseas. Copenhagen. How much then?'

'More.'

'So Angell or whoever has to have a lot of money behind him.'

'Or her,' she said.

'I don't think it's a woman,' said Rosslyn, 'but whatever the form is, we've no time to go back to Copenhagen on the off-chance of getting more evidence.'

'I wish we could.'

'But we can't,' he said.

'What do we do then? Wait until the bastard rears his ugly head again?'

'Not if I have anything to do with it. I'm not having this psycho running around my manor. He might get away with it in Copenhagen. But not here.'

'How will you set it up?'

'Gaynor's agreed to come in on it tomorrow morning.'

'I'd like to stay with it too, Alan. I was in with you at the start. I don't like unfinished business any more than you do.'

'Well, you can't indent for overtime on this one, can you? I know you like things tidy. But if you'd seen the inside of that sauna I think you'd change your mind.'

'I can handle it, I think,' she said.

'It's your life. Don't say I didn't warn you.'

Outside Green Park underground station she said, 'Take care.'

He watched her take the steps down to the underground two by two. Light on her feet.

20.05

He crossed Green Park on his solitary walk homewards to Eccleston Square.

Straub's warning was eating at him.

Thanks for telling me, even if you were a bit late.

He found himself searching the faces of the drunks on the benches, the eyes of veiled Arab women. Even a pair of women police officers. Scrutinized by figures he'd never seen before.

He took the long route around Victoria Station.

Straub must have known he was going to die.

Are you sure that I'm in the frame too?

You once told me, 'There's no harm feeling the fear in your spine. Makes you more alert.'

It also makes you feel sick in the stomach.

I wish you hadn't been writing the truth. But I have a nasty feeling that for once you were.

He hoped that an evening alone watching TV with a takeaway tandoori and two cans of lager would clear his head before the meeting at Custom House in the morning.

But home gave him little pleasure.

Wednesday 26 July

75°F/24°C. Sultry and hot with some hazy sunshine.
Threat of thundery showers later in the day. Wind
easterly to south-easterly, moderate.

08.00
Gaynor had driven fast from the east coast to be in his office
early. Rosslyn watched him read Straub's letter. Gaynor was
making careful notes.

'We're going to have to phone round, make a few visits,'
Gaynor said. 'I don't think we can make the connections till
we've done that. What does strike me, Alan, is that Straub or
whatever he called himself must have known, one, that he
was in considerable personal danger. Otherwise, why would
he have written this? Two, that if something did happen to
him he could rely on you to keep *Celeste* alive. And three, this
man Angell wants to kill the investigation. And, according to
Straub, you too. The first question really, Alan, is what made
Straub feel that matters were coming to a head? Given that
we know what happened to him, he was right to worry. Too
bloody right he was. That's what's persuaded me about what
he's said. There's nothing like a killing to sort everything out.
In one way, it makes life easier for us. In another way, much
harder. One of the questions that worries me most is this.
How watertight *was* the security surrounding *Celeste* when
you arrived in Copenhagen?'

'Well, it was all right as far as I was concerned,' Rosslyn
said.

'Don't give me that. It can't have been that brilliant, can it?

Two dead bodies lying around for a start.'

'Right.'

'You met him at his hotel. Then, if I remember rightly, you reported to the Visa Officer at the embassy. That's correct, isn't it?'

Rosslyn agreed.

'Between your seeing Straub and finding him in the sauna, what did you do with the rest of your time?'

'I stayed in the hotel and worked on the draft of my submission for the Annual Report.'

'You didn't see anyone else?'

'Other than Celeste, no one.'

'Made no calls?'

'None. Except after the sauna, when I got to Kastrup, I called Drew. Told her what had happened. No one could've been in on that call.'

'Well, if you didn't talk, someone must have done. Because they knew exactly where to find Straub. Who else knew the time and place of your RV with Straub?'

'As I told you, there was the Visa Officer at the embassy, the SIS man. Celeste knew, of course. Other than that, just our people here.'

'All these people knew the exact location before the RV with Straub?'

'Only me, Celeste, Straub and the man at the embassy.'

'No one else?'

'No.'

'And we don't know who Straub rang.'

'No.'

Gaynor started counting on his fingers. 'Now that we have it down in writing, more people are in the picture. The SIS officer. Home Office. Customs Team E. Ms Franklin. And we have this too.' He held up Straub's letter. 'This widens things even further. We have this man Angell. We have to find him. Or rather, you do.' He paused. 'Unfortunately, this whole thing's leaking like a fucking sieve. And it seems to me we're not just dealing with some contract killer who sticks a knife in someone's guts. We're dealing with a fucking maniac. Shouldn't we tell the Yard?'

'What the hell are they going to do?'

'Listen, Alan, if this loony can reach Straub in Copenhagen he can reach you or me in London or Suffolk. And what about that woman on the boat, Alan? I think you and I were a bit slow there. We thought she was out there fishing, but it isn't usual for women to be out fishing alone on the Alde with guns, is it? Even allowing for the local lads being a bit frisky in this heat. The skirts don't need that much protection. She was out there for a reason. Maybe she was on a recce or whatever. I think we're very likely going to see this Ms Angell again. You can bet your sweet life on that. You told me you saw her next at the motorway café. Then you're bloody nearly killed by a blown tyre. Next you come back down to London. There's SIS on Ms Franklin's doorstep saying: "No more *Celeste*, thank you very much." They have the photographs of the sauna. You know what I'm thinking? I'm thinking you were lucky SIS didn't find you in bed with Ms Franklin when they paid you and her that visit.'

'What's that got to do with it?'

'What, you sleeping with Franklin?'

'Yes, what does it matter?'

'Not a toss,' said Gaynor, 'when things are fine. You can sleep with whom you like. Even the bloody Chairman. I don't know what you two get up to. And I don't want to know either. But when the shit hits the fan, Alan, when questions are getting asked, when major operations are being aborted for reasons we don't know about, well, then there's a conflict of interest. One little visit from MI6 and then she aborts *Celeste*. This isn't exactly Stand By Your Man time, is it?'

'You don't need to tell me. Perhaps I was being unrealistic. I didn't think she'd throw the sponge in as quickly as she did. I think she's running scared of SIS and MI5. And I think there's one good reason. *Celeste*. It's hit a nerve that's making people very scared. And I'm not just talking about the paedophiles. I think it's friends of friends. There's a lot of people who are shit scared of it. And you know what, they can't come out in the open about it, can they? They don't want to say. They want the whole thing shoved under the carpet. Because if it isn't, we'll be investigating more than a bunch of perverts.'

Gaynor leaned back in his chair. 'Who have you been talking to, Alan?'

'No one,' said Rosslyn.

He watched Gaynor's eyes. Something in them told him that Gaynor knew he was holding back on him.

'Let's mark that file speculation,' Gaynor said. 'Put it in pending. Like my bloody retirement.'

'Do you want in on it?' Rosslyn said.

'I'd hardly have driven myself in here if I didn't. I think we ought to agree some ground rules, Alan. I'm not one of your bloody Straubs. I got the feeling a moment ago that you weren't being quite open with me.'

'I'm sorry,' said Rosslyn.

What I do not want to discuss is Milo.

'Is there anything else?' asked Gaynor.

'No.'

'So rule number one is, Alan, no holding back. Do you want to use Quinceau?'

'Celeste Quinceau. Fine. I'll call her. I'll pay a visit to Slaemann. Find out more about Angell's strength. We get one move ahead now. Even two. And we stay that way. And we let the rest of the world think we're doing what we normally do. This and that or sweet fuck all. We say I'm checking my submission for the Annual Report. We attend the fucking awful Annual Dinner tonight. In case you've forgotten, we're supposed to be presenting you with a retirement gift. And I have this feeling it'll be a video recorder you don't want so you can spend the rest of your days looking at dirty movies you've already seen.'

09.10

In his office Rosslyn told Celeste, 'I want you to inform the rest of Team E that the investigation's finished. Where are they?'

'Five are on surveillance at the Birmingham Conference Centre. Three have search duties at Heathrow. One's at the Yard. Three are still on early summer leave. And one's on maternity leave. Apart from you and me, that's it. And here's the list of Items Needing Your Attention.'

He glanced at the print-out she handed to him.

Celeste continued, 'There's no one to plan the Bristol operation. Or to interview suspects held in Manchester.'

'What's going on up there then?'

'It's magazines, photographs and videos. A couple of schoolteachers brought them in from Holland. They were filmed collecting them in The Hague. We've no one to attend the monthly liaison meeting with SO(1)4 at the Yard. Or to put the case for new computer equipment finance to Audit/ Budget. We have no one to send to Milan. And we have four more prisoners in maximum security units offering to do a deal. But everyone's showing up tonight for the Annual Dinner. Why don't I brief everyone quietly then?'

'Okay, then do it.'

His telephone was ringing.

A woman's voice said she was secretary to Dr Claudine Hecht. The appointment had been brought forward. 'Can you make twelve-thirty today at 76 Harley Street?' She reminded him to bring a copy of his curriculum vitae.

'You should know, Alan,' said Celeste, 'that we've been asked to destroy all records and traces of *Celeste*.'

'Then keep them somewhere out of sight. You don't have to tell me where. I don't want to know. Just keep them.'

'And if Sister asks what happened to them?'

'What will you say, Celeste?'

'I'll tell her they were shredded. And binned. And we never had this conversation.'

'We never had it,' he told her.

09.15

Before Rosslyn left for the West End and Slaemann's Brook
Street offices, he telephoned Gaynor.

He'd found nothing on Angell. At GRDA Associates in
Savile Row no one was answering the telephones. There
wasn't even an answerphone.

10.06

Fumes from a vat of boiling tarmac drifted across Brook
Street. The noise from road drills deafened him. A painted
sign apologized for any inconvenience being caused by the
installation of cable TV outside the door with a brass plaque.
SLAEMANN SOLICITORS it announced.

After he had pressed the bell a third time, the door was
opened by a stooped man wearing the tie of the Royal Air
Force Volunteer Reserve.

Rosslyn said, 'I'd like a word with Leonard Slaemann,
please.'

'I'm afraid that won't be possible, sir.'

Rosslyn showed him his ID.

The doorman checked it. He seemed satisfied. 'Perhaps if
you'd come in, sir, I'll ask one of the partners to see you
instead.'

He was shown into a small ground-floor waiting room.

On the table were the latest issues of *Country Life. The Field.
The Economist.* And that day's *Financial Times.*

He leafed through a luxuriously produced brochure out-
lining the services of SLAEMANN SOLICITORS. Slaemann
himself had provided the foreword:

> *Slaemann is dedicated to personal
> service of a high order in which
> commercial factors play a part but are
> not necessarily considered paramount.
> Ours is an international service.*
> *Our watchwords are threefold:*

Confidence
Consideration
Conciliation

SLAEMANN SOLICITORS, it appeared, offered Commercial, Family and Matrimonial, Litigation and Property Services.

'Mr Rosslyn?' The man was heavily built, in his late forties, sun-tanned, with short dark hair and a prominent nose.

He shook Rosslyn's hand firmly. 'John Fordyce. We can talk in the boardroom. Would you like tea or coffee?'

'Neither, thanks.'

He led Rosslyn to the next room and closed the door. 'Do sit down, please.'

'Is it possible to see Mr Leonard Slaemann?'

'I'm afraid you'll have to make do with me.'

Rosslyn loosened his tie. 'When will Mr Slaemann be available?'

'May I ask what this is about, Mr Rosslyn?' said Fordyce, turning up the air conditioning.

'We think he may be able to help us with some inquiries we're making.'

'Into what?' said Fordyce, returning to the table.

'It's classified. I need to talk to Mr Slaemann in private.'

Fordyce rubbed his chin. 'I can't imagine what sort of inquiries they might be. But whatever they are, Mr Slaemann won't be able to assist you.'

'May I ask why not?'

'Because, Mr Rosslyn, Leonard's dead.'

'Mr Slaemann?'

'Yes. I'm afraid I can't enlarge on it any more than that. You could always ask the police. They've only just left. I have the names of the relevant officers in my office.'

'Can't you tell me how Mr Slaemann died?'

'I'm afraid that the police are not at present prepared to offer an opinion.'

'Are you telling me he died in suspicious circumstances?'

'I didn't say that, Mr Rosslyn. I'm simply not in a position to help you, I'm afraid.'

'You mean you won't help me?'

'I'm not saying I won't. I'm saying I can't. But if there's any other matter we can assist Customs with, then we'd be more than happy to oblige.'

'Can you tell me, 'Rosslyn asked, 'did Mr Slaemann die at home or in hospital or somewhere else?'

'With great respect,' said Fordyce, 'I really do think that's a question you'd best put to the police.' He hesitated. 'May I ask if your inquiries are in some way related to theirs?'

'I've no idea,' said Rosslyn. 'Why is it so important for you to know?'

'It's not knowing what is happening that's so upsetting. Are you quite sure you wouldn't like some tea or coffee?'

'Tea, please,' said Rosslyn. 'I've changed my mind.'

Fordyce lifted a telephone and asked for tea: 'For my visitor and coffee for me, please. Thank you.'

'I don't know what happened to Mr Slaemann,' said Rosslyn. 'I wish I could help you. I wish you could help me.'

'You have, I imagine, come armed with specific questions you intended for Mr Slaemann?'

'I have.'

'Do you want to put any to me?' Fordyce asked. 'I can always try to assist you.'

A secretary brought the tea and coffee.

'Can you tell me anything about a man called Angell?' asked Rosslyn. 'Or his wife. Or anything about Mr Angell's dealings with Mr Slaemann?'

'Mr Angell?' He paused. 'Yes, I think I can. I did meet him a few times with Mr Slaemann. But in so far as Mr – I think he preferred to use his rank – *Major* Angell was employed by our firm, it was always on the basis that he dealt with Leonard in person.'

'Why was that?'

'I rather believe it was a personal matter between the two of them.'

'But you don't know what sort of services Mr Slaemann used Angell for?' Rosslyn asked. 'What sort of inquiries and so forth he pursued for Mr Slaemann?'

'I'm afraid I really don't.'

'Do you know when they last met?'

'No, I'm afraid not.'

'Or when Angell last visited these premises to see Mr Slaemann?'

'I couldn't tell you that either. Usually they met elsewhere. But I do recall that Major Angell did recently visit the firm. Possibly only a few days ago.'

'When would you say that was?'

'Let's see. I'd say it was on or about Friday the 21st. Last week. In the afternoon. I can check the diary for you, if you wish.'

'Did the police ask you anything about him?'

'Who, Major Angell? No, they didn't.'

'Well, what sort of records of meetings with clients or people like Angell did Mr Slaemann keep?'

'Very comprehensive indeed.'

'Would you be prepared to show me,' Rosslyn asked, 'last Friday's record of his meeting with Angell?'

'I'd say it's not so much a matter of showing you, more a matter of listening to it. Leonard tape-recorded confidential meetings in his office.'

'Can I listen to it?'

'Of course,' said Fordyce. 'So long as you treat the matter as strictly confidential. We must remember that the tape might just be adduced as evidence in connection with Leonard's death.'

'I'm happy to guarantee confidentiality,' said Rosslyn.

'If you'd wait here, I'll see what I can find in Leonard's office.'

'Didn't the police search it?'

'As a matter of fact they didn't. Certainly not when I was present. They simply asked if we had any sort of address book.'

'Did you give them one?'

'I had it photocopied. We arranged for a messenger to take it to the officer who'd requested it.'

'Who was the officer?'

'A WPC Helen Cliff at Paddington Green police station. D division.'

Rosslyn made a note of the WPC's name.

He was left alone while Fordyce fetched the tape, with nothing better to do than leaf through another of the Slaemann prospectuses. When the lawyer returned he brought with him a portable tape recorder loaded with a cassette.

'By all means listen to it here if you want. You appreciate that Leonard recorded interviews and so forth largely as a precaution against his being misrepresented. But I'm afraid I can find no other information on Major Angell. If you wouldn't mind, I must leave you. I have to make an urgent telephone call. I'll join you again when I've finished.' He waved at the tape machine. 'You know how to work that thing, of course?'

'Yes, I do. Thanks.'

'If there's anything further I can do to help you,' said Fordyce. He handed Rosslyn his business card. 'Please don't hesitate to ask. My home number's on the back.'

Alone in the boardroom, Rosslyn played the tape.

10.30

It was apparently Angell's voice that said:

'*For a start, there is the evidence of those bank statements . . .*'

There was a marked impediment in his speech: *w*s for *r*s.

'*They pwoove that she's substantially pwofited from her husband's involvement* [here a slightly stammered spit] *in child sex. I don't have to tell you that as a defendant, she could of course always stand up in court and say, "My husband deceived me. I haven't a clue where the money came from. I never asked." The media will have a field day.'*

And this must have been Leonard Slaemann: *Where should she start?* [ANGELL:] *Damage limitation, I suppose. Get a stop put to the authorities investigating her husband's private life. There aren't any other options available.* [SLAEMANN:] *Are you quite certain he's already a suspect?* [ANGELL:] *My sources tell me yes. Customs & Excise's investigation team doesn't need to collect much more evidence before they arrest Vratsides. Just enough to secure convictions. Most of it depends on what the usual run of informants tell the investigators. From a personal point of view, Lady Vratsides has to ask herself if she can handle the disgrace of being married to a man with form as a paedophile. His activities are pretty clearly demonstrated in child porn CD-ROMS. Several of the children, tiny defenceless girls, have been hideously abused.* [SLAEMANN:] *Is there any conceivable way whatsoever that this could be kept out of the public view?* [ANGELL:] *Only if we could gain control of the informants. It's possible. And I suppose the investigators could be sweetened.* [SLAEMANN:] *I very much doubt that Customs & Excise would play ball. I wouldn't be too hopeful about the police either.* [ANGELL:] *I suppose you're right. We'll just have to do it another way. But it's still going to be expensive.* [SLAEMANN:] *Money's not a problem here.* [ANGELL:] *If you're asking me to do it for her, it could be pretty expensive.* [SLAEMANN:] *How expensive?* [ANGELL:] *To abort this operation? This is going to come very dear. We'd be running an enormous risk. Several people are going to have to be taken out.* [SLAEMANN:] *What's your estimate?* [ANGELL:] *At least one million pounds sterling.* [SLAEMANN:] *She won't wear that.* [ANGELL:] *Then I'm afraid she'll have to lump it. Unless she and her husband are prepared to do time.* [SLAEMANN:] *I think I ought to telephone her.* [ANGELL:] *Fine, go ahead. But tell her from me, the price isn't negotiable.* [SLAEMANN:] *I'll tell her.* [ANGELL:] *And also tell her that, to be effective, I've got to start now.* [SLAEMANN:] *What do you need from her?* [ANGELL:] *She must*

*close her bank accounts right away. Then open new ones under
your direction.* [SLAEMANN:] *How do you want paying?*
[ANGELL:] *Electronic transfer. In advance. I recommend that you
use the services of a reputable currency dealer.* [SLAEMANN:] *And
when do you think you can secure the end of investigations into
Vratsides?* [ANGELL:] *Say by Friday 28 July.* [SLAEMANN:]
Friday the 28th. No sooner? [ANGELL:] *No. Simply arrange for
the currency transfer through your usual bank in the usual way to
my bank in Zurich. You have the relevant details. I guarantee you
completion by Friday 28 July. Then I'll be in a position to go ahead.*
[SLAEMANN:] *If not?* [ANGELL:] *Then we've been wasting each
other's time.* [SLAEMANN:] *Which reminds me. My charging rate
will be the usual. Fifteen per cent.* [ANGELL:] *Then I'm sure you'll
want her to agree. Don't get up. I'll see myself out.*

11.03

Rosslyn slipped the tape into his pocket and, without waiting
for Fordyce to return, saw himself out of Slaemann's place.

He had a call to make to Gaynor. To tell him there were two
days left.

11.04

Rosslyn telephoned Gaynor from a phone booth. He told him
about the Leonard Slaemann tape.

'We've got to build the case up yet,' said Gaynor.
'Statements have to be taken. And that's not going to be
easy with child witnesses, always assuming we can find any.
It's a bloody difficult area, you know, kids giving evidence on
video to be shown to the court et cetera. Or else from behind
a screen. We'll need to verify that any tapes or other exhibits
that we adduce as evidence are *bona fide*. Look at the kiddie
porn on the Internet thing. That took months before they
could make an arrest.'

Rosslyn looked out across the street from the phone booth.
Why was Gaynor stalling?

'This isn't the SFO, Chief. I want a result.'

'I'm not trying to put the boot in when you're down,' said Gaynor. 'But your track record recently *demands* that we get a result.'

'This man isn't any old toe-rag. I'm going for him.'

'But don't forget, there can't be any slip-ups.'

'I know that, Chief.' Rosslyn was irritated by Gaynor's cautious tone. 'I know he has friends in high places.'

'Yes, Alan, I know you know. Let's not rush our fences. This is going to take time.'

'I've got to speak to that policewoman. Then there's Vratsides's wife, God help us. And that's only just a start.'

'Landing the big fish takes time,' Gaynor said. 'You've got to play them. You don't just heave them on to the shore. Get to your Personal Appraisal Interview.'

'Oh, fuck it.'

'No, Alan, *you* fuck it. Get in there.'

'That WPC Cliff won't go away?'

'See her after.'

11.55

For his Personal Appraisal Interview he took a cab to Dr Claudine Hecht's consulting rooms in Harley Street.

Everyone said that at thirty-two he was too young to succeed the Sea Captain as Chief Investigation Officer. Everyone resents high-flyers. Jealousy, really. He had risen through the ranks too fast. Had he experienced failure, more people might have been rooting for him. His promotion when Gaynor finally retired would have been a foregone conclusion. Until last Saturday.

But Straub's death had altered everything. Straub was damage.

Maybe Drew's insistence that *Celeste* be closed was a Machiavellian move in his support. Nice thought. But wrong. Closing down *Celeste* might have been a way of covering her arse in the short term. But if she thought that it was anything other than papering over the cracks, then she was wide of the mark. SIS would know that they only had to snap their fingers and she'd dance to their tune. It was Danegeld.

Then there was Gaynor. The Sea Captain had made no secret of his support for him on a personal level. Though understandably, he showed scant enthusiasm for the nature of Team E's work. The watching of the repulsive evidence. The child porn. It might have been a necessary feature of the war against the scum. It got to you in the end. But someone had to face it. It had seemed like one area where he could have scored a quick success if he had the right intelligence. And he was getting it until Straub. *Celeste* had Gaynor's unwavering support. But soon Gaynor would be growing vegetables in Aldeburgh full-time. He wouldn't be a member of the Promotion Board. In fact, the Sea Captain was very nearly history.

The CV Rosslyn was taking with him to the interview with Dr Hecht seemed to reinforce the story.

In the cab he read it through.

My Life.

STAFF IN CONFIDENCE

ALAN HUTTON ROSSLYN
SENIOR INVESTIGATION OFFICER
CAREER HISTORY

1983   University Graduate Direct Entry to Higher
            Executive Officer Level

1983–85   Investigation Division: Drugs Financial
            Investigation Branch

1986–94   Appointed Senior Investigation Officer
            HM Customs Team A Division Arms &
            Explosives

1994–95   Appointed to HM Customs Team E Division
            Indecent & Obscene Material

HM CUSTOMS & EXCISE HEADQUARTERS AND OUTFIELD EXPERIENCE

Administration. Training. Technical tax policy. Legal Advice. Provision of Common Services. Service in the Outfield aboard vessels of the cutter fleet.

CAREER DEVELOPMENT

(A)   Extensive management experience and the handling of sensitive political intelligence. Specialized training in Firearms.

(B)   Surveillance and Undercover Operations in liaison with Police, Armed Services and the Security Services (MI5 and MI6). Postings in the UK, United States and Europe. Management of Liaison Officers in posts covering Europe, the United States, South America, the Caribbean, the Middle East, West Africa, South-East Asia and the Indian subcontinent. During 1992/93 duty with Liaison Officers on the increasing workload in Turkey and Pakistan, leading to arms and drugs seizures from Europe and the supply of information leading to seizures and arrests in Liaison Officers' own territories.

(C)   Identification and Investigation: drug smuggling, including tracing and recovering related illicit proceeds.

(D)   VAT and other revenue fraud including those concerning Customs Duties and agricultural levies of the European Community.

(E)   Fraud involving the evasion of import and export restrictions and prohibitions.

(F)   Collection, analysis, collation and distribution of international and national intelligence relating to Customs & Excise legislation.

(G)   Provision of advice, policy and training in relation to investigation.

(H)   Provision of support to local investigation activities. Co-operation and sharing of information about drug smuggling with other law enforcement agencies both at home and overseas.

(I)   Review of the Investigation Department requiring improved co-ordination of intelligence activities.

PERSONAL STATEMENT
1   Our work relies heavily on accurate intelligence.
2   The completion of the Single Market indicates that the opportunities for the distribution and manufacture of pornography involving children is increasing.
3   I believe that the links with the National Criminal Intelligence Service (NCIS) should continue to be strengthened.
4   Further expansion of resources is required to combat abuse of strategic export controls, concentrating on those contributing to the spread of nuclear, chemical and biological weapons, and closer co-operation is required with the European Commission and the Intervention Board on Agricultural Produce.

12.40
'It's impressive,' said Dr Claudine Hecht, peering at him over half-moon glasses with a smile that suggested he had nothing to fear. 'Have you ever visited a psychoanalyst before?'

'Once, yes.'

'Do you mind my asking why?'

'No. I saw my lover killed in a terrorist incident. Our people thought I needed counselling at the time.'

'Did it help?'

'Not really. That's why I gave it up.' He checked himself. 'No disrespect to you. Just that it didn't seem to help. I eventually realized that my reaction to her murder was a problem I had to handle on my own.'

Dr Hecht made some notes in pencil on a loose-leaf pad. 'So that's why you gave it up?'

'That's right.'

'Do you feel that you worked through it on your own?'

'What do you mean, "worked through it"? I suppose I *worked through it* as much as anyone works through anything.'

'It must still be painful for you.'

'Of course.'

'Yes,' she said, 'of course. But the pain doesn't stop you from functioning?'

'No, it doesn't. As I said, I dealt with it on my own.'

'On your own. It that how you handle all your problems?'

'No, it isn't.'

'I believe you're very skilled at interrogation.'

'I have to be,' said Rosslyn. 'It's my job.'

'Mine simply requires me to assess your general state of mind,' said Dr Hecht. 'Prior to your Promotion Board. Let me assure you, nothing of what you tell me here will be disclosed to anyone else.'

Then what's the point of it? Rosslyn wondered.

'First, I assess you in a general way,' she continued. 'Then mark you out of five in broad categories such as Aggression, Malleability, Suggestibility, Emotional Detachment. The degree to which you have a high or low opinion of yourself. Self-esteem. Those qualities which may sound like faults but very often are actually the opposite.' She reached behind her for a folder on a chair. 'I've been supplied with some general details of your personal circumstances by the people who've vetted you. Perhaps you can tell me more.'

He watched her leaf through the papers in her folder.

'If I may,' she said, 'I'd like to ask you, for example, about your personal and family relationships. Is that all right with you?'

'Go ahead.'

'I've been told something of your most recent investigation, which is called *Celeste*, isn't it?'

'Correct.'

'Pretty name, *Celeste*, isn't it? Why did you choose it?'

'I didn't. My assistant investigation officer chose it because that's her name.'

Dr Hecht made another note on her yellow pad. 'I'd like to move on to your personal life, your relationship with Verity, isn't it?'

He thought: *That's history. It'll do though. We don't want to rake up Drew. Stick to Verity. The truth is my relationship with her ended last Christmas. I'll fudge it.*

'Oh yes.' He paused. 'Verity. We have our ups and downs.'

'You don't live with her?'

'No.'

'She's financially independent?'

'Yes.'

I don't want to go into this any further.

'I gather Verity works at Vauxhall Cross. With MI6.'

'At their headquarters. Correct.'

She read on through her notes. 'Apparently she's failed to get promotion. How did she take it?'

'Pretty badly. The same as anyone would.'

He watched her making even longer notes.

I've heard all this confidentiality crap.

'Do you realize,' he said, 'your door's open?'

'Would you like to close it for me?'

'Why?'

'For privacy.'

'Privacy? What are you worried about? You've got a file on me. I haven't got one on you, Dr Hecht.'

He closed the door. *That's no marks for Malleability. What I should or could tell you, Dr Hecht, is this. I'm sure you'll appreciate, among other things, that she may have independent means but when it comes to spending money on herself, on Daisy, on furnishings for the cosy little love-nest – her long boat, the* Manchester Madonna, *on the Regent's Canal – on booze, she feels the pinch. So she complains to me. But I don't see why I should answer all your nosy questions.*

'Verity has a ten-year-old daughter, Daisy, I understand,' Dr Hecht asked. 'How do you get on with Daisy?'

'I get on very well with her.'

'Well, it isn't as common as you might think.'

'What do you mean?'

'Quite a lot of men find relating to young children, particularly girls as young as Daisy, rather difficult.'

'That's not been my experience.'

'When you're with her, what sort of things do you two get up to?'

'There's a lot of laughter. I tell her stories. She tells me her dreams. We have our little secrets.'

'Do these secrets exclude her mother?'

'She tells me she's the only one she's confided in.'

'What about the physical aspects? Do you kiss and cuddle?'

'Yes, doesn't everyone?'

'You kiss and cuddle?'

'Yes.'

'May I ask, when you first met Verity, did you know she had a daughter?'

'Yes.'

'How did you feel about that?'

'Well, I've always liked children. So if anything, it was an attraction. She's a sweet girl.'

Dr Hecht poured herself a glass of mineral water. 'Would you like a glass?'

'No thanks.'

'Don't drink or smoke?'

'Both sometimes. A little.'

'No drugs?'

'Drugs. What do you think, Dr Hecht?'

'I know this may sound as though we're dealing with minutiae. But every little helps when it comes to building up a psychological profile of you. Your relationship with Verity and Daisy may provide us with useful pointers. Tell me, what's her schoolwork like?'

'She's bright. Imaginative.'

'Takes after her mother and father?'

'After her mother, yes.'

'You don't know the father?'

'No.'

'Does Verity receive financial support from him?'

'I can't say.'

'Do you know who Daisy's father is?'

'No.'

'What, you've no idea?'

'It's not an issue Verity wants to discuss.'

'Why do you think that is?'

'It's something you'd have to ask her, Dr Hecht.'

I could tell you, he thought:

Until a year ago, MR A. N. OTHER, the absent father, was going to meet the cost of boarding-school fees. But it seems, so Verity said, along with a lot of other whingeing toffs, he lost a fortune at Lloyd's. Sold the family silver and a lot more besides. She refused to see the practical good sense of sending Daisy to a state school.

'You don't discuss money much with Verity, as a couple?'

'Not often.'

Again untrue.

When I offered to sell my flat in Eccleston Square, to move in with her and let her use the capital, she gave me a lecture about the need for a woman like herself to preserve her independence no matter what the cost.

'Are you still in love with her?'

Look, this is what I do all day long. I'm the one who's supposed to poke my nose into other people's business.

He smiled at her. 'Dr Hecht, we're adults.'

I sometimes wonder if that's true.

Verity also told me in a drunken haze that now I have to face a few home truths like, 'I am the rock and strength of Daisy's life. She comes first. You have to realize that actually she's resented all my

*lovers.' And throughout the early hours one morning, I listened in
silence as she unburdened herself with detailed recollections of her
affairs and her abortions. Booze coarsened her language.*

'You two are, if I may ask, faithful to each other?'

'Most of the time,' he said. He thought of Drew. 'Depends
on what you mean by faithful. I'd say I was faithful, yes.'

'Would you know if she was unfaithful to you?'

'Dr Hecht, I think that's out of order.'

'I sense a lot of anger in you, Alan.'

If you keep saying that, I'm off out of here.

'May I call you Alan?'

'Whatever.'

'Do you feel that Verity is open with you?'

'Not particularly. We don't discuss her work, for instance,
what she does at Vauxhall Cross.'

'What about your own? Do you find it easy to unburden
yourself about your work, about your having to deal with the
darker side of human sexuality?'

'No, I don't.'

'Why do you think that is?'

'Let me give you an example.'

'By all means.'

'Take my present investigation. It involves some of the
worst instances of child abuse. Paedophiliac pornography.
Sex acts against children. Killing in cold blood for the benefit
of very rich and twisted minds. Celebrities even. I can't think
of anyone, including my own officers, who wouldn't be
deeply affected by it. You should know, you're the mind
doctor. I dream about it. I wake up sweating in the night. I
wake up screaming. Now do I make myself clear? You said
something about me being angry.' He lowered his voice.
'You're right. I am very angry. I'm very angry that someone
somewhere is trying to block my investigation. Now, these
darker sides of sexuality you talk about. Maybe people like
yourself, Dr Hecht, might or might not have some fancy
ways of sorting them out. What I care about is stopping these

animals from doing any more damage. What I care about is that somewhere in London or in Europe there are people who actually want to stop me nailing the people responsible. Why could that be? Why would they want to stop it?'

'To avoid being sent to prison, I imagine.'

'There's more to it than that, let me tell you. The truth is they don't want anyone to cut off their supply of filth. To have their appetites denied. And there's something else you won't have thought about. They have their position to consider. Reputations. They can't afford that sort of exposure. That's why this man, the man we think we're going to nail, is shit scared, desperate. Who knows, maybe he wakes up sweating and screaming in the night.'

'Who is he?'

'A man called Sir Achilles Vratsides. Ever heard of him?'

'Vratsides?'

'You know him?'

'I've read about him in the papers.'

'So you see my point?'

'Yes, it's much clearer than it was.'

'Good.'

Now she's going to tell me some bullshit about us all being prisoners of our history.

She was interrupted by a telephone call. 'Excuse me a moment,' she said to Rosslyn.

He watched her lift the telephone.

She said, 'I'm afraid I'm with a patient.'

So I'm a patient, am I?

'Very well, I'll take it in another room,' she said.

As she left the room she turned to Rosslyn. 'I'm so sorry. I won't be long. I'm sure you'll be all right on your own. There are still one or two points we have to cover about your relationship with Verity.'

He thought back to her.

Verity a little the worse for wear. Wandering about the Manchester Madonna naked and laughing. Threatening to throw him into the canal. And Daisy had come in dripping wet from the shower and Verity had yelled, laughing at her, to put her clothes on. Lunch that went on way into the night. The 'family photos'. The fun of home video making.

Dr Hecht returned, offered her apologies for the interruption, and began again. 'Would you say Verity was a happy woman?'

'Yes, I would say that.'

Liar. In the New Year her failure to gain promotion had really hurt. Even though she wouldn't admit to it, my own probable promotion made things worse.

Silence. Except for the scratching of Dr Hecht's pencil.

'Is there anything else you feel I should know about?'

I need to get out of here and find WPC Cliff.

The list of Slaemann's friends.

I want to know where and how Leonard Slaemann died.

And Vratsides. Bank statements.

Angell. I need to know the why and the wherefore.

Dr Hecht was saying, 'Mr Rosslyn.' She had caught him looking at his wrist-watch.

'Nothing else.'

'Do feel free to contact me,' she said, 'if you feel there's anything you've left unsaid.'

'How have I scored?'

'Let's wait and see.'

14.13

WPC Helen Cliff, small, trim and blonde with a wide smile, was waiting for him upstairs at the Porchester Spa. She was relaxed after a massage, Thalgo body wrap, facial and pedicure. Wearing rubber flip-flops and wrapped in a large white cotton towel, she was eating a tuna mayonnaise sandwich and drinking an iced yoghurt.

Rosslyn felt overdressed in his lightweight blue linen suit. 'You're WPC Cliff?' He showed her his ID.

'That's me,' she said. 'Helen Cliff. Pull up a chair.' She

adjusted the towel above her breasts. 'Don't mind me like this?'

'It's fine by me.'

'So you've come to ask me about Mr Slaemann?' she said.

'Yes,' said Rosslyn. 'I'd really appreciate you telling me anything you can about him.'

She looked around cautiously. Rosslyn could tell she was anxious not to be overheard.

'It has to be on this basis,' she said, 'that what I tell you is treated as privileged. Before I tell you anything, let's get one thing clear. I don't want any bloody awkward comebacks.'

Tough girl, Rosslyn thought. *Hard one to crack. Win her round. Slowly.* 'You needn't tell me anything you don't want to.'

'What makes you think that I might?'

'You're not pissed off with me for interrupting your beauty session?'

'Don't know about the beauty,' she said, 'I chose this place because it's easier to talk in here off the record.' She brushed breadcrumbs off the table with her hand. 'You've got it in one about my being pissed off, though. That's to put it mildly. I'm not sure of anything. I can't trust anybody after what happened last weekend. In fact, I'm not sure of anything or anyone any more.'

'I know the feeling,' Rosslyn said. 'I get it about four times a day usually.'

'Look I haven't been in the force long. I don't know if I can handle this sort of shit.'

'Do you want to talk about it?'

She gave him a watchful look. Still unsure of him. She seemed to waver. 'How much do you know about Slaemann?' she asked.

'A lot less than you, I should think,' Rosslyn said. 'Otherwise I wouldn't be here. All I know is that as a result of an investigation we're pursuing, I leg it round to Slaemann's office to see him. Then someone tells me he's dead. When I ask his partner, man by the name of Fordyce, what's happened, he says your lot's been busy. First off, they want a list of Slaemann's acquaintances. That's what you asked for, wasn't it? Had his address book sent round by messenger, didn't you? Your people also said you weren't prepared to disclose the cause of death. So I figure that the circumstances are distinctly suss.'

'Suss? You should've seen it. Fuck a duck. I don't know how many stiffs you people deal with. But I'm telling you these were the pits.'

'Was it Slaemann you saw?'

'See him? I fucking found him. Plus his lover boy. Matter of fact, lover boy was both boy *and* girl. Arthur and Martha. He and she. Dressed in a nightie. Tits and a dick. First time I've ever seen that combination. Total fucking chaos. Blood all over the shop. You couldn't have seen anything like this, my friend. And I hope you never do. The place was a bloody shambles. I don't know if you can even half imagine what I'm talking about.'

Rosslyn thought of the public sauna at Sjellandsgade and resisted the temptation to tell her that he knew exactly what she was talking about. He let her go on.

'In the bedroom Slaemann's body was sprawled out on the bed bollock naked. I could see straight off that he'd been shot. This blood frothing out of his mouth. Next to the bed there were panties and nighties still wet with blood. I looked around. Found a Visa card with Slaemann's name it. There were other bills and stuff lying all over the kitchen. Some Chink name or something on them. Kim Sang Park and Jeong-Kyu Hang. There was this terrible stench in the place. Like they must have thrown up and shat themselves. Jesus Christ Almighty, never again.'

'Then what happened?'

'I tried to call for assistance and the fucking transmission failed. You know how you don't touch anything at the scene of crime. Well, I managed to find a dog in the living room and called in.'

'Hang on,' Rosslyn said. 'What dog?'

'Dog and bone. Where were you dragged up then? The phone. After that I went downstairs, stood in the fresh air in the street, and waited. Believe you me, I needed the fresh air.'

'Then the SOC officers came?'

'Yes. I had to wait to make sure the place was secure. No unauthorized bodies in and out.'

'Did you see anyone try to come in or leave?'

'No.'

'Did you see anyone in the street?'

'Only the usual passers-by at that time in the morning. You know the sort of scum you get round here in Bayswater and fucking Notting Hill. You've no idea. Fucking hell on earth. No, I didn't see anyone except some tom loitering in a doorway opposite. I couldn't be bothered to nick her.'

'What did the tom look like?'

'I only clocked her for a second. Between forty and fifty. Slim. Dark-haired. I only noticed her because I felt she was watching me too. I remember thinking, "Christ, this place reeks of toms." They make me sick.' She shook her head. 'Just what the fuck's wrong with men nowadays? Present company excepted, of course.'

'What happened to the tart in the doorway?'

'I don't know for sure that she was a tom. That was just the sort of feeling I had at the time. But when the Scene of Crime Officers arrived she'd legged it.'

'Pity,' said Rosslyn.

'What?'

'I said that's a pity. Shall I give you my opinion, for what it's worth?'

'If you want.'

'I think that tom of yours might've been the killer.'

'You must be joking.'

'I'm not joking. Any sign of forced entry?'

'No.'

'Then my guess is that she was known to Slaemann and lover boy. You should hang on in there, Helen, and get the fucker in for questioning.'

'I would do if I knew who I was looking for,' she said. 'Except that it doesn't matter now.'

'Why not?'

She was breathing deeply. 'The investigation's got a funny feel about it.'

This one too? Here's an investigation that's been going on for a bloody sight less time than Celeste, and it's already begun to smell.

'What's odd about it?'

'I know it doesn't make any sense,' she said. 'And as I told you, I'm pretty new to this business. But even I can spot Special Branch or MI5.'

'How do they come into it?'

'I'm not sure. They were through there like a dose of salts.'

'In where?'

'In the investigation.'

'Doing what?'

'Just about everything, I should say. They started with Slaemann's offices. I was there. You know what, the only reason they wanted me there was not for me to find out about Slaemann. No, they wanted me there to find out what I knew. Two gits from the security services.'

'MI5?'

'My boss thought they were from MI6. Which was odd. What the hell they were doing poking around in a double murder was anybody's guess. There was this man and woman.'

'There usually is. What were their names, do you remember?'

'The man was called McEvoy. The woman I can't remember her name. I'd have to check it. Smelled of mouthwash.'

'Not Hughes by any chance?'

'Yes, I think that was it. Right cow. Hughes. Do you know her then?'

'Only slightly.'

'You surprise me.'

'You mean amaze,' he said.

'So what's the difference?'

'There's a big one. You're screwing someone's old man when the wife walks in. You're surprised. She's amazed.'

'Let me buy you a yoghurt,' she said. 'Surprised?'

'Thanks all the same, Helen. Tell you what, would you like to come to our Annual Dinner Dance tonight?'

'I don't think so, thanks. I feel really washed out.'

'I think it'd do you good, Helen. Take your mind off last weekend.'

'What sort of party is it?'

'Dinner dance. The usual.'

'What do I wear?'

'Semi-formal. At the Connaught Rooms, 19.00 hours.'

She tightened the towel around her. 'I might *just* amaze you, Alan,' she said.

20.00

Including staff and guests, several hundred people were at the Investigation Division's Annual Dinner Dance.

Madonna on the disco: 'Like a Virgin'.

Rosslyn was on the dance floor with Helen. She was in a black silk dress.

She'd noticed he'd noticed. 'How do I look?'

'Great.'

He had called for Helen at her flat in Stockwell. In the cab crossing the river she had said, 'I won't know any of these people. Are you sure this is a good idea?'

'You'll like my boss.'

'Yes? I hope he's easier than mine. What's his name?'

'Richard Gaynor.'

But now, there was still no sign of the Sea Captain. It

wasn't like him not to show up for the annual party. In about
an hour's time, at nine, there was supposed to be a speech by
Drew, then the presentation of the Sea Captain's retirement
gift.

Celeste was at a table with her two brothers. They were
austere for Jamaicans, unsmiling. Erroll Quinceau, a prison
officer on leave from HMP Whitemoor. The other, Junior
Quinceau, wore the collar of a Baptist minister. They didn't
drink. They hardly ate a mouthful of the Coronation Chicken
and glutinous summer pudding. When Helen offered them a
cigarette it turned out they didn't smoke either. 'Blimey,' she
said, 'what do you two do for fun?'

Erroll said, 'I keep them in and stop them getting out.'

Junior the Baptist minister said, 'I can't get them in.'

'Where's Gaynor?' Rosslyn asked.

'He left with Franklin,' said Celeste.

'Do you know why?'

A waiter was approaching them between the tables.

'Mr Alan Rosslyn?' the waiter shouted above the music.
'There's a phone call for you.'

In the manager's office he lifted the telephone.

Gaynor's voice at the other end said, 'Sorry to spoil your
fun, Alan. Would you mind coming over here?'

'What's happened?'

'I want you to set that CD-ROM thing for me.'

'Which?'

'*Celeste* Item CD-ROM 87/1 in the fleapit. And the draft for
the Annual Report, we need to look at it now.'

He went back to the table. Erroll was dancing with Helen.

'I have to go,' Rosslyn told Celeste. 'I don't know how long
this is going to take. Gaynor wants me at the office. If I'm too
long, Celeste, can you look after Helen?'

'What do you mean by long?'

'An hour maybe. Perhaps longer.'

Erroll brought Helen back to their table. 'I'd like to go
home,' she said. 'I'm on earlies this week. And I'm shattered.'

'What's your home phone number?' Rosslyn asked her. 'In case I have to get back to you on the Slaemann business.'

She gave him her number.

Rosslyn gave her his. 'Let's keep in touch,' he said. 'I'll find you a cab.'

21.05

Rosslyn unlocked the secure door to the viewing room. Known to the headquarters staff of HM Customs & Excise as the fleapit, the ground-floor viewing room is no more than an airless cubicle equipped with video machines and a Compaq Presario for playing CD-ROMs.

He set up the Compaq Presario to show the Sea Captain a CD-ROM, the record of the worst example of child pornography he had ever seen.

Waiting for Gaynor, he had redrafted his text for the Annual Report. He worded the amended draft in such a way as to argue that Team E was managing to stem the tide of filth. He knew that it was really only window-dressing, but it had to be done to justify next year's budget.

Celeste might be in bad shape. But as Gaynor would say, 'Ours not to reason why.' Rosslyn knew the score. The facts about the spread of the multi-million pound industry were indisputable. It was finally impossible to argue a case that Team E was winning.

SECRET

To: Ms Drew Franklin, CB
           Chairman
           Board of HM Customs & Excise

From: A. H. Rosslyn
           Senior Investigation Officer
           Team E

Draft Submission
HM CUSTOMS & EXCISE ANNUAL REPORT
Indecent & obscene material
Contravention of import & export prohibitions
and restrictions.

KEY RESULT AREA ACHIEVED IN PART
Enforcement of prohibitions and restrictions
relating to paedophile material through
intelligence-led selective checks and the use of
key informants.

RESULTS
The results overall are broadly comparable to
performance last year and previous years and
indicate that improved targeting has
maintained the effectiveness of our
enforcement of paedophile pornography
prohibitions and restrictions in the completed
Single Market.

FIGURES
(Figures in brackets show last year's
achievement.)
PAEDOPHILE PORNOGRAPHY MATERIAL:
Seized: 31,073 items (45,901)
CRIMINAL PROCEEDINGS:
We prosecuted 29 people, of whom 3 received
custodial sentences totalling 2 years 10 months,
and 2 received conditional discharges. Fines and
costs were imposed totalling £21,438. (51 people
received custodial sentences, of which one was
suspended, and fines and costs of £41,651 were
imposed.)
COMPOUNDED SETTLEMENTS:
131 cases for a total of £19,063 (365 cases, with a
total of £55,298).

REDUCTION IN DETECTIONS
The reduction in detections of importers and
exporters of paedophile pornography material is
in part due to the removal of certain publications
from control as a result of standards applied in
this area.

We are seeing a steady change in the types of
items seized as a result of technological
developments.

Although magazines still predominate, we are
now finding a growing number of computer
disks and CD-ROMs.

Computer disks are of particular concern
because they are extremely easy to copy, and a
small number of imported disks can form the
basis of a significant trade in pornography. Team
E is making significant progress and looks
forward to major success in the immediate
future.

21.10

Out of 162 cases the previous year, Team E had initiated only
twenty-nine prosecutions. As a result of these, three people
received custodial sentences totalling a paltry two years and
ten months.

The punishments hardly fitted the crimes.

These people, mainly male, included teachers, charity
workers and desk-top publishers. On average they had been
fined about £1000 each. The sums hardly acted as a serious
deterrent.

Okay, Team E had impounded and destroyed large
quantities of serious hard-core SM videocassettes from
Korea; a batch of necrophiliac magazines printed and
published in Amsterdam; and colour photographs from 'an
artist's studio' in Frankfurt showing sex acts involving
humans and dead animals.

Old Team E investigators faced the horror with black humour.

QUESTION: *Do you admit to the practice of flagellation, necrophilia and bestiality?*

ANSWER: *Yes, I'm flogging a dead horse.*

There was an ever-increasing quantity of child pornography and murders on CD-ROMs. What Team E saw on the easy-to-copy computer disks profoundly disturbed them. Some officers even had to be monitored for stress. And as their workload increased, they had suffered serious psychological damage, depression and memory loss, culminating in some cases in complete breakdown.

The Annual Report told the truth.

Yes, I'm flogging a dead horse.

21.30

Gaynor called from his office to say he was still 'tied up variously with Drew and two people from the Home Office'.

Rosslyn reminded Gaynor that he had his Promotion Board to face next day. He badly needed an early night.

'Any idea how long you'll be, Chief?'

'Can't say exactly. I'd like you to wait on for me.'

Then Rosslyn remembered that he had agreed to be with Verity to celebrate her birthday. Never mind a present, he'd even forgotten to send her a card. He set aside the draft report and telephoned her.

'Happy birthday.'

'Thank you, Alan. You forgot.'

'I know. I'm sorry.'

'When are you coming over?'

'Late, if that's okay.'

'It's past nine, Alan.'

'I know,' said Rosslyn. 'You know what it's like, Verity. How do I know when Gaynor will be through?'

'At the party? You don't sound as though you're at the Connaught Rooms.'

'I'm not. If you must know,' said Rosslyn, 'I'm in the viewing room at Custom House.'

'Viewing what?'

'Another very sick CD-ROM.'

'Instead of having the decency to turn up on time on my birthday? I think the kiddie porn's got to you.'

'Perhaps,' said Rosslyn, knowing that she could be right. The thought of what he was about to look at with Gaynor nauseated him.

'I'll see you later,' Verity said.

He could hear her voice was slurred. She must have been drinking hard.

'You may have forgotten my birthday,' she added, 'but I bloody haven't. And it's very important you come to see me here tonight. Do you understand me? Before your Promotion Board tomorrow? Okay? It's in your own interests.'

The phone went dead. Immediately he hung up, it rang again. It was Gaynor: 'On my way,' he said. 'Got it ready?'

'Yes.'

Rosslyn's hands shook as he withdrew the disk from the plastic case. Even the sight of the label made his mouth dry.

HM Customs & Excise
STRICTLY RESTRICTED VIEWING
Team E Investigation Officers Only
Operation Celeste
Item CD-ROM 87/1

21.50

He pressed the eject button on the Compaq Presario player and inserted the CD-ROM, then closed it. The icon appeared on the screen.

I don't think I can stand having to examine this filth much longer.

He was opening his file of written notes on Item CD-ROM 87/1 when Gaynor arrived in the fleapit.

'Draft finished?' he asked, pulling up a chair in front of the screen. 'Is it good?'

'As good as it'll ever be.'

Gaynor looked exhausted. 'Remember it's the bloody minister who'll be viewing this and reading your analysis. Always assuming the stupid shit can manage to move his finger across the page.'

He offered no apology for having kept Rosslyn waiting. He seemed distant and preoccupied. 'What's wrong?' he said, glancing at Rosslyn's shaking hands.

The old boy never misses a trick.

'You really want to know?'

'Of course. You look bloody terrible.'

'I don't think I've got the stomach for this paedophile shit much longer.'

'You haven't? That's tough on you. Whether we like it or not, Alan, someone has to look at it. That's you and me for starters. Do you think I like it?' He motioned for Rosslyn to start. 'Okay, let's see it. Transcription and analysis. The Home Office says it wants to see if this filth is as bad as we say it is. We want to make the right selection. Show them the worst we've got. Talk me through this thing with your analysis notes, would you. Show it to me, then we'll talk over your draft report. Right, let's start.'

Rosslyn double-clicked on the icon.

He read his analysis aloud. His tone of assumed indifference seemed to offer some protection against the horror which appeared in full colour on the screen.

21.55

SIO A. H. Rosslyn
Continuation of Commentary and Transcription
Including Observations and Recommendations for
Further Analysis

WARNING
UK & EC Council Directive (EC 788 – EC)
These sequences show acts of extreme indecency
and sexual violence towards small children.
THEY ARE PROVEN TO CAUSE VIEWERS SEVERE
PSYCHOLOGICAL DAMAGE.
Under UK Reg. 78xx/9v they are NOT to be viewed
by personnel without prior authorization from the
relevant case officer or senior officers.

SEQUENCE 21: 2 MINUTES, 35 SECONDS
It shows an unidentified unclothed white female
child of about 10 years of age, CHILD X.

Her hands are tied to her head with white
nylon chord. The cord may possibly be a clothes
line.

CHILD X has long fair hair braided in pigtails
on the top of her head with a coloured tartan
ribbon. The material of the ribbon seems to be
of a synthetic type, as if taken from a gift
wrap.

Note: check gift wrap manufacturers, wholesale
suppliers and distribution, retail outlets and
distribution.

CHILD X is being subjected to genital abuse by penile penetration by an unidentifiable white male possibly aged between 20 and 50, MALE 1.

It is possible to see that the victim's genitalia are underdeveloped and therefore prior to puberty.

It is suggested this sequence also be shown to Medical Adviser/Paediatrician with reference to:

(a)   check of onset of puberty in victim CHILD X to assist identification. (95 per cent of girls begin between 9 and 13 years?)

(b)   check on signs of skin tears, redness, sores, swelling, scars and possible marks to be seen on the skin of the victim immediately behind the opening and between it and the anus or posterior fourchette.

(c)   partially obscured anal verges for defects, damage to anal canal folds, prominent veins &c.

SEQUENCE 22: 5 MINUTES, 11 SECONDS
It shows a second unidentified unclothed female of mixed, possibly white–Asian, race of about 10 years, CHILD Y.

CHILD Y is tied with cord similar in manufacture to that seen previously in Sequence 21. She is being subjected to penile genital penetration by an unidentifiable white male, possibly aged between 40 and 70.

SEQUENCE 23: 3 MINUTES, 37 SECONDS
It shows CHILD A and CHILD B, both female, who appear to be aged between 8 and 10, being forced to masturbate MALE 1 and MALE 2.

In this sequence it would appear that MALE 2 is operating the video camera. Therefore it may be assumed that in sequence showing MALE 2, the video camera is being operated by MALE 1.

SEQUENCE 24: 4 MINUTES, 16 SECONDS

It shows what seem to be a woman's hands (FEMALE 1). A gold wedding ring is visible on one finger and a white band of skin next to it indicates where maybe another ring is normally worn. FEMALE 1's face is not shown.

She would seem to be kneeling at the edge of a private swimming-pool. Various tiles are patterned indigo (blue), white and post-box red. A pair of rubber flip-flops may be seen to the right of several frames. Also a bottle of lubricating gel of Swiss manufacture. The location of this swimming-pool is not identified and may not be in the UK.

FEMALE 1 is seen, in close-up, lubricating CHILD A's anal passage and inserting the end of a plastic broom handle.

FEMALE 1 is then seen inserting a studded vibrator into CHILD A's vaginal passage. FEMALE 1's hand is then seen turning a switch. The switch would seem to be attached to a battery-powered vibrator. The tip and full length of the vibrator are seen at the end of a length of white plastic-coated wire.

FEMALE 1 is then seen lowering CHILD A into the water.

A distorted woman's voice, presumably FEMALE 1, is heard on the sound-track repeating: 'Swim, pussy baby. Be a good girl. Enjoy, Enjoy. Swim to Daddy to make him happy, honey baby.' The woman's accent sounds American.

FEMALE 1 is then seen holding the brush end of the broom handle with her right hand.

FEMALE 1 pushes CHILD A through the water.
CHILD A is seen to be attempting to swim while
holding on to a small plastic or rubber inflated
ring.

Note SEQUENCE 24 also includes a sound-track
on which choral music is being played. This may
be (check)

The child's fear seemed to be exciting the men and woman
committing the atrocities.

César Franck's *Panis Angelicus?*

The girls looked so vulnerable, so helpless, so terrified.

At this point a man's voice is heard to say: *'We
know what's going to happen now, don't we, dearie?'*
and *'You trust Daddy, don't you, darling dearie?'* The
accent is British/educated.
   CHILD A says: *'Please. No. Not that.'*
   MALE 1 or MALE 2 says: *'The dog will have you.'*
   CHILD A says: *'No.'*
   MALE 1 or MALE 2 says: *'Then you will die.'*
   CHILD A says: *'Yes.'*
   In the final part of SEQUENCE 24 CHILD A and
CHILD B are shown bound together being led to
the edge of a small swimming-pool.
   There is a break here. Then the two girls are
shown in the water in which is a FEMALE, face
not shown, who appears and holds the heads of
both girls beneath the surface.
   From one side two males, who would seem to
be identical to the ones already seen, appear and
each penetrates the girls.
   A short sequence of bubbles is followed by

shots of the girls, open-mouthed, with eyes open. They seem to have been held beneath the water until dead.

END OF COMMENTARY FOR TRANSCRIPTION

Rosslyn hit the STOP button.

However often you watched it, you never got used to it. He would have liked to be the one who killed these bastards.

'They're appalling.'

'Okay, Alan. I understand.' Gaynor's voice softened. 'Where did you pick this up?'

'Same place as the others. The Felixstowe batch.'

There was a satisfied smile on Gaynor's face. 'Then it must be a Vratsides disk, Alan, mustn't it?'

22.31

flickered on the digital wall clock in Gaynor's office.

Looking at him now, Rosslyn saw the veteran of a thousand office battles. Whoever the Sea Captain may have confronted in his time outside Custom House, they were probably less dangerous than the opponents he had faced within. Very rarely had he seen Gaynor vacillating quite so obviously. His face was grey with fatigue. He put the CD-ROM next to the slim black leather Freemason's case open on his desk. A glass of whisky which usually mellowed him was next to the telephones. 'Right, let's take a look at the draft of the report.' He handed Rosslyn the whisky bottle. 'Help yourself.' Lifting the transparent plastic folder from his desk, he noticed Rosslyn glancing at the digital clock. He seemed to have read Rosslyn's mind.

I don't want to be here all night.

'You must be tired,' Gaynor said. He turned over the pages of the draft report. 'Why don't we shelve this till morning?'

'Fine.'

Gaynor got out of his chair, ambled unsteadily like an overfed bear to the door, and opened it sharply, as if expecting to surprise someone listening in the corridor. Rosslyn waited for the Sea Captain to speak.

'I know that you're thinking I ought to be more involved in this one myself,' Gaynor said. 'But it's not as simple as that, is it? Whatever anybody else might say to you about me, what no one can take from me is that Customs has always come first in my life. But what you learn in this game, Alan, if you don't already know it, is that not everyone plays it my way. And what I learned fairly early on here is that the name of the game is look after number one. Self-preservation.'

He looked towards Rosslyn uncertainly.

Oh no, Rosslyn thought, *he's making a bid for sympathy*.

Gaynor continued, 'I'm not going to beat about the bush, Alan. I've been leaned on heavily. Economic sanctions have been applied. That's what that meeting was about. I've been told, in words of one syllable, that if I want my pension I must be very careful that my hands are completely clean.' He shifted pens and pencils around his desk nervously. 'I can't be seen to be helping you.'

'I can't pretend that I like what you've just told me,' Rosslyn said.

'I didn't expect you to.'

'But I suppose if I were in your shoes,' Rosslyn said, 'I'd have done the same. You don't owe me anything. In fact, it's the other way round.'

Gaynor looked grateful. 'Thank you for that, Alan,' he said.

'Obviously I have to keep a low profile.' Gaynor fingered the CD-ROM. 'Nice, isn't it? Never seen anything as bad as this before, have we? Could've earned the filth hundreds of thousands of pounds already. Probably encouraged some other perverted scum to do the same to others. We can't let it go on, can we? I'm prepared to do what I can, though, Alan.'

'I appreciate that you've got to protect your pension rights,' Rosslyn said. 'But I'm not used to seeing you toe the line in this way. It must be pretty big pressure that's been applied.'

'It is,' said Gaynor. 'Once the Establishment decides to get you, there's no limit to how shitty they'll make things for you. By the same token, if they decide to protect one of their own, believe me there's no limit to the lengths they'll go. Listen, I don't think it's only my pension they'll take away. Given half a chance they'll take very much more than that. Just so long as you realize you can't rely on me to put in any man hours on your behalf.'

'What can you put in then?'

Gaynor reached inside the slim black Freemason's case.

'Just one other thing. Keep this.' He handed Rosslyn a business card. 'Although I'm sure you've got one already.'

Rosslyn read:

Aiko Holland
US Customs Senior Special Agent
United States Embassy
24 Grosvenor Square
London W1A 1AE
tel. 0171 499 9000
ext. 7899

He seemed on the verge of speaking in confidence, and then had second thoughts. 'You'll have good reason to be grateful to her,' he said. He was leaning over his desk, rummaging among pens and pencils in a wooden tray. He wrote something on a yellow Post-it slip. 'One other thing besides, Alan. I'm not putting you in a position to quote me. A name that came up in the meeting I'm not supposed to refer to. Just read this.'

Rosslyn looked at the Post-it slip. The Sea Captain had scribbled down: VRATSIDES.

'She may be able to give you a whole new package deal,'
Gaynor said. 'The Americans have stuff they never share,'
he added at his most paternal. 'They only tell us what they
want us to know. Usually it's fuck all. Still, that's the way it
goes. But they hate filth as much as you and I do. I believe
they really want a collar as much as we do. Even if they
appear to be interested in only what affects them. Think of
those kids. Ruined lives. Dead even. If our eyes are to be
believed. You said you'd like to kill the filth who destroyed
those little girls. You and me both.'

22.50

In the silence of his office Rosslyn checked his in-tray for any
urgent messages. He found none that couldn't wait until the
morning.

He locked a pile of classified papers in his safe along with
his summary, transcription and analysis of the *Celeste* CD-
ROM, and a copy of his CV he'd shown to Dr Claudine
Hecht. The yellow Post-it slip with the name Vratsides he
transferred to the inside pocket of his jacket, along with Aiko
Holland's card.

What he needed was a few moments alone. To collect his
thoughts.

Straub.

*Now Gaynor, hamstrung by unnamed visitors abandoning the
ship like the proverbial rats.*

His promotion. Before Straub's death in Copenhagen it had
seemed worth the toss. 'Full steam ahead. Piece of cake,'
Gaynor had said. 'Just a steering job,' was the racing
metaphor he'd used. There were so many appointments to
be filled. 'Young blood,' said Gaynor, 'young blood's what's
needed now. This is leap-frog time.'

Then came Copenhagen and now his prospects didn't just
look to be burning dimly.

Looked more like lights out.

The corridor to the lift took him past Gaynor's office. A

shaft of light showed beneath the door. He walked on past and took the lift to the ground-floor foyer.

Custom House had an atmosphere of neglect. Dreary pictures of the Thames hung lopsided above a line of plastic furniture and wilting rubber plants. One more exercise in the management of decline. The cracked notice-board headed State of Vigilance said NIL.

'Sorry, Mr Rosslyn, sir,' the duty security guard said, 'your cab-driver woman said she couldn't wait.'

'I haven't called a cab.'

'She said you called half an hour ago.'

'Did she just?' Rosslyn snapped. 'Then why didn't you call me?'

'Sorry, sir. She said not to bother you.'

'That's okay. Forget it. Good night.'

Traditionally, the security guards enjoyed being the bearers of bad news. Bemedalled former servicemen and women. Coppers from the beat. Ex-ratings from the Royal Navy. They claimed the world had been a better place in their day. Going about their duties sustained by some vague pride in being in the service of Her Majesty, they were the last subscribers to the idea that Her Majesty's Customs & Excise upheld the spirit of Commonwealth and Empire. *Honi soit qui mal y pense*. Sometimes one of them was rewarded with an MBE.

He pushed through the revolving doors with unnecessary force.

The Thames smelled sour. In the Custom House windows the only lights still burning were Gaynor's.

He wondered about that woman cab driver. It was very odd.

23.01

In Monument Street he heard the sound of footsteps.

Glancing back through the yellowish light, he made out the indistinct figure of a woman.

At the Fish Street entrance to Monument underground station he looked round a second time. The woman hesitated for a second, as if she had changed her mind, and turned towards an otherwise deserted Gracechurch Street.

In the ticket hall at Monument, near the barriers, the only other travellers were two men huddled together making a call by cell-phone.

The eyes of one of them met Rosslyn's briefly. Rosslyn was alerted to a flicker of expectancy. The man turned his back with a studied and casual air to show a key chain dangling from his belt.

His companion had apparently ended his telephone call. And when he carefully returned his cell-phone to the inside of his leather jacket, he laughed and Rosslyn clearly heard him say, 'No reply.' Odd, because seconds before he had seen him engaged in conversation.

He was used to picking up such trivial inconsistencies of behaviour at airports or railway termini. Even here in the underground station late at night. The nose for deceit. The hunter's instinct. These days, late-night travellers needed to be particularly alert for muggers known to carry portable phones and offensive weapons. Or maybe they were on the look-out for casual pick-ups.

Down through the two levels, on the escalators and along the echoing pedestrian tunnels leading into the station at Bank, they stayed behind him and then boarded the train.

23.16

On the seats next to him, jammed between the armrests, two women feasted on fried onions and chips. There was an overwhelming stench of vinegar. They were reading aloud from a tabloid. Its headline took up most of the page: MPS DEMAND EXECUTION FOR PAEDOPHILES. Smaller letters said: 'Customs Fail to Stem Tide of Filth'.

Splashed across another page was a photograph of a

minister with his wife and three daughters looking bewildered beneath a headline: BI-SEXY MP – 3 IN A BED.

Rosslyn looked at the other passengers. All of them, young and old, cramming their faces. Kebabs. Crisps. Ice-cream. Empty beer cans rolled across the floor. Four white youths with shaven heads and Nazi tattoos on their cheeks slouched opposite him. One, with his legs wide apart, had a felt-tip drawing of a penis in the crotch of his torn jeans. Another's T-shirt announced: RATS HAVE RIGHTS.

Half-drunk and sullen, the hostile quartet stared at Rosslyn with contempt.

Without warning the train squealed and juddered to a halt, its lights flickering off then on. The youths were on their feet, swaggering down the aisle, deliberately treading on people's shoes. Rosslyn noticed the youth with the crotch drawing was toying with a flick-knife. He felt relieved when they left the train at the next stop. But the two men he had seen at Monument were still in the next carriage.

It has to be coincidence. Keep one eye on them though. Better safe than sorry.

He turned his attention to the draft report.

It's bad news. He wondered how he could dress it up to make it more acceptable.

Say:

Delete ACHIEVED IN PART *from* KEY RESULT AREA *and leave it as* ACHIEVED?

Insert LESSONS LEARNED.

Insert STRATEGIES FOR A BETTER FUTURE?

By the time the train had reached King's Cross most of the passengers had left.

Okay, let's paint a rosy future. Team E will succeed.

From where he was sitting he could see that the two men were still in the next carriage. And they were still there too when he left the train at Camden Town.

He'd run too many street surveillance operations of his

own not to recognize the techniques of shadowing.

If they were common street muggers they'd have pounced on me by now. So why are they tailing me?

Outside the underground station at Camden Town there was another worrying sign.

An empty black cab, its FOR HIRE sign unlit, set off at a slow pace ahead of him northwards up Camden High Street. And there was another cab apparently following behind him. He reckoned that if he kept up a steady pace he should easily make it to Camden Lock Place inside ten minutes. A few more and then he would be safe aboard Verity's canal boat, the *Manchester Madonna*.

In the street, car stereos pumped dub music full blast. It clashed with other music coming from flats above closed and barricaded shop fronts. He noted police cars parked across the street in front of the Fusilier and Firkin pub. Police officers were hauling a shoeless derelict to a van, her feet dragging across the pavement. She was screaming 'Fatwa, Fatwa, Fatwa.'

Opposite Castlehaven Road, at the corner of Camden Lock Place, he stumbled over a pile of smashed wooden vegetable crates. A sad voice spoke to him from a darkened doorway. A little further on, he paused in the entrance to a flower shop.

The men.

They can't see me now.

He glanced back down the street, then at his watch.

23.37

They may want to chance their arm and attack for the sake of the twenty quid and credit cards in my wallet. Probably now is their best chance to score against me.

He had temporarily lost sight of them and was tempted to walk back the way he'd come, to return to the Fusilier and Firkin and those police cars, or to the relative safety of Camden Town underground station.

Ahead, Camden Lock Place was in darkness.

Glancing back, he saw the men again. This time he saw them standing in the flower-shop doorway. One of them was speaking into the cell-phone.

At his feet something began to scratch at the bottom of a pile of garbage bags. What was it? *Rat? Cat?* He couldn't tell.

A police siren sounded in the distance, then faded.

As he reached the entrance to West Yard he was certain that the men were following him. And now a new figure appeared, illuminated by the lights across the canal. A man in a hooded running suit.

Though exposed, the narrow footbridge across the canal somehow promised safety. *Once I reach the top of it I'll make a run for it to the other side. To the* Manchester Madonna. *And* Verity.

He told himself, *Keep walking. Across the bridge. Don't look back. Don't run. Don't let him know I've seen him. Don't show you're scared.* But the figure in the hooded running suit kept on coming.

The path to the footbridge over the Regent Canal rose steeply. At the top of it, he saw the lights from the warehouses. Here the sour air became a little clearer.

Male. Wearing training shoes. Not out here running on the night streets of north London for the sake of fitness.

To his left, where the view of Camden Lock should have been, the lights were a dull electric blue. Ahead and to his right, he could make out the glow of lights in curtained windows. There was less than fifty yards or so downhill to the footpath on the other side. The figure was still there ahead of him, the face a dark oval in the hood.

Wait. Retrace my steps. See if it doesn't vanish.

From the towpath, he saw the low outlines of the *Manchester Madonna*.

At the entrance to Middle Yard, music thundered through smashed windows of Georgian glass, Jule Nagel Band: *'Wir sind wie besinnung-slos! Wir kussen uns – kissen uns ins All!'*

Headlights came on: low, then at full beam. For a second he stopped. The man had gone. To the accompaniment of the butch German singer Jule Nagel's 'Lieb' mich, oh my Baby!' he walked quickly across the footbridge. Along the footpath. To the rickety gangway and the *Manchester Madonna*.

Thursday 27 July

84°F/29°C. Dry and bright. Isolated thunder later.
Wind south-easterly, becoming southerly to south-
westerly, mostly light.

00.01

'Happy birthday,' Rosslyn said.

Verity, wearing her bright blue silk dressing gown, kicked
aside a pile of unclaimed mail and circulars on the wooden
floor. She looked younger than her thirty years. She smelled
of musk. Strands of her platinum-blonde hair were caught up
in the links of her heavy silver neck chain, his gift to her.

'That was yesterday,' she said. Her breath smelled faintly
of whisky.

'I'm sorry.'

'Yes.'

'How's Daisy?'

'Fine, Alan. Just fine. Tucked up and fast asleep. Sit down.
There's something we have to talk through. We should get it
over with.'

'Go ahead.'

Long legs astride the captain's chair back to front, she
faced him with The Look.

It always heralded some kind of intimidation, following a
brusque Miss Strict instruction such as *'Sit down, there's
something I want to tell you.'* In or out of bed, before, after or
during love, always the born interrogator, she delivered
attacks or bad news or both only when she had you at her
mercy. In the same way she began rows.

'Something you need to know, something I'm not supposed to tell you,' she said. 'You've probably suspected it anyway. That's why I asked you to come and see me. I had a visit at Vauxhall Cross.'

'What visit?'

'Some people looking into you.'

'I hope they're not the same bastards who followed me here.'

'When?'

'Just now.'

'I wouldn't know anything about that,' she said.

'Then who are these people "looking into me"?'

'I can't tell you,' she said.

'Why not?'

'Well, I can't.'

'My people?' Rosslyn asked.

'No.'

'MI5?'

'I wouldn't know.'

'When was this?'

She hesitated a moment. 'Let's just say they weren't your people. Not their plodding style.'

'I see,' said Rosslyn. 'So what did they want to know about me?'

'More, actually, about us. The usual sort of thing. How permanent things are between us. About your frame of mind. Stable or otherwise. Sexual history.'

'You told them.'

'Up to a point,' she said. 'Yes, I did.'

'You didn't think to ask my permission first?'

'Why should I?'

'They didn't ask *my* permission, Verity.'

'They didn't have to. Or so they told me,' She sucked her teeth. 'They wouldn't, would they?'

'What exactly was it about?'

'Your promotion,' she said. 'To replace Gaynor as Chief

Investigation Officer.'

'What did you tell them?'

'I told them that, in my view, you're perfect for it.'

'Thanks a lot.'

'No need to thank me.'

He thought: *Come to the point. No more games.*

'Is that why you've asked me to come here in the middle of the night?'

'I asked you to join me for dinner.' She said. 'On my birthday.'

'And I've said I'm sorry I couldn't make it,' he said. 'And what else did you tell your visitors?'

'I told them that our relationship had ended.'

Perhaps she read my thoughts. 'Fair enough.'

There was a faint smile on her lips as though she had gained the upper hand.

'I've been overdoing the drink,' she said. 'That's always a bad sign in my love affairs.'

'I know.'

'For Christ's sake,' she snapped, 'don't start the jealousy all over again. I thought we'd grown out of all that. Anyway, did it come out at the shrink's? I really do hope I can trust you to have left me out of things. I've got Daisy. Daisy's got me. Women and children first.'

'If you say so.'

'I can keep secrets, Alan. That's my job. I'm paid rather well to do it. I hope you've done the same.'

'Have you told Daisy that we've ended things?'

'Ages ago. She's actually rather happy about it.'

That hurt.

He missed Daisy. The kite flying. Home video making. Peter Pan, *even the dreadful Christmas pantomime. Tea at Fortnum's with blue rinses and Japanese. The fancy-dress party for her little friends. Endless bedtime stories of his own invention. The videos:* Wizard of Oz, Snow White and the Seven Dwarfs.

'I hope you won't be bitter,' Verity said.

'I'm not. I'm just thinking of the countless times you've said how you hate living alone.'

'Yes, well.' Slowly she stretched her arms above her head. 'I thought you'd understand, Alan. It's in your nature to be generous about people.'

'You didn't give me much choice, did you?' he said. 'Do you mind my asking if you said anything else to the spooks?'

'Just what I told you. Just that we had come to an amicable arrangement.'

'You mean an understanding?'

'No. An arrangement's what I said. Everything's settled. We're the best of friends.'

'That's all you told them?'

'Yes, Alan. That is all I told those creeps about you and me.' She unfastened the silver chain from around her neck. 'Here, take this. You always said this turned you on.'

'I'd like you to keep it,' he said. 'It's yours.'

She placed it on the table. 'The thing I loved about you most,' she said, 'is your complete lack of sentimentality.'

She was interrupted by the sound of Daisy calling out 'Mummy?'

'We've woken her up,' said Verity. 'Wait here. I'll see to her.'

He thought he heard Daisy asking, 'What's the matter, Mummy?'

'I have a visitor. It's all right, darling. Settle down.'

'Who's here, Mummy? Is it Alan? Or is it You-Know-Who? YKW? Is it YKW?'

Who's YKW?

'Get to sleep, darling,' Verity was saying softly. 'I won't be long.'

Who's You-Know-Who?

He felt the *Manchester Madonna* nudge the canal wall.

Verity's eyes were on him. She had come back into the cabin. 'She's frightened. I'm going to sleep with her.' She lifted the telephone. 'Why don't I call a cab for you?' She was

standing legs crossed, her arms folded. 'Alan, I'm sorry about
the things I've said. You have to admit they needed saying. I
just want you to go on trusting me.'

The trust went months ago.

'As a friend. I need that, Alan. Tell me about *Operation
Celeste*.'

The need to know everything. Some things will never change.

'Another time.'

As she was dictating the directions for the cab, he saw
Daisy in her pyjamas standing in the doorway. Her eyes were
puffed with sleep. She was holding a small envelope. 'Have
you got to go?' she said.

'Alan has got to get home,' Verity said. 'Come on, back to
bed.'

'I mean, are you *leaving*? I mean, *for ever*?'

'Alan will be back, won't you?' said Verity.

'Yes,' he said.

Daisy looked unconvinced.

'We're rearranging things,' Verity said.

Daisy was holding out a small package. 'I want you to
have this,' she said. 'It's my present to you.'

She handed him the package. Her writing on the label said:

FOR DARLINGEST ALAN
LOTS AND LOTS OF LOVE
DAISY

'Mind if I open it in the morning?' he said.

'That's all right,' she said.

'Thanks, Daisy. You know what I think? I think it's a
video.'

'You're not allowed to *guess*,' Daisy said.

'It's not *The Wizard of Oz*,' said Verity.

'It's much better than *The Wizard of Oz*,' said Daisy. 'Please
come back, Alan. Soon.'

'If you invite me.'

'We will, Daisy, won't we?' said Verity. 'Once you're back
from Granny's. Now, into bed.'

The cab driver was at the door.

'Time to go,' said Rosslyn.

'Keep in touch.' said Verity. 'Good luck at your Promotion Board.'

He kissed her on both cheeks. 'Thanks.'

01.05

In the cab bound for Eccleston Square he told himself, *Think of a question:*

'Why, Mr Rosslyn, do you want the job of Chief Investigation Officer?'

Because I believe we have earned our reputation as the best and most successful Customs investigation organization in the world.

'What values will you instil in the members of your staff?'
Integrity, professionalism and courtesy.

'Do you feel, after ten years' service in Customs & Excise, at the relatively young age of thirty-two, that you may, at the end of the day, be rather too young to take on the challenge of the appointment as CIO?'

I realize I will be the youngest officer ever to have been given the job.

I prefer to let my record speak for itself.

What had Dr Hecht made of what he told her?

Inevitably, his relationship with Verity would become an issue. It was not unknown for Promotion Boards to request an interview with a candidate's partner. If the relationship was long-standing. Even the category of ex-partner sometimes received the treatment. The medical test for HIV was obligatory. So too was the question about his having ever contacted sexually transmitted diseases. The number of sexual partners had to be recorded also. Care + Welfare = Interference + Manipulation would sooner or later earn its place on some flow-chart like Drew's Egg Timer.

Plausibility + Reliability = Success.

A trick learned from years of experience in dealing with deceitful subordinates and criminals.

Eccleston Square was empty. Nevertheless, he was careful to look up and down the street before he let himself into the house. He took the stairs to his flat two at a time.

Ten minutes later he was in bed and asleep.

07.30

said the digits on his bedside clock and the telephone was ringing.

Celeste was saying, 'Can we talk?'

'Yes. Go ahead.'

'I can't talk over the phone.'

'Why not? We're on a secure line.'

'Something terrible happened last night.'

'You don't say,' Rosslyn said.

'I have to talk to you in private, Alan.'

'I'll be right in.'

08.31

He entered Custom House in Lower Thames Street by the western and nearest entrance.

'I'm sorry, sir,' said the guard. 'We're doing our best to scrape it off.'

'Scrape what off?'

'You haven't seen it then?'

'Seen what?'

'I wouldn't look at it if I were you, sir.'

'Would you mind telling me what you're talking about?'

'What's on the wall outside. You can't miss it. They used paint that the bricks absorb.'

'What are you trying to tell me?'

'The graffiti. Outside. We know it isn't true, Mr Rosslyn. It's on the wall, sir. Some people won't stop at anything, will they? If it were me, sir, I wouldn't look at it.'

He ignored the guard's advice.

And outside, in Lower Thames Street, along the rear wall of Custom House, he saw the maintenance men scraping away at four-feet high letters painted in thick red:

rosslyn is a paedophile

'We'll get it off by lunchtime,' said one of the maintenance men.

Said another, 'Don't you worry, sir. Sooner or later the cops'll get the bastards who did that. The closed circuit TV should show who did it.'

Said a third, 'Unfortunately, it didn't pick them out.'

He was about to add some further words of reassurance when the duty guard interrupted. 'Mr Rosslyn, sir.' He was shouting and waving from the corner of the building. 'The Chairman wants to see you, sir.'

Said one of the maintenance men, 'Don't you worry, sir. We'll fix it.'

'The Chairman wants to see you, Mr Rosslyn,' said the duty guard with a smile.

'I heard the first time.'

'Sorry, didn't mean to shout. She's in her office, sir.'

They walked together to the western entrance.

'It's a tragedy, sir.'

'I wouldn't go so far as to say that,' said Rosslyn. 'I'm afraid it goes with the territory.'

Sweating in his office, he hung his jacket behind the door.

On his desk was a note from Drew asking him to see her in Gaynor's office at nine. *Neutral ground*, he thought.

09.01

Rosslyn waited for her in Gaynor's office.

Everything had already been rearranged. Presumably Maintenance and Removals had been in very early in the morning because there was a stack of Custom House cardboard packing-cases filled with Gaynor's office stuff marked FOR STORAGE and COLLECTION.

Exhibits: Two open packing-cases. A kelim, his personal property, is rolled up. Tied with red nylon cord. On the top of one packing-case is a framed family photograph.

There's a stack of current papers on his desk.

Unfinished business for approval.

Someone's stuck small red paper squares on the most important items.

Exhibits: Outfield Reports on current investigations with requests for recommendations and authorization for surveillance.

Exhibit: Counter-signature requests for cash payments to informers.

Exhibits: a copy of my own CV drafted for the Promotion Board.

On the top of the pile was a draft of the Bad News letter to be sent to all Investigation Division's officers from Drew.

STAFF IN CONFIDENCE

To: CIO Richard Gaynor, CBE
From: Chairman

TO INITIAL AND RETURN

There are going to be major cuts in personnel comprising a reduction of about 4000 in our staffing levels. This means that, taken together with reductions which were already planned, by the year 2000 staff will reduce to about 20,800.

Contrary to some press reports, the reduction of staff will be phased over 5 years. This will allow us to make maximum use of natural wastage and voluntary early release, in line with our commitment to avoid compulsory redundancies wherever possible.

I do not want to understate our staffing problems.

We have to face a very difficult task which will require all our skill and co-operation to manage.

We will place greater emphasis on areas of high risk and more complex work to achieve the best results, giving less priority to routine control where risks are low.

I know that change on this scale can be painful.

She's pinned a note to it.

PERSONAL & CONFIDENTIAL

To: CIO Richard Gaynor, CBE
From: Chairman

SUBJECT: ALAN ROSSLYN Team E

If there is a case for NOT making an appointment for your replacement at CIO level?

I'd like to be able to say I have your agreement.

The view is that Alan Rosslyn is too junior in terms of length of service to take over.

I gather there is a mood of resistance to his being appointed your successor. (A history of some unreliability/instability in his personal and domestic arrangements.)

I tend to think John Thornley-Miller will be the wiser appointment and I gather he will be prepared to undertake the role on the same salary scale.

I'd like to talk this over with you, and whether you might be prepared to leave the Department earlier than planned?

Subject to final approval and assessment, your pension arrangements will not be affected.

Please initial and return if you approve.

I don't believe this. Gaynor has initialled it.

Rosslyn remembered Gaynor saying, *'All I've got is my pension.'*

Drew came in while he was reading her note. He stiffened. She said, 'It's in the hands of the police.'

Behind her was the view of the river and Tower Bridge in the morning sun, its shape defined sharply against the clear blue sky.

'I've given immediate instructions for its removal. No matter what the expense. Or what it takes. To have it removed without trace. I have asked the police to make every effort to find those responsible.'

'I very much appreciate that,' said Rosslyn. 'But with all those security guards wandering around and the CCTV, I just don't believe someone didn't see the bastards who did it.'

Drew looked downriver at Tower Bridge. A million miles away. 'I don't know what to believe,' she said.

He was about to confront her with her letter when she said, 'Leave that for the moment, Alan. I have to warn you. It's about *Celeste*. I have to warn you that if you continue with it, I am under orders to suspend you from duty. You're playing with fire. On a purely personal level, just between ourselves, I think you should go back to Verity, God help you.' She pointed at the packing-cases containing Gaynor's property. 'As the previous occupant of this office would say, "You're in danger of burning your boats." It's a pity, Alan, don't you think?'

She turned on her heel.

Rosslyn saw her slam the door.

09.28

There was a message in his office from Thornley-Miller, asking Rosslyn to call as soon as he was free. The note continued: PLEASED TO TELL YOU WE'VE UPDATED THE EQUIPMENT. GIVE IT A RUN-THROUGH. LET ME KNOW WHAT YOU THINK. J T-M.

He hung his jacket behind his office door and felt the package that Daisy had given him.

09.35

In the fleapit he viewed Daisy's video.

The title was:

♥

Daisy Cavallero
aged 10

There were shots of himself when he'd had toothache. Some of him smiling. The Regent Canal in the winter sun. The *Manchester Madonna* docked at the Camden Basin. Daisy was saying:

'Here is the *Manchester Madonna*. This is home, where Mummy lives with me. The *Manchester Madonna* was built about sixty years ago. It was given to Mummy by a friend and is worth a lot of money.'

There were close-up shots of ducks, followed by others of Daisy's cabin. Daisy said: 'This is my little cabin, which has a very comfy bunk and a duvet and several teddies who sleep with me cuddled up. There is my favourite nightie.'

Then the main cabin and Daisy's commentary:

'Here's what Mummy calls "Lounge Out". The stove is wood-burning and when we burn apple-tree branches it gives off a lovely smell. There are some nice pictures on the wall from Mummy's travels. Some are of Greece and Lake Como, which is in Italy, where Mummy used to go on holiday with boyfriends.'

Now Verity's cabin, with Daisy saying:

'Here is Mummy's great big bed. She has goose-feather pillows, which isn't fair to geese. On Saturday mornings we all get into bed together and *I try not to leave croissant crumbs* in the sheets. Once I left some honey there by mistake.'

Now the camera was exploring his flat in Eccleston Square and Daisy was saying:

'The flat doesn't look lived in because it's not.'

Rosslyn saw himself and he was saying, 'And who am I?'

And Daisy was laughing. 'MY GREAT BIG BEAST.'

Now Verity was reciting to camera:

> There was a little girl
> Who had a little curl
> Right in the middle of her forehead,
> When she was good
> She was very, very good
> And when she was bad she was horrid.

Daisy laughed and said, 'That's not what Alan says.'

'What does Alan say?' asked Verity.

And Daisy recited:

> There was a little girl
> Who had a little curl
> Right in the middle of her forehead,
> And when she was good
> She was very, very good
> And when she was bad
> She was very, very POPULAR!

After the music-hall joke was another sequence taken in the *Manchester Madonna*.

Daisy undressed for bed, slipped on her nightdress and jumped into bed.

'I hope,' she said, 'that makes you very happy, Alan.'

That was the end of it.

Sad to think she's almost out of my life, he thought. *Nearest I've ever got to having a child of my own.*

When I was a kid I used to make drawings of the woman I'd marry and the children we'd have together. Daisy's the sort of child I drew. Big dark eyes. Quite different from her mother's. Fair olive skin. A flirt. The sweetest child. Easy come, easy go. In a few years'

time she'll be a heart-breaker. Like her mother. Perhaps like the
father who can't know what he's missing.

09.55

From the open window of Gaynor's office he looked across
the Thames at low tide.

Some small children, treasure-hunters with a metal
detector, were searching the mud and yellow scum at the
river's edge. He could hear their distant laughter above the
hum of the City traffic. One of them, a girl with hair
bleached white by the sun, was wearing a long and rather
old-fashioned white dress. Her dark glasses looked too large
for her small face. She was carrying a mongrel dog in her
arms. Not far from the derelict Tate and Lyle warehouse
moorings, someone had lit a small fire. Its single plume of
bluish smoke drifted upwards fifty feet or so, spreading out
slowly, until it blurred the edges of Tower Bridge. The
familiar squareness of the structure for once looked strange
and out of place against the blue cloudless sky and the khaki
and grey colours of the river. Set against his anger and
resentment, inspired by Drew's decision, the stillness of the
morning seemed unreal.

The graffiti on the wall of Custom House could not have
been the sole reason for her bitter outburst. Only a fool would
believe the grafitti's message; and everyone at Custom House
knew there had been plenty of others like this morning's
directed at individual officers. Splashed in bright red, white
or black paint across the old brick walls of Lower Thames
Street, not one had contained a single shred of truth.
Paradoxically, they always worked against the perpetrators
by encouraging an involuntary closing of the ranks at
Custom House and a temporary boost to morale. Unfortunately, the City police had never caught a single perpetrator
of the previous slurs. Common sense and precedent
suggested that the chances of them nailing these particular
lying daubers were zero. Drew's personal animosity and her

opposition to his promotion, to say nothing of Gaynor's endorsement, preoccupied him more.

And why hadn't she spoken to him about it herself? Strangely, her confidential memorandum to Gaynor was undated. Had she sent it to Gaynor before or after the end of their affair?

He couldn't work it out. Yet he felt sure that its content somehow originated in her buried bitterness rather than in any professional strategy.

Except.

He looked again at the memorandum.

The working of her mind was plain. Here it was in black and white.

She wants Thornley-Miller as her CIO.

And she's added that comment about the protection of Gaynor's beloved pension arrangements.

He remembered Verity once commenting wryly and with a touch of *Schadenfreude* on the Peter Wright damage. When the irascible and eccentric old MI5 agent's memoirs, *Spycatcher*, were finally published in the UK, Verity had said, 'All they had to do was pay the old fart his pension and he'd have kept his mouth shut.'

A greenish crack like a prism's edge in the window glass caught sunbeams and formed the colours of the rainbow. He saw a large wasp squirming in its death throes on the window-sill. He carefully crushed its head with his thumbnail to end whatever misery it was suffering.

He remembered Drew saying, 'I don't know what to believe.'

You know exactly who's given the orders to see to the termination of Celeste.

You know why the order to abort it has been given, and exactly why they have threatened my suspension from duty if I continue with it. Who are They? Home Office, Paymaster General's Office, Attorney-General, MI5, even MI6? Take your pick. If I were in your bed, would you tell me, Drew?

What pressure's been applied to you of a more personal kind?
What's your problem? Scared about the future of your pension too,
are you? I heard you sneer at me:

'On a purely personal level, just between ourselves, I think you
should go back to Verity.'

And, *'God help you.'*

What's eating you, Drew? Don't tell me it's jealousy. That
you're covering up rejection. I hate to tell you this. But that's the
sort of crap Verity would say lies behind this volte-face of yours.

From below, down by the riverside, he heard one of the
children yell a warning to the small girl in the white dress to
keep away from the water. He watched her turn and saw her
smiling at the blue sky. With a shock, he realized she was blind.

It must have occurred to Drew weeks ago that there was no
point in continuing their clandestine affair. It was also
something of a minor miracle that news of it had not spread
further. It had always been necessary to surround it in
secrecy. In the early and headier days, there was an
undoubted attraction to the late-night rendezvous, the sense
of conventions flaunted and the conservative proprieties of
the Customs service undermined. It had seemed like a
harmless, romantic and adulterous affair they'd both needed
and deserved.

You, to forget the husband.

Me, to put Verity out of mind.

'Like having a long drink of cool water,' she had put it rather
clumsily, *'in the dry deserts of our hearts.'*

And he'd imagined Verity laughing with delight at this
bash at lyricism on Drew's part. Verity would have had a
name for Drew's image, culled from some 'handbook of
psychological awareness'.

Rather paradoxically, Verity did her ideological causes
little service by reserving most of her bile for attacks on other
women's emotional outpourings and problems. Had she
been a man, Rosslyn sometimes thought, she might well have
been accused of misogyny.

Suppose his affair with Drew had ever become public knowledge?

We'd have had to handle corrosive gossip and silent censure.

There would have been the inevitable comments about favouritism and the difference between them in rank and power, to say nothing of age.

We were lovers pitted against the petty office gossips, the secretaries huddled on the pavements of Lower Thames Street snatching a hurried smoke away from the No Smoking zones. The messengers in the corridors. The infield officers bringing outfield pals up to date in Waxers and in the bar at Custom House.

Maybe it had been selflessly, for the sake of both their interests, that she had decided to end it so abruptly.

But why put the boot into my promotion prospects?

Thornley-Miller is salt in the wound.

When he turned away from the view of the Thames, he noticed Maintenance and Removals had forgotten to pack Gaynor's favourite reproduction: Turner's *The Fighting Temeraire*.

The framed reproduction was still hanging where Gaynor had preferred it, on the wall behind the door. Its imitation gold frame was cracked. A fine grey and pink dust veiled the glass. A small label was peeling from the false gold leaf. The quotation beneath it, affixed to the frame by browned Sellotape, was in Gaynor's hand and came from Thomas Campbell's poem *Ye Mariners of England*:

'The flag which braved the battle and the breeze / No longer owns her.'

You're right, Drew. Gaynor would've said to me, 'You're in danger of burning your boats.'

Turner's painting seemed to be as much about breaking up a way of life as the scrapping of the veteran warships of the Napoleonic wars.

Drew had once said, 'My work is my family, my children, my stability, my life.' To have let the end of the affair influence her judgement about the future of *his* career seemed unreasonable, though he could believe she must have been thinking hard about her own.

He felt tempted to call her in her office straightaway.

Give it to her straight.

'*In the light of Straub's last fax, to ditch Celeste is as unjust as the timing was wrong. Just at the moment when there's at last a fighting chance Team E can nail the scum involved. We have a name. Why block the investigation now? Who's calling the shots, pulling the strings? To add insult to injury, you're even spreading the word that I'm PERSONALLY unsuitable to be appointed Chief Investigation Officer. Out of order, Drew. Who else have you told that I'm no longer the best candidate for promotion to CIO? Is it just because we're no longer lovers? Are you that crass?*'

It was, he felt, ironic that he had been simultaneously involved with two such ambitious women, Verity and Drew, who inhabited two different secret worlds. Odd too that both were without friends; unless, in Verity's case, you counted Daisy, who was much more.

His thoughts were interrupted by Celeste, who was standing in the open doorway of Gaynor's office.

He didn't hear what she said at first.

He realized that there was now no turning away from *Celeste*.

'Alan, I'm sorry,' Celeste was saying.

He had no idea how long she had been standing there.

At first he thought she was sympathizing about the graffiti.

'I've seen worse,' he said. 'It's bullshit.'

'Drew's been throwing her weight around,' Celeste said, closing the door.

'She likes to save face,' he said. 'I don't blame her. Likes to show who's number one.'

'I've just come from her office,' Celeste said. 'She's in a foul temper. She told me to tell you about your Promotion Board.'

'What about it?'

'It's been postponed indefinitely.'

'*She* told you *that*?'

'She told me to tell you.'

'She was here a while back,' Rosslyn said. 'She could've told me herself. What's she trying to do, make sure that the world and his wife knows before I do?'

'You know what she's like,' Celeste said. 'Likes to twist the knife.' She looked at the reproduction of *The Fighting Temeraire*. 'She's been asking for the *Celeste* files.'

'Did you tell her they'd been shredded?'

'Yes, I did,' said Celeste. 'And, guess what, she didn't believe me. And did she blow her top! "Fuck it," she said. And started telling me there's a conspiracy around to keep *Celeste* alive and that you're behind it. Something's eating *her* alive.'

'What did you say to that?'

'I said it was the first I knew about it. That anyway we have to close ranks. That the staff will support you. Especially in the light of that graffiti. I told her it'll have the reverse effect to what was intended. "I fucking hope so," she said. She seemed, well, threatened, you know. Sort of cornered.'

He watched another wasp squirming on the sill.

He pointed out to her the children still standing in the morning sun at the river's edge. 'Lucky little bastards, aren't they? Wouldn't you rather be playing around down there instead of in here? Without a care in the world.'

She nodded.

'Me too,' said Rosslyn.

He sat on the edge of Gaynor's desk. For a moment he wondered whether Drew had got Celeste to sound out his intentions. He decided this was not the appropriate moment to ask her. He had to make the leap of faith. Trust her.

'You need to know,' he said. 'I didn't tell her that we're continuing with *Celeste*.' He looked her straight in the eye. 'You want to stay with it, don't you?'

'I do, Alan,' she said. And then added, as if she were making a solemn vow, 'Yes, I do.'

'For Drew to have given the order to abort it,' Rosslyn said, 'may turn out to be the worst career move of her life. I think that's why she's so angry. Not with me. Or us. With herself. And with whoever's putting the squeeze on her. Whoever's blocking us. Angry at herself for not having the nerve to stand up to her superiors. So in love with her career. And herself. The two are inextricably connected. Anyhow, she mustn't know we're continuing with it. I know too much. Sooner or later, I think, what happened to Straub could happen to me anyway. So fuck it. It may not be possible to carry on out of here. And, if we have to, we'll handle it without Gaynor.'

He changed his mind now.

Ask her the main question.

'Celeste, I need to know something. Did Drew ask you to report back to her after this conversation?'

She shook her head. 'I thought you'd ask me that. The answer's no. And I want you to know that even if she had done, I'd have refused. I want to continue with it just as much as you do. Deep down, I think Gaynor really wants you to go on with it. He told me as much.'

'What else did he tell you?'

'You mean, *asked* me. What I thought of Straub's fax to you.'

'He showed it to you?'

'Yes, but I'd already seen, hadn't I? I didn't let on. He said, "I think this time an informant's been worth his twenty grand." Gaynor thinks you won't give up either.'

He showed her the note that Gaynor had initialled. 'Does it surprise you?' he asked her.

'No.'

'Why not?'

'I'd say he's freed you up, Alan. He knows you'll win.'

'Did he tell you that?'

'As a matter of fact, he did. Yes.'

The telephone was ringing on Gaynor's desk. Celeste

looked at Rosslyn with a look that said 'Aren't you going to answer it?'

He gestured at her to pick it up and watched her.

'He's not here, Ms Franklin,' Celeste said. 'No, I don't know where he's gone. I'll tell him you'd like him to call you. But what are you saying?'

There was a pause while she listened further.

'You say he's to take indefinite leave until he hears from you.' Celeste was repeating Drew's instructions: 'He's to take no papers or files from his office.'

Another pause.

Then Celeste said, 'I honestly don't know where he is, Ms Franklin. I think he's already left the building.'

She put the telephone down. Rosslyn watched her take a long breath.

'I didn't know I was such a convincing liar,' she said.

'Neither did I,' said Rosslyn. 'Thanks.'

'You'd better get out now without her knowing,' she said.

'If they won't interview me,' he said, 'you and I will interview someone else. You meet me in forty minutes. At the Notting Hill entrance to Palace Gardens. Bring a miniature cassette recorder. Indent for a handgun and rounds. And on the way buy a large bunch of flowers. The best you can buy, almost more than you can carry. One fine day you can charge it to expenses.'

'Where are we going?'

'I told you, Celeste. Notting Hill Gate entrance to Palace Gardens. Next to the Russian Embassy. We're going to see a woman about a dog. We've got to pull a stroke with Lady Vratsides. We don't want her refusing to see us. There isn't time for that.'

Before leaving Gaynor's office he slowly closed the window on the view of the Thames.

He thought: *I wonder if I'll ever be standing here again.*

He could see the small blind girl in white kneeling beside the water and the two small boys laughing at the mongrel.

The dog had caught a sewer rat.

The boys were trying to wrench the rat free from the dog's jaws.

11.30

'Yes,' said the porter in Palace Mansions to the caller on the telephone, 'Lady Vratsides is a Palace Mansions resident.'

The caller, a woman, had a pleasant voice. 'I'm an old friend from her modelling days. I have some flowers as a surprise which I'd like to deliver in person. Is she in?'

'Yes,' the porter said. 'I can put you through.'

'That won't be necessary,' the woman said. 'I'd rather it were a surprise. She hasn't got visitors or guests by any chance?'

'Not as far as I know.'

'You've been very helpful,' the woman said. 'Thank you.'

'Who shall I say called?' the porter asked.

Before the woman replied the line went dead.

11.41

The Crown Estate gatekeeper at the north entrance to Kensington Palace Gardens glanced cursorily at the visitors' IDs. 'You'd be better off using the other entrance next time,' he said as if he were reprimanding them for wasting his time.

'Palace Mansions is at the Kensington High Street end.'

He was looking at the bouquet of lilies and orchids wrapped in cellophane that Celeste was carrying.

'I'll call the Palace Mansions porter and tell him you're on your way.'

'No you won't,' Rosslyn said quietly. 'This is official. You won't call anyone unless it's the Protection Unit Officers.'

'I understand you, sir.'

'If it makes your life easier, I can speak to them for you.'

'That won't be necessary, sir,' said the gatekeeper. 'You'll find the gates at the other end.'

'What's the porter's name?' said Rosslyn.

'The day shift? Ronnie. Ronnie always does the day shift.'

'Don't call Ronnie either,' said Rosslyn. 'Otherwise it could be trouble. Understand me?'

'Very good,' said the gatekeeper.

Rosslyn and Celeste headed down Kensington Palace Gardens in the shade of the trees.

'First move,' Rosslyn said, 'is we introduce ourselves to Ronnie the porter. Warn him it's official. Show him ID. I don't want any awkward hold-ups. We don't give the Vratsides woman a chance to stall. The porter is not to call her in advance. I ask him where the CCTV control unit is. If there's a scanner then we don't go through it. Then we get him to phone Lady Vratsides himself. He's the one who tells her she's getting a nice surprise. A woman friend is bringing flowers. That's you. You go up with the flowers. If the maid answers and says she'll take them on behalf of Lady Vratsides, go straight past her. Do the talking inside the apartment, not in the corridor. You stay there until I get there.'

'Why aren't you coming up with me?'

'I'm staying with Ronnie until I know you've got inside the apartment.'

'How will you know that I have?'

'We'll turn on the CCTV. You stay in the hallway near the camera so I can see you.'

'If there's no CCTV?'

'There's bound to be. Just stay put until I get there.'

'And if she gives me grief?'

'She won't. Show her ID. If she makes any other threats, move out of view of the CCTV so there's no recorded trace. Get your gun out if you have to. Anyhow, I don't think it'll come to that. She'll be surprised all right. They always are. Then, second move. You play hard. You make sure she thinks we have enough evidence to send her down. And her husband, unless she co-operates. Offer her a deal.' Play the Angell card.'

They walked on in silence.

Plainclothes guards of several nationalities eyed them from the gateways to embassies. Uniformed gardeners directed water hoses across ordered flowerbeds. A French family passed them. The children were on roller-skates. Above Kensington Palace, to their left, a red kite dived and swooped, a splash of shining red against the blue which briefly reminded Rosslyn of the colours he'd seen in the sauna in Copenhagen last Saturday.

Garden sprinklers played across the trim yew hedges, flowerbeds and moist green lawn in front of Palace Mansions. Elsewhere in Kensington Palace Gardens Terrace, on Kensington Palace Green, even outside Kensington Palace itself, the grass was brown and scorched, dry as the dust covering the pavements of the avenue.

11.49

Rosslyn studied Celeste's progress on the hall porter's CCTV screen with one eye on Ronnie the porter, who he could see was itching to lift his telephone.

Things had not gone quite according to plan.

Ronnie had kicked up a fuss about the visitors' refusal to subject themselves to a body search. He was, he said, 'under the strictest orders to check all visitors for firearms and explosives. No matter who.' He said that if Rosslyn and Celeste were Customs officers, he wanted 'to confirm the fact with Customs headquarters'.

Which, had circumstances been normal, Rosslyn would not have prevented him from doing.

Instead, he muttered something about there being no time. It was a matter of 'Customs operational policy'. He'd commend the porter for his diligence. Whereupon Ronnie embarked on some long-winded explanation of the security policies 'specifically laid down by the managing agents'. And during the brief exposition of what Ronnie called 'chapter and verse' and the dangers of 'the managing agents reading the bloody Riot Act', Rosslyn saw the key in the lock which protected the surveillance systems. While he kept Ronnie engaged in the discussion of security formalities, Celeste took her cue and headed for the lift.

Rosslyn moved closer to the terrified porter, who flinched and stepped back from his desk. Perhaps he suspected, as would indeed have been true, that if he didn't step aside Rosslyn might use force against him. For Rosslyn made a show of slipping one hand inside his light blue linen jacket to where his handgun was in its holster. A Sigsauer P226 9mm automatic, loaded with thirteen rounds.

He was familiar with the surveillance system, the infra-red and tilt-and-turn cameras of Japanese manufacture, the guard wires, the banks of CCTV monitors housed in the plain pine cabinet beside the porter's desk. A second before Celeste called the lift, Rosslyn reached down for the key in the lock and switched the system off.

Ronnie protested vainly.

Rosslyn had by now wedged himself between the surveillance systems control panels and Ronnie, whose furrowed brow was pouring nervous sweat.

To one side of the desk was another CCTV monitor. Once Rosslyn had seen Lady Vratsides open the door, he turned the CCTV system on again.

Now it showed Celeste inside the Vratsides apartment.

'We're not going to be more than forty minutes,' Rosslyn told the porter. He waved a printed slip of paper in front of the man's eyes just long enough for him to blink at it. 'See this. Search warrant. This is a routine security operation. There's no need for you to know about it. When we've finished, we'll give you a clearance note. You don't have to feel in any way responsible for having acted contrary to whatever security regulations govern this place. Understand?'

Ronnie blinked.

'I hope you're on the level, he said.

'I hope you are too,' Rosslyn said firmly. 'Do you have any questions?'

Ronnie said he didn't.

'You understand,' said Rosslyn, 'don't lift those phones, right? I'm staying with you. If we get any visitors, let me handle them.'

'What will you tell them?'

'To go away.'

11.52

'I assume, officer,' said Lady Vratsides, 'that you have the necessary authority to come here unannounced?'

'It's normal procedure,' Celeste said. 'I'd be grateful for your co-operation.'

They stood in the entrance to the living room. Celeste thought her a striking woman. Tall and sleek, a little too thin perhaps. But with fine long legs. Her skin was very pale.

On the other side of the room, on a long window-seat upholstered in crimson silk, a boy who looked about twelve was playing with two china dolls. He was twisting their heads back to front and pressing their stomachs to produce a howl.

Celeste saw the display of framed photographs of the Royal Family, the US President and the UK Prime Minister among others.

'My son is autistic,' said Lady Vratsides. 'I would be grateful if you didn't upset him.'

'Perhaps he should play elsewhere,' Celeste suggested.

'I'd prefer not,' said Lady Vratsides. 'He's uncomfortable on his own. Perhaps you'd care to take a seat?'

They sat on deep couches forming three sides of a square. The open side faced the tinted windows with the view of Kensington Palace.

'Will this take long?' Lady Vratsides asked.

'I don't think it should,' Celeste said.

'I can't imagine why you've come. Why the flowers? I don't imagine Customs officers usually bring people flowers?'

Celeste avoided the question. 'I'd like to ask you some questions about Sir Achilles,' said Celeste.

'You'll understand he's out of the country at present,' Lady Vratsides said. 'I'm afraid I can't help you if this is connected with his business affairs.'

'Do you mind me asking where he is?' said Celeste.

Lady Vratsides leafed through an open diary on the table. 'At this very minute with business associates in Nassau. He leaves tomorrow for New York and a committee meeting at UNICEF.'

'How long's he been abroad?'

'Some weeks,' she said. 'On and off. You'll appreciate that business requires him to travel a great deal.' She ran her fingers slowly through her hair. A free as air gesture, Celeste thought, to give the impression she was untroubled.

'But I can always reach him by telephone,' she said. 'If you really do need his assistance.'

'Yes, I would like to talk to him,' Celeste said.

'You only have to say the word. I rather think, however, he might have preferred a little prior notice. His diary is usually fairly full for at least six months ahead. I hope you understand.'

'I hope you'll understand that, as undercover Customs officers, most of our work deals with matters of a criminal nature. Most of our intelligence is received from well-placed and long-term informants. Here. In Europe. In the States and elsewhere. In fact, ninety per cent of our work depends on our informants for its success.'

'You want me to help you?' said Lady Vratsides, looking at Celeste with a smile. 'With *what*, supplying you with *what*? Drug cartels? Is that what you're asking me?'

Celeste watched Lady Vratsides spread out her hands, her fingers pressed flat against the cushions of the couch. 'Someone has informed on you.'

'Informed about what?' Lady Vratsides asked. 'Who has *informed*? I'm very curious.' She looked at Celeste, her head on one side, her dark eyes wide. '*Informed* about what?'

'About aspects of your husband's business in Scandinavia.'

'You'll have to discuss that with him yourself,' said Lady Vratsides. She stared at Celeste in apparent innocence. She was adjusting the folds in her black silk skirt. 'My husband, as far as I know, has no current business dealings in Denmark.'

'Why do you say Denmark'? Celeste asked.

'It's in Scandinavia,' she said, as if the question was absurd. 'Norway, Sweden, Denmark. All the same thing. Scandinavia.'

'And he has business contacts in the Middle East?'

'Like any substantial and highly influential international businessman,' said Lady Vratsides.

'With Libya?'

'I really wouldn't know. If you're suggesting he may have any injudicious contacts with the Libyans, you're much mistaken. Bear in mind, however, my husband enjoys an intimate, if not privileged, relationship both with the US State Department and the White House. To say nothing of the Foreign Office here. As well as Downing Street. You only have to read the papers to know that. You'd be well advised to speak to my lawyer. A Mr Fordyce is dealing with my affairs.'

'I'll speak to him then,' said Celeste. 'He has an associate, I think you know him. A man called Angell, Lady Vratsides.'

'I've never heard of him,' she said abruptly.

'I thought Mr Slaemann arranged for him to be of help to you.'

'With what?'

'Some accusation that had been made about your husband.'

'About what?'

Celeste hesitated. Then she said, 'There are allegations that he has connections with a paedophile ring.'

'With a *what*?'

'A paedophile ring. A group of men involved in the

manufacture and sale of pornography involving young children.'

Lady Vratsides took a deep breath. 'Look, officer,' she said. 'Miss?'

'Quinceau.'

'Miss Quinceau, I don't know what sort of people have been spreading these lies about my husband. But you'd better be terribly sure you've got your facts right. I'm telling you that what you've said amounts to a very serious and slanderous allegation.'

'You're saying it's totally without foundation?'

'I've never heard anything so fantastic and repulsive in my life. Surely you're obliged to explain what precisely this is about?'

'I'm not obliged to do anything,' said Celeste. 'Except establish the facts.'

'What facts?'

'That your husband may or may not be involved in offences of a serious nature involving sex with children.'

'It's patently untrue. You can't just walk in here and make such deeply unpleasant insinuations about my husband behind my back.'

'Maybe you'd let me ask him about it in person, then?'

'I don't think you should be wasting his time.'

'Perhaps you should allow me to be the judge of that,' Celeste said. 'What about this man Angell?'

'I expect,' said Lady Vratsides, 'that, like myself, you have given undertakings from time to time to keep professional matters confidential.'

'Yes.'

'This man Angell is known to me. He's a well-known private investigator on an international scale. In the same class as Kroll or Salamander. I've used him in the past in connection with various patent arrangements connected with a small company my husband and I have set up in Los Angeles. V-Two offers its digital scanning services to the film and television industry in Hollywood, New York City and, more recently, in Seattle.'

'Why did you employ him?'

'If you'll be patient, I'll explain. We had occasion to believe that the progress of various experimental research projects had been revealed to our main competitors in San Rafael. Angell was able to investigate the matter. There was nothing unfortunate happening in California. Rather, Angell's work led, I'm happy to say, to several successful prosecutions in San Diego, Dallas and Chicago. He was worth his weight in gold. Highly effective, reliable, discreet and professional. My lawyer can provide you with any papers, or anything about our dealings with Angell, you may wish to see. We're an open book. I hope that satisfies your worries.'

'I'd like to see the papers.'

'Simply make an appointment, Miss Quinceau, with my lawyer.' She got to her feet. 'Now, forgive me, with your permission I have various matters to attend to which I cannot defer any longer. Why don't you take the trouble to see Angell yourself?'

'I will.'

'Why not call him now, Miss Quinceau?'

'Because we already have. And he didn't answer.'

'Like my husband, he spends a great deal of time abroad,' said Lady Vratsides from the doorway. She used the pad on the telephone to make a note. 'That's Angell's number in emergencies. Call him. And please don't think it's impertinent of me to say so, Miss Quinceau, but Major Angell only deals with major players in the international business and social networks. On the other hand, do by all means feel free to mention my name. I'm sure he'll give you a helping hand. Please, I don't mean to sound offensive, but you might find him to be more than a little interested to know about the ludicrous suppositions you're being silly enough to entertain about my husband. I see no reason why you shouldn't speak to him too.'

She smiled wistfully at the silent Elias playing peek-a-boo with the dolls he'd smothered in the silk cushions on the window-seat.

'Being a mother and a housewife is a full-time job, you know.' She smiled at Celeste. 'You'd understand.'

Celeste shrugged.

She was staring at the paintings on the walls.

Maybe I'm reading too much into this arty-farty stuff. The mother-and-child sketches look like Michelangelo. Maybe they are Michelangelo. A young girl sprawled out exposing herself next to a little girl in frilly silk knickers. What looks like a Picasso of a blind girl with a dove. She was wearing a white dress and reminded her of the blind girl she'd seen with Rosslyn from Gaynor's office window playing by the river. Then there were small oriental prints which, even from a distance, looked to be strong stuff.

'If you wouldn't mind waiting. I have to see to Elias's midday meal. Settle him down. Then why don't we telephone my husband and Major Angell? Do have a look at the paintings. Feel free. Make yourself at home, won't you? Take your time. You're not in any great hurry, I suppose.'

Celeste said she'd wait.

12.40

'Let me get them on the telephone for you,' Lady Vratsides offered.

There was a delay before Sir Achilles came on the telephone to his London apartment. He had called straight back from Nassau.

'I appreciate you letting me know of these allegations,' he told Celeste. 'They are, you may not be aware, not the first to have been made against me. On the whole, I am inclined to ignore them. Though I am bound to say none has been so unpleasant and far-fetched. This is totally without foundation. In my position, one has to inure oneself against petty jealousy. Envy and so forth. I'm afraid that's the nature of the world we inhabit.'

Celeste could hear him gasping for breath.

'You deny any association with Lund of Copenhagen?'

'Never heard of them.'

'You do business with the Danes?'

'I do business in the financial sector with anyone who'll do business with me. Does that answer your question?'

'For the time being,' said Celeste.

'You must forgive me if I sound breathless. I've just completed my mandatory twenty lengths. Doctor's orders. I need my sleep. We're five hours behind you, as I'm sure you're aware. And I haven't yet had breakfast. Thank you for your call anyway. Would you put my wife back on again?'

Celeste watched her smiling, listened to her telling him to take care. Think about becoming a vegetarian. Telling him to send her a transcript of his talk to UNICEF from New York City.

12.48

Major Angell, whose line had been busy the first time Lady Vratsides put through the call, came on second. He had a languid voice. Celeste noticed the *r*s came out as *w*s.

'I've been happy to work for the *Vwatsides* family,' he said. 'Exclusively on the West Coast. A confidential matter I'd *wather* not go into over the telephone.'

'I'd like to meet you,' said Celeste.

'I'm afraid it'll have to wait a few weeks. I'm due to fly to the Middle East tonight. I'll be more than happy to assist you, Miss Quinceau. I trust you'll have no difficulty in *dispwooving* the allegations.'

The calls were at an end. Lady Vratsides smiled.

'I hope that satisfies you,' she said.

'Thank you,' said Celeste.

Little Elias was walking towards his mother.

'He wants to use the bathroom,' said Lady Vratsides. 'If you'd wait here a moment, I'll show you out.'

Celeste thought: *Straub was wrong.*

She crossed the room quickly to the telephone. Keyed in 1471 for BT's redial service.

She listened for a few moments.

Then slowly replaced the receiver.

13.15

Hand in hand with Elias, Lady Vratsides returned to say goodbye.

'I appreciate your co-operation,' said Celeste.

'Any time,' she said. 'You're welcome. Let me show you out.'

'Its okay, thanks,' said Celeste.

She gently ruffled Elias's dark and curly hair. He clung to his mother's skirts.

'Those big sketches,' said Celeste by the lift. 'Do you mind me asking, are they really by Michelangelo?'

'Yes,' said Lady Vratsides, 'they are. I'll let you into a secret. One of the few advantages of being very rich is to be able to buy great art. It makes up for all the awful persecution that comes your way to make life hell. Like what that scum told you about Achilles. Yes, these are Michelangelos. Two of the last great sketches left in private hands. Do you know the painting they're for?'

'It's in the National Gallery,' said Celeste, preventing the lift doors closing.

'Right,' said Lady Vratsides. 'Clever of you. For the *Manchester Madonna.*'

As the doors slid quietly shut, Celeste felt the blood rushing to her head.

13.19

'Don't speak till we get outside,' Rosslyn told Celeste in the Palace Mansions entrance hall.

'All in order?' asked the porter.

'Thanks,' said Rosslyn.

Outside in the heat, he left Palace Mansions with Celeste in the direction of Kensington Church Street.

'She kept her cool,' Celeste said. 'Started off by saying her husband is abroad.'

'Where?'

'In Nassau. But I think she's an arrogant lying snob.'

'Shouldn't be hard to check where her husband is.'

'Maybe not. I said that someone had informed on her. Leaned on her. She hesitated. Tensed. I had the feeling my finger was pressing on a nerve. She denied he has any business dealings in Scandinavia.'

'I thought you said she claimed not to know about his business affairs.'

'That's what she said. She admitted that he had dealings in the Middle East. But she claimed she didn't know whether that included Libya. And she said I should speak to her lawyer, Fordyce. And then I went for her about Angell. At first she denied any knowledge of him. Finally she shifted ground. Said she did know him. That Angell had worked for some branch of the Vratsides business in California. That the lawyers can show us any documentation we need to see.'

'What happened then?' Rosslyn asked.

'She suddenly suggested I speak directly to Angell. And Vratsides.'

'You spoke to them?'

'Yes,' said Celeste. 'First Vratsides. He denied everything. Claimed not to know what I was talking about.'

'You believed him?'

'Yes.'

'And Angell?' Rosslyn asked.

'He confirmed what Lady Vratsides said. Said he couldn't meet me. That he was going to the Middle East tonight.'

'You believed him too?'

'Yes,' said Celeste. 'I did. Until I thought, well, I'll check where the call was made from. So I dialled 1471. You'll love this. It was – wait for it, I checked the number – it's the Porchester Spa.'

'She called the Spa and had one of them call back?'

Celeste corrected him. 'Had *Angell* call back. It's irrelevant that he may or may not be working for Vratsides in California. I believe she's covering up for the fact that Angell's working on *Celeste*. Covering up for her husband. She almost succeeded in persuading me. And take this on board. Didn't you once say what the *Manchester Madonna* is?'

'Verity's canal boat.'

'And besides, Alan? It's a painting in the National Gallery. Vratsides has some sketches for it.'

'Well, the call establishes that Lady Vratsides can be added to the list of liars. What I need to know is why Verity lied to me as well.'

'What do you mean, she lied to you?' Celeste asked.

'I've only just realized what that was all about last night,' said Rosslyn. 'She told me that MI6 had been asking her a load of questions about her relationship with me. As they've presumably got this all on file anyway, it doesn't make sense. If the Visa Officer in Copenhagen knew about me and Verity, you don't honestly believe that this was some kind of revelation to either MI5 or MI6. I didn't think enough about it at the time. And I'm afraid that like a lot of things Verity's said to me in the past, it went in one ear and out the other. There was every reason for Drew, Gaynor and myself to receive a call from MI6. But Verity was never part of *Celeste*.'

'Verity may be imaginative,' said Celeste. 'But she wouldn't have invented the visit. The question you have to ask is what they actually talked to her about.'

'What has she got to cover up?'

'Cover up?' Celeste said.

'What else other than a cover-up is happening here?' said Rosslyn. 'Straub is killed. And then MI6 lean on Drew. *Celeste* is killed off. And Drew goes along with it. Straub was going to give me Vratsides's name. If you recall, the Visa Officer at the Embassy had also approached Straub with a deal. What does that add up to? MI6 wanted to know how much Straub really knew. Because, let's face it, Straub was killed because of what he knew. And, in the fax Aiko gave you, only two names really count.'

'One is Angell,' said Celeste.

'The other is Vratsides.'

'So if Verity is involved in this, it's because she's tied up with either Vratsides or Angell.'

'MI6 had no need to kill off Straub,' said Rosslyn.

'They only needed to offer him more money to keep his mouth shut,' said Celeste, 'than you offered him to open it.'

'It looks as if Straub was killed by Angell,' said Rosslyn. 'I'll tell you why I think this. If you remember, you said Lady Vratsides claimed that Angell was working for her husband. Some set-up in California. Vratsides has no need to do his dirty work for himself. He would hire muscle. Anyway, Straub said in the fax that Angell was a professional killer. A man that our people would be wiser to avoid. Straub had knocked around a lot. If he said that, then you can take it from me Angell is a loose cannon.'

'Suppose we take it for granted that Straub was killed by Angell,' Celeste said, 'this still leaves open the question why Slaemann and Park were murdered. Lady Vratsides never implied that Slaemann had done anything other than act as His Master's Voice.'

'When I spoke to WPC Helen Cliff,' Rosslyn said, 'she told me that, to use her expression, Special Branch or MI5 were "through there like a dose of salts". So it seems that they were as interested as the Met in finding out who'd done it to them. Here, on the face of it, is a double killing carried out by either a psychopathic homophobe or a jealous ex-lover. But they're not content to leave it to the Met to solve it. I don't think Park knew anything worth knowing, unless you count the ability to pick up rich boyfriends as important. Not that Angell was that loaded. That's what puzzles me.'

'What would Slaemann have known, Alan?'

'Just about everything. That is, everything to do with Vratsides's affairs. Which he did.'

'Someone still knew where to find Slaemann and Park,' said Celeste. 'If Angell wasn't the killer, who knew where to find them, Alan?'

'I'm no wiser than you on that,' he said. 'What was that you were telling me about the *Manchester Madonna*?'

'That Vratsides has sketches for it in his apartment.'

'Later on,' said Rosslyn, 'I want you to find out more about that. After we've been to the Porchester Spa.'

13.41

The Porchester Spa supervisor had gone out for a few minutes.

They waited in the Cypriot café across the street for him to return.

Celeste, the sweet tooth, ordered a cold chocolate drink and a jam doughnut. Rosslyn, an occasional smoker of the filter cigarettes he bought in packs of ten, held a moist cigarette between his thumb and forefinger. She leaned across the greasy plastic table-cloth. 'Alan,' she said. 'Get yourself sorted out. You're too bloody obsessive. You should enjoy yourself more. The porn's got to you. It's like an acid.'

'I know.'

'It's corrosive. You have to learn to clock off sometimes.'

'What are you suggesting?'

'Take your mind off it. Get rid of PPP. Get yourself a proper woman.'

'Like who?'

'One you can really trust. You think there's safety in numbers.'

'Did I ever tell you that?'

'Yes, you did. I'm telling you, though, it leads to chaos. Look, forget Drew Franklin. She was just out to get laid by a

younger man. Professionally, I have to admire her; personally
I can't stand her.'

'Don't let it worry you.'

'Me worry? Why should I? Anyway, I reckon you're well
shot of her. Verity, now that's different. At least you had a
commitment to her. And to Daisy. You really liked her, didn't
you?'

'Yes.'

'Back to shop again. The thing is, we'll eventually get
rumbled. Someone's going to say we went to see Lady
Vratsides. You leaned on the porter. And there's Lady
Vratsides. She's well able to use the phone. She's probably
already been through to Custom House to check us out. And
let's face it, as far as Sister's concerned, the operation's
closed. We've been given strict instructions to lay off *Celeste*.
And here we are. Knee-deep in it. Then they'll say, "Piss off
out. *Arrivederci*." And you and I'll be spoiling the government unemployment stats next month.'

'Thanks for the advice,' he said. 'Let's go and check the Spa.'

13.53

'There's no way anyone who isn't staff can use this phone,'
said the wheelchair-bound supervisor at the Porchester Spa.
'See that?'

He pointed at the STAFF USE ONLY notice stuck to the
telephone. 'There are public payphones, BT and Mercury, for
the use of punters.' He wheeled himself in close to his desk.
'And as I've told you, there are no punters today. Or
tomorrow either.'

The Spa, its pump system and water-heating unit requiring
replacement, had been temporarily closed to the public. This
combination of circumstances shot a hole in Celeste's theory
about the origin of the call from Angell. He had asked Celeste
to question the workmen, to see if they had noticed any
stranger in the place this morning.

The supervisor tried to be helpful. 'There's only the

plumbers and electricians around this morning.'

'You've had no other visitors?'

'Only the copper we had in here earlier.'

'What was it about?'

'Just a routine visit. The Spa has been known to attract some people who aren't, shall we say, of the normal kind, if you get my drift. Most punters are fine.'

'How often do the police visit then?' Rosslyn asked.

'About once a week usually,' said the supervisor. 'Sometimes one or two of them use the place. They're mostly the women.'

'Couldn't one of the coppers have used your phone?'

'Not without my authority,' said the supervisor. 'Anyhow, they have their own phones on them. What would they want with mine?'

Rosslyn remembered WPC Helen Cliff's problems with her Storno on the night she discovered the corpses of Slaemann and Park nearby.

'They don't always work,' he said.

'I wouldn't know about that,' said the supervisor.

'Could anyone have taken an incoming call on one of the phones?'

'I'd have known if they had.'

'You're sure.'

'Sure.'

'You never left here *more than once* during the past two hours?'

'No.'

'Not even for a few minutes?'

'No. Just the once.'

'It's important you tell me if you did.'

'I didn't. And if there's one person who knows about the phone, that's me. Why? Because it's my lifeline.'

Unless, Rosslyn thought, *you were paid* to keep your mouth shut.

Paid to let someone make and then take a call.

Celeste was standing in the passage beckoning him.

She took Rosslyn to one side, away from the supervisor's cubby-hole.

'The workmen say they saw no one,' she said. And then: 'Come here.' She led him to the end of the corridor. The sound of Capital FM drowned out the rest of their conversation until they were in the caterer's office. 'Look.' She pointed to a telephone on top of a large refrigerator. 'There's your phone, Alan.'

'The wheelchair man's been bullshitting me,' Rosslyn said. He keyed in 1471. The affected tones of the recorded voice: *'The telephone number'* . . . then the number . . . *'is stored.'*

Lady Vratsides's number.

'Let's make sure.'

He keyed in Lady Vratsides's number. After a few rings he heard her voice: 'Hello? Hello? Who is this?'

He silently replaced the receiver.

Celeste was in the doorway.

'Hold it,' she shouted over the Capital FM din.

Rosslyn stepped into the corridor to see the supervisor propelling himself towards his cubbyhole.

'Someone used the phone,' Rosslyn said. 'Someone who conned the supervisor. We're going to search this place, Celeste. Just in case there's any trace of who it was or might have been. You take this floor. I'll do below.'

14.06

The engineers on the lower floor had completed the installation of the new heating system. An inspector in white overalls was peering at the control panels. And a team of cleaners were at work. A concrete passage linked the main steam rooms to the lines of showers and the toilets for Men and Women. Beyond those the renovation work was incomplete. There was a warren of small rooms that had been newly divided by brick walls. And beyond those, Rosslyn found two workmen sharing a box of sandwiches.

One of them was reading the *Sun*. Beside them was a pile of broken cardboard boxes and black plastic bins.

'This your gear?' Rosslyn asked them.

'Nothing to do with us, mate,' said the *Sun* reader. 'Fucking squatter bastards. Doss in here of a night. Get in like rats.'

Rosslyn rummaged in the contents of a bin-liner.

'Won't find anything in there,' said the *Sun* reader. 'What are you looking for anyway?'

'Just checking,' Rosslyn said evasively.

Two more black bags contained rags, old towels, empty soap-boxes and cleaning material. Then he opened a green bag. And it was the scent that drew him to look at the contents more closely. Issey Miyake for Men.

He lifted the plastic bag by the neck and took it over to one corner of the room. The workmen ignored him. He found flat and partly crushed boxes containing women's clothes. The labels read Comme des Garçons. Donna Karen. Whistles. Dolce and Gabbana. A large Marks & Spencer carrier contained tights and a black and white chequered scarf.

Last Monday. He remembered the view from Gaynor's Suffolk garden.

The woman fishing.

This is her. She has to be Angell.

And here was the source of the scent. The open, pyramidal scent bottle and the black and white Issey Miyake carton.

A sponge bag contained razors, soap and a battery-powered tooth brush.

In another he found make-up. Eye-liners. Lipsticks. Face creams.

When he emptied the last of the contents on the floor he saw a brown John Dickinson bubble bag. Inside he found a collection of colour photographs. Most were of a semi-clothed, demurely smiling Kim Park. Among them, in a small transparent folder, were four small photographs of himself leaving Custom House. Each one had been savagely defaced by a razor-blade.

He put everything back in the bag.

Angell had literally left his scent and more besides.

He wondered whether Angell would come back. And if so, when.

He replaced the bag where he had found it and noticed a heavy oblong plastic box. When he opened it he saw it contained Siebe Gorman breathing apparatus. A cylinder. A rubber mask. A torch. And there was a new canvas bag. Inside he found a long Nomex fire coat, a flash hood like a white balaclava. Leather boots.

Was all this stuff Angell's too?

14.23

On the pavement outside the Spa, Rosslyn said, 'He's been here. I think he's holing up here.'

'Will he come back?' Celeste asked.

'We'll find out about that tonight.'

They divided up the immediate tasks and agreed to meet later.

Celeste had the rest of the afternoon in which to research the ownership of the *Manchester Madonna*.

Rosslyn called Aiko Holland for a meeting.

She suggested that they meet privately in the Executive Club of the Mishibura Corporation in the Strand.

15.01

Aiko Holland was a *Sansei*. A third-generation Japanese-American. Her hair was cut in a fringe. It was hard to tell her age.

'I have arranged a private room for us,' she told Rosslyn with a nervous smile.

The windowless room in the Mishibura Corporation's Executive Club was furnished with a small conference table and hard wooden chairs.

Aiko Holland sat opposite him, downcast. 'Jack may not have been a fine man,' she said. 'But I loved him.'

'You have my sympathy, Mrs Holland.'

She leaned her head to one side. 'I still can't believe what happened. I think –'

A knock at the door interrupted her. 'I've asked them to bring us tea,' she said.

The Mishibura bar steward set two cups and a china pot of green tea with a bamboo handle on the table. After the bar steward had left, she took a photograph from her shoulder bag.

He saw a colour snapshot of a teenage girl.

'My daughter, Mitsuko,' she said. 'Jack's daughter.'

'I never knew he had a child. Is she involved?'

'She was involved. Jack used her as a courier.'

'Where is she now?'

'In Germany. Under US government protection. *Operation Celeste* has cost enough lives, don't you think? Jack's enemies are yours now. Too many of those he thought were friends have turned out to be enemies. He couldn't see the truth. He grew a little careless. You should also know that there are a lot of people who want your investigation dead and buried.'

'I know. But I need the proof. Who's giving the orders?'

'Jack's death is proof. They had him murdered because he was closing in on Vratsides for you. Now you're the only one left.' She took a sealed envelope from her shoulder bag.

'You have to see this,' she said, 'in the context of Jack's fax to me. I think it will explain what's happening to you.' She hesitated. 'I think . . .'

'What do you *think*, Mrs Holland?'

'That the people who want your skin are the same as those who killed Jack.'

'Have you discussed this with anyone at the embassy or Alconbury?

She shook her head.

'Why not?'

He opened the envelope.

'You'll see that I have underlined certain passages,' she

said. 'But before you read it there's one important thing I
have to tell you. Jack never betrayed you.'

'Why do you say that?'

'You realize that he could have done, in a manner of
speaking.'

'How?'

'Vratsides was his man. There was not much that Jack
didn't know about him.'

'Like what else?'

'Verity Cavallero,' she said, then paused.

'What about her?'

'She was her informant's lover.'

'Whose lover?' said Rosslyn. 'What are you trying to tell
me?'

'Vratsides's,' said Aiko Holland. 'Verity has been Vratsides's long-standing mistress.'

Rosslyn struggled to focus on the Xeroxed pages.

SECRET

National Security Agency Monitor
United States Air Force
RAF Alconbury United Kingdom
Cambridgeshire PE17 5DA
Federal Bureau of Investigation Liaison
Central Intelligence Agency Liaison
US Customs Liaison

SUBJECT
UK Customs & Excise Investigation Division
OPERATION CELESTE
Computer Surveillance Intercept Transcription
Internal E-Mail Communication
New Century House, Vauxhall Cross, London

Indentifications

V. Cavallero (VC)
J. McEvoy (JM)
M. D. Hughes (MDH)
E. Robertson Jones (ERJ)

CSIT

ERJ: Can you put your hands on the AV file?
VC: Go ahead.
ERJ: We stick to the story. But if we find ourselves
pressed, then we distance ourselves as before.
VC: If matters can't be contained, what is it you
personally have decided to say?
ERJ: As little as possible.
VC: What are you getting at?
ERJ: What do you think? You used a man who turns out
to be a manufacturer of paedophile pornography.
VC: With respect, we weren't unaware of his activities.
Certainly, he was told that he was not allowed to get
away with anything against the law. AV's no different in
that way from anyone else we use. On the other hand,
we took the view that, on balance, the quality of the
Middle East intelligence he had been providing was
exceptional and highly valued by our American friends.
All right, we took a calculated risk. C is also of the view
that it is not in the interests of national security that he
be prosecuted.
ERJ: The Americans aside, I think it's a bit unreasonable
for you to equate national security with plastering over
personal cracks.
VC: You can't always calculate a risk. This was an
operational matter. And again, with respect, it seems to
me you're trying to have your cake and eat it. Bear in
mind that a deal was offered to AV through his solicitor.
ERJ: What exactly was on the table?
VC:The prosecution would offer no evidence against
him. AV's end of the bargain was that he would take up

residence abroad in due course. Obviously, we have too many people in place for us to have him exposed. That's what he threatened to do if Customs decided to bring charges against him. We're not dealing with some second-rate informant. His connections are invaluable.

ERJ: If he's prepared to keep quiet and you are too, then who's going to blow the whistle?

VC: Customs & Excise.

ERJ: Can't they be squared? I was under the impression that we'd spoken to them.

JM: MD and I have spoken to the relevant officer in the presence of Drew Franklin.

ERJ: So what's the problem?

VC: There is a rogue element here.

ERJ: Go on.

JM: An inquiry agent called Angell.

ERJ: What's his connection with AV?

MDH: Professional. Through AV's solicitor.

ERJ: Why can't it be handled then?

VC: When I spoke to AV about Angell he'd never heard of him. Or so he said. I can hardly expect AV to control someone he claimed he'd never met.

ERJ: What we have, in short, is the fact that AV's solicitor has taken to employing people without AV's consent. Am I right?

VC: Yes. And now the man is dead.

ERJ: What are you talking about?

JM: A Mr Leonard Slaemann. AV's solicitor.

ERJ: What did AV say when you told him Slaemann was dead?

VC: Not much. Expressed sympathy in a rather offhand way, I thought.

ERJ: Do you think he was in any way responsible?

VC: Shouldn't be surprised. Not the sort of man you'd readily cross.

ERJ: I can accept that you couldn't have anticipated

Angell or what he might do. But surely you've kept fully
in the picture? If anyone knows what's in AV's mind, you
should.

VC: Yes.

ERJ: You told me that Customs were prepared to keep
the lid on this thing.

VC: Correct. Except for a continuing problem. Operation
Celeste is very much the operation of the customs
officer who leads their Team E. Alan Rosslyn. He
believes AV to be at the core of Operation Celeste. He
wants to secure AV's conviction and all that entails.
Moreover, he probably has a fair idea who killed his main
informant in Copenhagen. The American, Straub.

JM: We believe Straub had some long-standing
connections with Angell. By all accounts, Straub sailed
close to the wind, but Customs officers have the usual
relationship to their informants. It's a case of he may be a
bastard but he's my bastard. Straub's widow, a woman
going under her late husband's real name, Holland, a
Customs officer on secondment to NSA at Alconbury,
understandably feels aggrieved. Rosslyn's taken very
real objection to his informant being killed and that,
coupled with the fact that he regards all paedophiles as
vermin, hasn't exactly made him amenable to effective
persuasion.

ERJ: This investigation into AV is continuing?

JM: In so many words, yes it is.

ERJ: What do you propose to do?

JM: I'm reasonably confident that we can handle
Rosslyn and Mrs Holland.

ERJ: The man Angell?

JM: Angell presents us with rather more serious difficulties.

15.51

As they discussed the mention of Verity, Aiko Holland
watched Rosslyn's battle for self-control.

'I'm sorry I had to show you this about your girlfriend,' she said. 'I had no choice.'

'In a way I'm glad you did,' he said. 'I can't pretend that discovering what Verity's been playing at is anything but painful, but this transcript helps to explain a whole load of things that didn't add up. I think the trouble was that both Verity and I had been trained in deception. It gets to be a habit.'

'I know.'

'I suppose the signs were there. The pressures. The stress. She'd been drinking heavily to deal with it lately. I did ask her where she got the extra finance from to pay for her daughter's education and other things. She was always evasive. Nothing unusual in that in her case. I don't think either of us took the occasional infidelities that seriously. I think what hurts is the feeling that she could divide up her loyalties so easily.'

'You told me she didn't get the promotion she wanted so much.'

'That's right,' agreed Rosslyn. 'To believe that she could apportion herself out between her people at Vauxhall Cross, Vratsides and me. She must have been crazy.'

'What if they'd promoted her?' Aiko asked. 'She couldn't have carried on as Vratsides's case officer. SIS knew that. It's a matter of who's using who. However bitter the pill, perhaps you'll come to see that she was used more than she used other people. With the exception of you.'

'I can't see it like that.'

'You were probably the most constant element in her life. She knew that whatever else happened she could always rely on you.'

'She could rely on me not to have seen through this,' he said bitterly. 'I don't want to reopen old scars, Aiko. Do you know what I think?'

'What?'

'That what Verity had in common with Jack was an inability to play things straight. I can't tell you why some people are like that. It's just the way they are. They can't play it straight. You know this as well as I do. Our time is spent dealing with shits who devote all their energies to crime. I really sometimes wonder if there isn't a gene that makes people simply dishonest. If there is, it goes right to the top. They're prepared, as far as I can see, to let Vratsides off the hook. He isn't just some Scoutmaster with his hand on the troop-leader's knee. He's made a fortune out of the misery and abuse of children. And Verity's his mistress. Which is what the sum total of all this is. Am I supposed to believe that she knew nothing of what he was doing?'

'I know it's not easy for you,' Aiko said. 'Give yourself some breathing space. You haven't got the full picture yet. You're not really sure what Verity does or doesn't know. What we've got here is bad enough without you jumping to more conclusions.'

'It's good of you to be concerned,' Rosslyn said. 'Especially as you're having a bad time too.'

'We've both lost someone,' she said. 'I lost Jack. And it looks like you've lost Verity.'

'Yes,' said Rosslyn. 'What are you going to do now?'

'I've got some leave. I'm thinking of going to Germany. At least I still have Mitsuko. I think we both need to spend more time together.'

Rosslyn moved his chair back from the table. 'Thanks for your help anyway, Aiko. Can I give you a lift anywhere?'

'No thanks,' she said. 'I'll find my own way.'

Rosslyn got to his feet. 'See you around.'

'I hope so,' Aiko said.

Leaving the room, Rosslyn turned. Aiko Holland was still sitting at the table. She looked very vulnerable. Yet, he felt, someone who could survive life with Jack Straub could survive anything.

16.10

Delayed shock hit him in Trafalgar Square.

He watched the hands on the two visible faces of Big Ben blurred by the haze of dust and fumes. The maple-leaf flag dangling against the mast on the Canadian Pacific Building.

A pigeon tried to settle on Nelson's hand.

A crowd of sightseers on top of a red and cream bus were taking photographs.

Yobs in Union Jack T-shirts were imitating sex acts at the rear of one of Landseer's lions.

Children were playing in the water of the fountains.

Children chasing pigeons.

Children being photographed by happy parents.

Children laughing. Shouting. Screaming.

Children whose minds were a million miles away from those of the participants in the transcript Aiko had just shown him.

The shivering had spread downwards from his arms and hands to his legs and feet.

It was as though Straub had delivered from the grave.

16.14

The dishevelled figure standing with his back to the CCTV camera in the lift ascending soundlessly to the top floor of Palace Mansions controlled his breathing.

He fingered the contents of his snakeskin wallet, including the photograph of Straub a.k.a. Morton Damm a.k.a. Jack Holland, now torn into quarters. Likewise, he glanced at the photograph of Leonard Slaemann he had defaced with a razor blade. Two other small photographs were intact. That of Senior Investigation Office Alan Rosslyn. That of Kim. When he looked into Kim's shining eyes, his chest began to wheeze.

Two sharp squirts from his Ventolin inhaler eased his breathing difficulties and helped calm him. But when he looked at the knob on his hand where his thumb should have been he saw it was raw. Some strange connection of brain and nerves registered pain in that missing thumb.

He heard the echo of Kim's voice in the Porchester Spa last

Friday: 'An eye for an eye.' And the sweetness of Kim's voice in his ear singing 'Say A Little Prayer For Me'.

And then the notice in the lift, headed EMERGENCY, reminded him again of the other he had seen last Friday at the Spa and the small print that explained how a computer would monitor the heat for the comfort of future visitors. '*And* their pain,' he thought.

It seemed to him as though Kim was by his side. Some ghostly and almost holy presence guiding him to fulfil his lover's promise, saying, *I am your blood. I am your body. Be yourself.*

The words of his howling alcoholic mother. He saw the lipstick stains on her yellow teeth that he had thought was blood. The thought flashed in his head like part of a waking dream.

The day of the blood. When his blood had flowed from his freezing hand in the school playground in Great Yarmouth. When the teacher had solemnly placed his bloodied little thumb in a matchbox with a view to its being stitched back on at the local hospital.

Such memories of childhood fired him up.

Hated memories gave him strength. The assaults on him by his stepfather. His weeping grandmother. And the memory of saying prayers with her. The fierce grip of her blotched and bony hands had offered a moment's comfort and seemed like love. Until she crooned Bing Crosby songs to him and piped 'The Day Thou Gavest Lord Hath Ended.'

Kim seemed to be crooning to him: *Kill Rosslyn. Boil him alive. Cut him. Watch him boil. You are an artist. Give a deeper meaning to the word Deface.*

The pain of Kim's death was temporarily assuaged by the imminence of slaughter, and he delighted in it.

Kim will not have died in vain.

'At the going down of the sun,' his grandmother used to whisper, 'we will remember them. They're on God's list.'

And I have my list too, thought Angell. *And they will be*

*remembered on Earth. The only point of Art is that it affords you
immortality.* He had often tried to explain his view to Kim,
who had not seemed to understand what he had been
driving at.

'Say a Little Prayer' was echoing in his head as he left the lift
for his appointment with Lady Vratsides at a quarter past four.

He was on time. To the minute.

16.15

Once he was inside her apartment, Lady Vratsides found it
hard to believe that this was the same Major Angell who had
visited her the week before. Little wonder it had proved so
difficult to persuade both the Crown Estate gatekeeper at the
south entrance to Kensington Palace Gardens and the Palace
Mansions porter to allow her nameless visitor to enter. The
smooth presence had been replaced by a dishevelled figure,
unshaven and with an almost demoralized air.

His anxious eyes darted past her, as if he was half-
expecting someone else to step into the room. 'Are you
alone?' he asked.

'Quite alone,' she said uneasily.

'Are you sure this place isn't being watched?'

'I don't see why. Who by?'

'The police,' he said impatiently. 'Hence the rather changed
appearance.'

'They're not looking for me,' she said. 'They could hardly
believe that I had anything to do with your boyfriend's
death. I put the television on for the lunchtime news. Both
sides were showing shots of your flat with a police guard
outside. They gave your name.'

'What did they say?'

'The usual guff about their being anxious to interview
you,' she said, 'to assist them in their inquiries. There was
some speculation about motives for the killings.'

Angell nervously fingered the collar of his grubby shirt. 'I
suppose I couldn't stay here?'

'Not here.'

'I thought you said this place *isn't* being watched?'

'It may not be,' she said. 'But I'm getting altogether too many visitors for comfort. The black customs officer, the one you spoke to. What's her name? Quinceau. She's the officer working in tandem with Rosslyn. You told me his Team E would be dangerous opponents. You were supposed to have contained this investigation. You're not succeeding, are you? My God, I only have to look at you to see you're a loser.'

'I keep my bargains,' Angell said quietly.

'What bargains?' she almost shouted at him. 'Now you're asking me if you can stay *here*.'

'My deadline is tomorrow.'

There was a silence.

'Tomorrow,' she said. 'I can imagine what my friends would say if I recommended you. If they asked me for your address. What do I say? You have no office. No flat. What do I suggest? Call you at some public baths? Dear God.'

'You know it would be unwise to return to my place.'

'That's your problem.'

'I can understand your disappointment,' Angell said. 'I do wonder whether I could just ask for one small favour.'

'If it's money, no.'

'It isn't money, Lady Vratsides. And I also understand your impatience. What, however, you seem to be forgetting is that if anything goes wrong for me it will go wrong for you too. What's the expression Slaemann used? Something about putting one in an embarrassing position. I don't want to do that. I suggest you continue to do what you've done so far. Leave the technical matters to me. Chief of these is to end this investigation within twenty-four hours from now. I have lived day and night with Mr Rosslyn. I most probably know his mind better than he does himself. I am one, possibly two moves ahead of him. I've made it my business to stay close to him. By close, I mean very close. I was there last night when he left Custom House. And there in the background when he visited his girlfriend at Camden Lock. If I may just make use of your kitchen.'

'You're asking me to turn a blind eye, are you?'

'That's what I'm asking, Lady Vratsides. If you'd just excuse me.'

In her kitchen he found the Shoudai Masayoshi blades on the counter. Untouched, still in the same place where he had seen them a week ago. He wrapped them in a tea-cloth and slipped them inside his jacket.

Back in the main room he said, 'I will be able to report a satisfactory outcome to you within twenty-four hours.'

She watched him walk slowly in the direction of the lift. 'I hope you do,' she told him. 'If not, you'll feel the full force of my husband's anger.'

16.25

It took Rosslyn some time to find a vacant telephone.

Dead time. In the sour heat of the London afternoon there was dead and then there was dead.

He finally found a telephone in Charing Cross Station and called Celeste.

'Where are you, Alan?' she asked.

'At Charing Cross. I've just been with Aiko Holland.'

'How did it go?'

'As well as can be expected – i.e. not very well. I've learned a few things this afternoon that I wish I hadn't.'

'What about?'

'Look, I can't talk about it now. I've no change. In any case, this is far too public. We'll talk about it later. See you shortly.'

Walking out of the station, he looked for a taxi in the forecourt.

The feeling of numbness that had stayed with him since Aiko's disclosures seemed, if anything, to have intensified. After he had left her he had been almost oblivious to his surroundings. Had he been asked for a description of any of the passers-by he would have been unable to give one. He felt an urgent need to get back to Celeste.

He had to wait some time for a taxi. It was the wrong time of day, he thought, to get one quickly. Businessmen flushed with lunch had got there first. Eventually, a taxi pulled up. Its passenger got out and Rosslyn seated himself whilst the fare was still searching for change. Rosslyn told the driver to take him to Lower Thames Street and Custom House.

Roadworks and failed traffic lights delayed them for what seemed to be an eternity.

And when they did reach Lower Thames Street, he found himself paying off the taxi driver in the middle of a traffic jam.

The duty security guard glanced briefly at Rosslyn's ID. 'Looks as if it's going to rain at last,' he said.

'Could be,' said Rosslyn.

'By the way,' said the security guard, 'Mr Gaynor said for you to see him as soon as you got in.'

'What's he doing here?' Rosslyn asked.

'Can't keep away.'

Rosslyn headed for the lift. Perhaps Gaynor had got something new for him. Although he doubted it. For some reason, Gaynor seemed to have allied himself with Drew. The initialling of Drew's recommendation of Thornley-Miller remained almost incomprehensible. He wondered if he had ever really got Gaynor right. Perhaps he was just the same as the rest of them. All right until the crunch came and then: Low profile. Protect your pension. Cover your arse.

On the fourth floor, he found Gaynor standing in the corridor looking grim. 'If you have tears,' he said, 'prepare to shed them now.'

'What's up?'

'Just about everything,' said Gaynor. 'Sister's waiting for you. Come into the office.'

17.13

Drew was standing by the window of what had been Gaynor's office. On the desk, now Thornley-Miller's, was a new Compaq Presario. So recently delivered and set up that the packing-cases lay in a pile in one corner of the room.

'You got here then, Alan,' she said.

'Sorry I couldn't get here any sooner.'

'That's all right,' she said. 'Where's Thornley-Miller?'

'Said he'd be here in a minute,' said Gaynor. 'Don't think he'll be long.'

Rosslyn saw Drew glance at the clock. Nobody will ever steal the clock while you're around, he thought, you've always got one eye on it.

Thornley-Miller came into the room.

She nodded at him. 'Now you're here, John, we can get on.' She handed him a CD-ROM. 'Can I leave the technology to you?'

'Yes,' said Thornley-Miller.

Rosslyn watched him prepare the Compaq Presario for the CD-ROM

'I think I ought to tell you, Alan,' said Drew, 'that what you are going to see is pretty unpleasant.'

'I'm supposed to be used to it.'

'This is rather different.'

'Very different,' said Thornley-Miller, who somehow managed to seem ingratiating and aggressive at the same time.

'If you would, John?'

Rosslyn recognized the title:

As innocently as the original video, the CD-ROM began.
Some shots of the *Manchester Madonna*.
Sunlight reflected in the canal water.
Daisy's voice was saying:
'Here is the *Manchester Madonna*. This is home, where Mummy lives with me. The *Manchester Madonna* was built about sixty years ago. It was given to Mummy by a friend and is worth a lot of money.'
Rosslyn watched the video shots of himself with toothache.
Some of him smiling.
There were close-up shots of ducks, followed by others of Daisy's cabin. Daisy said: 'This is my little cabin, which has a very comfy bunk and a duvet and several teddies who sleep with me cuddled up. There is my favourite nightie.'
Then the main cabin.
Daisy's commentary: 'Here's what Mummy calls "Lounge Out". The stove is wood-burning and when we burn apple-tree branches it gives off a lovely smell. There are some nice pictures on the wall from Mummy's travels. Some are of Greece and Lake Como, which is in Italy, where Mummy used to go on holiday with boyfriends.'
Now Verity's cabin.
He remembered Daisy handing him her gift.
The written label:

FOR DARLINGEST ALAN

LOTS AND LOTS OF LOVE

DAISY

Now Daisy's voice was saying:
'Here is Mummy's great big bed. She has goose-feather pillows, which isn't fair to geese. On Saturday mornings we all get into bed together and *I try not to leave croissant crumbs* in the sheets. Once I left some honey there by mistake.'
Now the camera was exploring his flat in Eccleston Square.
And Daisy said:
'The flat doesn't look lived in because it's not.'
He saw himself. And he was saying:

'And who am I?'

And Daisy was laughing. 'MY GREAT BIG BEAST.'

Now Verity was reciting to camera:

> There was a little girl
> Who had a little curl
> Right in the middle of her forehead,
> When she was good
> She was very, very good
> And when she was bad she was horrid.

Daisy laughed and said, 'That's not what Alan says.'

'What does Alan say?' asked Verity.

And Daisy recited:

> There was a little girl
> Who had a little curl
> Right in the middle of her forehead,
> And when she was good
> She was very, very good
> And when she was bad
> She was very, very POPULAR!

After that was another sequence in the *Manchester Madonna*.

Daisy undressed for bed, slipped on her nightdress and jumped into bed.

Rosslyn saw himself. Naked and erect.

The blood beat in his brain.

He saw Daisy. Naked.

A penis gorged with blood.

Her eyes were wide open.

Then the pair of them.

A naked man seen from the rear.

The small vagina prised open.

A smear of lubrication.

Penis.

Its red tip.

Its opening like an eye.

Inserted.

Red wetness.

Her face in agony. Her cries:

'NO NO NO.'

And Daisy's commentary:

'*I hope,*' she said, '*that makes you very happy, Alan.*'

That was the end of it.

Rosslyn stared at the screen in silence. His fists clenched, he was holding his breath.

'I think I'm going to throw up,' he said. 'You'll have to excuse me.'

17.57

He made it to the toilet just in time before vomiting.

Afterwards, sweating profusely, he sluiced his face in cold water. And then, for the first time in many months, he wept uncontrollably.

18.10

'Are you all right, Alan?' Drew asked. 'Do you feel well enough to go on?'

He cleared his throat. 'Yes.'

Drew turned to Gaynor. 'Perhaps you'd like to start?'

The Sea Captain shifted awkwardly in his chair. 'Right,' he said. He was trying to avoid Rosslyn's gaze. 'This came into our possession earlier today.'

'Where did you get it?' Rosslyn asked.

'From our friends at Vauxhall Cross,' said Gaynor. 'Their version of affairs is that they broke into your flat and very conveniently found it there.'

'What else do they say they found?' Rosslyn asked.

'Nothing else,' Gaynor. 'Or at least if they did, they didn't bring it along here.'

'Wait a minute,' Rosslyn interrupted. 'That's not enough. I want to know who the fuck is behind that filth. *You* tell me,

Drew. "They" – just *who are* "they"?'

'We've been told not to name names,' she said.

'You know who "they" are,' Rosslyn snapped. 'Hughes, was it, or McEvoy?'

Drew was toying with the cord to the Venetian blinds. 'It's okay, Alan,' she said. 'We don't for one minute think it's genuine.'

'You don't,' said Rosslyn, enraged. 'Great.' The colour was returning to his face. 'Thank you very much.'

'Let's not lose our heads,' said Gaynor. 'On the face of it, Alan, we're confronted with the sort of evidence which would make us take you into custody with no possibility of bail. And that's the way Vauxhall Cross are playing it. We would need a pretty good justification for not acting in the face of evidence like this disk. What are we supposed to do? Go back to SIS and say we don't believe it?'

'It doesn't matter that we believe,' said Rosslyn. 'It's what the public believe. The jury. Scotland bloody Yard. The whole crew. What matters is what they'll believe. So what happens? Some expert in multi-fucking-media is called in to adjudicate on the authenticity of this disk. What am I supposed to be doing in the meantime? Sitting banged up somewhere while some nerd faffs around?'

There was a silence.

Thornley-Miller broke it. 'Why don't we visit Verity Cavallero and her daughter and quite simply ask them to support you?'

Rosslyn turned on him. 'Why don't you just shut the fuck up? Why in God's name should a totally innocent ten-year-old be asked her opinion? Are you suggesting she look at this? What planet are you living on?'

'The mother is SIS,' said Thornley-Miller, trying to limit the damage.

'So what?' said Rosslyn. 'Once and for all, get this into your brain. If SIS say anything, which I very much doubt, they'll say, "Does any reasonable person believe the service would waste its time with this sort of fakery? We've better things to do." They'll deny all knowledge of it.'

'I doubt they can now,' said Thornley-Miller. 'It's gone too far.'

'You're telling me *that*?' Rosslyn almost yelled.

'Calm down, Alan,' said Drew. 'This is generating more heat than light.' She turned again to Gaynor. 'What do you think we should do?'

A smile formed on Gaynor's face. 'Isn't all this a bit late in the day?'

'I don't follow you,' said Drew.

'Well, you seem to be asking for my opinion,' Gaynor said. 'I've never understood why you caved in so easily over *Celeste* in the first place.'

Rosslyn intervened. 'You know, Drew, that's what I think too. As far as I can see, the minute SIS decided that they didn't like it, you went along with them. You didn't consult either me or Mr Gaynor in any real sense. We were just confronted with a *fait accompli*. We lost Straub, a key informant. Killed in Copenhagen. So what? It wasn't the first time. We had a name, Vratsides. But you just wanted to wave goodbye. Goodbye *Celeste*. You've never called off an operation like this before. There's something different about this, something you're holding back from us.'

'I've been very open with you,' said Drew. 'I'm on your side.'

Rosslyn shook his head. 'Can I tell you something off the record, Drew?'

'Yes.'

'I'd like you, Thornley-Miller, out of the room, if you don't mind.'

'I do mind, Rosslyn.'

'If you'd wait outside,' said Drew.

'This is my office,' said Thornley-Miller.

'For Christ's sake,' said Gaynor. 'It's an order. Move it. Get the fuck out of here.'

18.31

'What is it you want to tell me,' Drew asked, 'off the record?'

'That you're out of your depth,' said Rosslyn.

'Even by your standards, Alan, that's a pretty impertinent thing to say in front of a third party.'

'Far from being impertinent,' Rosslyn said, 'it's highly pertinent.'

'Are you saying you're in possession of information that I haven't got?'

'Yes.'

'Perhaps, then, you'd do me the courtesy of telling me what it is,' she said. 'And where it came from?'

'I'll tell you what it is,' said Rosslyn. 'Not where it came from. Let's not waste any more time playing silly buggers. You can't seriously have believed that SIS were that worried about Straub's corpse. Did it have anything to do with them? In any case, I doubt if any body-count of ours could match theirs. Why were they suddenly becoming squeamish? I'll tell you about that. Vratsides is one of theirs.'

'Go on.'

'He's one of their main men in the Middle East and fuck knows where else besides. He's of no use to them banged up in some sex-offenders' wing.'

'Is this on the up and up?' said Gaynor.

'More so than that poxy CD-ROM,' said Rosslyn. 'I learned something else. Something I wish I hadn't heard. I know who Vratsides's case officer is.'

'Who?' Drew asked.

'It's Verity Cavallero.'

Drew tugged at the cord to the Venetian blinds and they clattered down. 'So what?'

'How long have you known?' said Gaynor.

'Only for a few hours,' said Rosslyn. 'Though I should've guessed something of that sort.'

'Take stock,' said Gaynor. 'What happens now?'

'Some of it depends on you, Drew,' said Rosslyn. 'Are you

prepared to stand up and be counted? Because if you're not, then you're going to have to live with the idea that you've allowed one of the most evil men we've ever dealt with to peddle his filth in the name of some cause you can't even tell us about. I'll tell you where that disk came from.'

'Are you saying it didn't come from SIS?' Drew interrupted.

'No. I am saying it came from Vratsides. You know why? You've read my analysis and transcript of that CD-ROM, Item 87/1. The one I showed Mr Gaynor in the fleapit yesterday night. This one bears all the same technical and stylistic hallmarks. I am saying that SIS planted it. They didn't need to manufacture it.' He looked at Drew. 'Take the risk. Let me finish it.'

'If I don't?'

'Make your mind up.'

'If you go ahead –' she began.

Rosslyn interrupted, 'You don't want to know about it?'

'Would you mind, Alan,' she said quietly, 'returning your handgun?'

'If you need it.'

He unfastened his gun and holster. Handed them to Gaynor. Who handed them to Drew.

For the second time that day she turned on her heel.

Rosslyn and Gaynor watched her slam the door.

'Plenty more where they came from,' said Gaynor.

'Guns too, Chief. I want you to lay your hands on one. Now. And three mobile phones. And that, with respect, is an order.'

18.39

According to Celeste, because the police had by now established the ownership of the flat where Park and Slaemann had been murdered, they were on the look-out for Angell. 'But they've found no traces of his fingerprints,' she told Rosslyn. 'Nothing that would make him a leading suspect.'

She looked at him apprehensively.

Rosslyn was waiting for Gaynor to give him the handgun. He had explained the contents of Aiko Holland's transcript to Celeste. She had been sympathetic about Verity, whilst not seeming particularly surprised. *Celeste*, he told her, was alive and would stay that way until he had finally confronted Vratsides, Verity and Angell. The investigation had taken on what he called 'a kind of circularity'. It was like approaching a black hole. You could calculate its power and rage by the chaos of the ripples around its edge. Fall in, and you'd be shredded and cooked alive.

Waiting for Gaynor, she said, 'You want to know what Milo thinks?'

'What's that?' Rosslyn said, his thoughts elsewhere.

'That we can't beat the opposition.'

'He's wrong.'

'He asked me to warn you off. In the interests of the general good.'

'How do you know all this?'

'He rang me.'

'What did that woman Satomura come up with?'

'Nothing that you don't already know. What Aiko Holland said is pretty well correct. Satomura says we shouldn't move. "Don't scare Angell," was the last thing Milo told me. I'm only quoting him, Alan.'

'Tell me what you've got on the *Manchester Madonna*.'

She opened her notebook.

'It was last sold by a man named Jozef Spoto, originally Maltese, with vice convictions way back. He was the previous owner. Before Verity.'

'Did she really buy it from a villain?'

'Didn't she tell you?'

'Like hell.'

'Jozef Spoto kept the boat in Little Venice. It was subsequently renamed. When Spoto owned it he called it *Spice Girl*. He has a kebab house in Marylebone now being run by his wife, Ruth. She's a buck-toothed, bitter divorcee obsessed by her old man's refusal to come up with a once and for all divorce settlement. Ruth Spoto tried to get possession of *Manchester Madonna*. Ten years ago Spoto sold it for cash. A few thousand. No questions asked. So what Ruth Spoto reckoned to be her divorce settlement disappeared. She had an investigation agent look into the background of the sale. He followed the money. He turned up Spoto's past, when he was earning big money from girls in Bayswater. Until he got busted by the Vice Squad. And who was Spoto's lawyer? None other than Slaemann.'

'Is this for sure?'

'It is. The agent got hold of a clerk in accounts at Slaemann's. There's a record down in black and white of a big cash payment. And where do you think the money came from?'

Rosslyn stared at her.

'Vratsides,' said Celeste.

'Are you sure of this?'

'Ruth Spoto wanted to tell me the truth.'

'Why are you so certain?'

'Because she's angry. She has scores to settle. And she'd have no need to invent a story like this.'

'Who was her inquiry agent?'

'A man called Ghulam Singh.'

'Where is he?'

'He had offices in Tottenham.'

'What do you mean,' Rosslyn asked, ''had''?'

'Singh was murdered three years ago.'

'Mrs Spoto tell you that?'

'She did,' Celeste said.

'Then that's him ruled out,' said Rosslyn.

'I thought you'd already know some of this, Alan.'

He remembered the interview with Dr Hecht.

I could tell her. *Verity, as the single parent of ten-year-old Daisy, with no support from the absent and unnamed father, is soon going* to have to carry the burden of paying her daughter's school fees. To say nothing of the expense of paying for Daisy's nanny.

Until a year ago, MR A. N. OTHER, the absent father, was going to meet the cost of boarding-school fees. But it seems, so Verity said, that along with a lot of other whingeing toffs he lost a fortune at Lloyd's. Sold the family silver and a lot more besides. She refused to see the practical good sense of sending Daisy to a state school.

Maybe little Daisy's father is nameless because Verity put herself about so much she was unsure exactly which of her lovers had got her pregnant.

He thought he heard Daisy asking:

'What's the matter, Mummy? Who's here, Mummy? Is it Alan? Or is it You-Know-Who? YKW? Is it YKW?'

Now he knew.

19.11

Gaynor returned with the mobile phones, a holster and a new Sigsauer P226 9mm automatic. 'Loaded,' he said, 'with thirteen rounds.'

'We've got enough on them to bring them in,' said Rosslyn. The evening sunlight seemed to increase the hollowness of his eyes. 'You understand what I'm saying? That's what we're going to do.'

He looked at Celeste. 'I want you to go back to Palace Mansions. Bring in Lady Vratsides. I don't want her talking to anyone else before you interrogate her back here. Don't let her make any phone calls. Particularly to her solicitor. If there's a problem with the kid, get on to social services. Take your shooter with you just to be on the safe side.' He turned to Gaynor. 'We're going to bring in Verity and Vratsides. Then Angell.'

'If we can't locate them?' said Gaynor. 'What do we do then?'

'Wait for them to get home,' said Rosslyn. 'Wait all night if needs be. We have to get cars. Unmarked.'

'Leave the car pool to me,' said Gaynor.

'If you run into any problems, call me,' Rosslyn said. 'We'd better get going. We're not even supposed to be here.'

19.15

Verity heard someone at the door to the *Manchester Madonna*.

Must be Daisy, she thought, back with Granny.

Barefoot in a pale blue tracksuit, and with a glass of chilled vodka in her hand, she opened the door and found herself looking at a man wearing a white mask.

Had she immediately kicked the door shut in his face, she might have delayed Angell's entry. She could have gained enough time to telephone for assistance. But the sight of his white mask like a balaclava petrified her. In one gloved hand he carried a can of lighter fuel. And when she saw the long thin blade he carried in his other hand she seemed to freeze to the cabin floorboards.

'What do you want?' she asked.

'Is he here?' asked Angell.

'Is who here?'

'Vratsides.'

'No, he isn't.'

'Don't lie to me,' Angell said. 'I've seen enough fucking photos of him to last a lifetime. I saw his face at the window.'

'I don't know what you're talking about,' she said.

'Lock the door,' Angell told her.

She followed his instructions.

'Put that glass down. Now raise your hands above your head and turn around.' Again she did what he said. And once she had turned round, Angell deftly sliced through the fabric, beginning at the collar, then tore off her tracksuit top.

'Now take your pants off.'

She turned, shivering, to face him again. 'If you're going to . . .'

'What makes you think I'd ever want your body?' he wheezed. He slowly pointed the blade at her face. 'This is what I want.'

She tried to turn away from him. 'Achilles,' she yelled. 'HELP ME!'

As she shouted, Angell, infuriated, sprayed a streaming arc of lighter fuel into her face. 'Don't make me have to set light to you,' he said.

She turned away too late and screamed.

Blinded, she began to blunder towards the table. She crashed into it and screamed.

'Stupid bitch. Shut up.'

Angell went to the cabin and listened. Tried the door and found it locked from the inside.

'Unlock it.'

He beat his fist against the plywood panels.

No answer.

He took two quick steps backwards. Glanced to one side at Verity cowering at the table before kicking in the door just beneath the lock.

The plywood splintered and cracked.

Inside the cabin he saw the slim figure standing by the low bed. The cabin was hot. The bed disordered. He smelled sex.

Vratsides must have dressed hurriedly in his fawn light-weight suit. He was slipping on brown loafers over black silk socks.

Angell caught a momentary flash of terror registering in Vratsides's hollow eyes. The thin voice betrayed his nervousness. 'What are you doing to her?' Vratsides said.

'Just lift your hands above your head,' Angell said, stepping back to allow Vratsides to leave the cabin. 'Move towards her. Sit down.'

'What's this about?' Vratsides said, squatting on the floor next to Verity.

'My eyes,' Verity said weakly, her face buried in her hands. 'I can't see.'

'Fuck your eyes,' Angell said.

'Is it cash you want?' Vratsides asked. He began to feel inside his jacket as if for his wallet.

'Don't move,' Angell snapped. He jabbed the blade near Vratsides's face.

'For Christ's sake, Achilles. *Pay him.*'

'If you started counting from now until fucking Doomsday –'

'Counting what?' Vratsides interrupted.

'It wouldn't be enough to pay me off.'

'Pay you off?' said Vratsides. 'Pay you off for what?'

'Why don't I let you guess?'

'I haven't time to play games,' said Vratsides.

Given half a chance, Angell thought, Vratsides would gain the initiative.

'You haven't got much time to play anything.'

'Then tell me what you want.'

'Straight answers.'

'What's the question?'

'Why you killed my partner and your lawyer in my flat?'

'I did not.'

Angell stamped heavily on Verity's knee. 'Don't tell me it was you.'

She moaned.

'Leave her alone,' Vratsides said, leaning as far back as he could to avoid the end of the blade that was now touching his nose.

'If you want her left alone,' Angell wheezed, 'then all you've got to do is give the answers I'm looking for and give them to me fast.'

'I don't know who killed them.'

Angell leaned down to Verity and made a small, sharp cut in her back. Blood trickled down between her shoulder-blades.

'I'll cut her until you answer.'

'For Christ's sake,' she said, 'tell him what he wants to know.'

'If I tell you who killed them,' said Vratsides, 'will you leave at once?'

'It depends on who it fucking was,' Angell said. He smeared some of Verity's blood across Vratsides's face. 'And also, fucking why. See? I'll cut her nose off next.'

'Leave her alone,' said Vratsides. 'Whatever happened to Slaemann and your partner, it had nothing to do with her.'

'Good . . . If we leave her out of it, then that leaves you or your wife. Good. The pair of you. Did you do it together?'

'It was Giselle. My wife. Not me.'

'You're trying to save your skin, Vratsides.'

'I'm telling you the truth.'

'No, you're not. She doesn't call the shots. She only does what you tell her to do. Even if she did fire the shots, it was only because you loaded the fucking gun.'

Clusters of sweat had formed on Vratsides's forehead. 'I honestly did not know anything about it until I was told.'

'Are you telling me that when I visited her and asked for a million to keep your name out of things, she never contacted you? That she never phoned up and said, "I've got a phone bill, and by the way, somebody wants a million pounds from your account?" Is that what she said? Is that what your bloody wife said? She must have said something. Or does she have your say-so to draw out the odd million from the bank?'

Angell suddenly grabbed Vratsides by his jacket collar. So hard that Vratsides almost choked. The blade was so close to Vratsides's face that he closed his eyes. 'Don't fuck with me, Vratsides. Or I'll chiv you here and now.'

'Why would I lie to you?'

'I'll tell you why,' said Angell. 'Because you haven't even got the balls to cover for your wife.'

He saw Verity was trying to crawl sideways towards the door.

'DON'T MOVE!' Angell bellowed at her.

'LEAVE HER ALONE!' Vratsides shouted. 'I've told you what happened.'

'I don't want any more of your fucking lies,' Angell said. 'Let me tell you what happened. She wouldn't pay a million pounds out off her own bat. She *did* get on the phone to you, *didn't she*?'

Vratsides nodded.

'And there and then you decided that Slaemann and Kim would have to die. Isn't that it? And the plan was to kill me there as well.' He was slicing the air with the blade in fury. 'At *my* flat, you fucking PSYCHO!'

Verity had begun to weep. She cowered against Vratsides, whose eyes were wide open at the horror.

The shout turned into a scream. 'ONLY I WASN'T THERE, WAS I?' His eyes filled with tears. 'YOU DIDN'T HAVE TO KILL KIM!'

The blade stabbed and sliced. In and out. To the rhythm of his chanting.

'You didn't have to kill Kim!
You didn't have to kill Kim!
YOU DIDN'T HAVE TO KILL KIM!'

19.37

Angell, carrying a crumpled Sainsbury's carrier bag, crossed the footbridge.

He passed a woman in a floral dress holding hands with a small girl carrying an overnight bag and a red plastic Snoopy lunch-box.

'Good afternoon,' the woman said.

'Good afternoon to you,' said Angell.

'Say good afternoon to the gentleman, Daisy,' the woman said. 'We shop at Sainsbury's too.'

'Good afternoon, Daisy,' said Angell.

'Good afternoon,' said Daisy, letting go of the woman's hand. 'Race you home, Granny! Last one back's a chicken.'

Angell headed away in the direction of the nearest telephone kiosk with a euphoric smile.

He had a final call to make to Lady Vratsides.

19.50

And in what had been Gaynor's office the telephone rang.

Gaynor lifted the receiver.

The switchboard operator said, 'Mr Gaynor, I have a call for Mr Rosslyn.'

'He's in a meeting. I'll take it.'

'The caller insists on Mr Rosslyn.'

Gaynor's tone became one of irritation. 'What's their name?'

'She won't give it. She just insists on Mr Rosslyn.'

'All right, I'll see if I can get him.' He placed a hand over the mouthpiece. 'Alan, there's a call for you. Do you want to take it? Switchboard says whoever it is won't give her name. Except to you presumably.'

'Give it to me.'

Gaynor passed him the receiver.

'Alan Rosslyn.'

'Giselle Vratsides.'

'How can I help?'

'I've been thinking matters over. And if you want me to, I'm prepared to make a statement.'

'Hold on a second,' Rosslyn said. He put the telephone on voice stand-by mode, motioning Gaynor and Celeste to listen in. 'Please go ahead, Lady Vratsides.' He glanced at the caller display screen. Her number. 'Do you want to make your statement here and now?'

'I don't think it's wise to do this over the telephone,' she said.

'Do you want to meet then?' Rosslyn asked. 'Where do you suggest? Your place?'

'No,' she said. 'I'd rather we met somewhere else.'

'Where then?'

There was a pause.

It seemed she had her hand over the mouthpiece.

She's got company, he thought.

'Do you know the Porchester Spa?' she asked.

'I do, yes.'

'Can you meet me there?'

But the Spa's closed, he thought, *for renovation*.

'When?' he asked.

'In about two hours' time,' she said.

'I'll meet you there.'

'Can I have your undertaking that you'll be alone?'

'You can, yes. Do you need to contact your solicitor? Will you be bringing anyone with you?'

'No, that won't be necessary.'

He detected a faint tremor of nervousness in her voice. *She's not alone*, he thought. *I wonder who's standing alongside her*. 'I'll be there, Lady Vratsides. I look forward to seeing you.'

The line went dead.

'That alters the picture a bit,' said Rosslyn.

'Why?' Gaynor asked.

'Because when you passed the phone to me,' Rosslyn said, 'she had no reason to know who she was talking to. I could've been the tea-boy for all she knew. She didn't ask for Celeste, did she? You'd have thought Celeste was the obvious one for her to speak to. For all she knows, Celeste could be running this operation.'

'Are you thinking what I'm thinking?' Gaynor said.

'If you're thinking that this is a set-up,' said Rosslyn, 'and that it isn't Lady Vratsides who wants to see me, then we're on the same wavelength.'

'How do you want to play it then?' said Gaynor.

'I think it's best if I go to the Porchester Spa,' said Rosslyn. He looked at Gaynor. 'I'd like to leave Vratsides and Verity to you. Is that all right with you? You happy about doing it on your own?'

'It's all right by me,' said Gaynor.

Rosslyn turned to Celeste. 'I think Lady Vratsides is lying, just as she has been all along. In which case you'd better be bloody careful, girl. Why not take somebody with you?

There's a couple of people from Team E, surely. Get hold of them. This is a three-pronged operation. What's important is that we don't have any slip-ups due to lack of liaison. I want immediate phone contact the minute anything occurs. Good or bad. Stay close to the phone.'

20.45

Gaynor was the first to find himself thwarted. He was quite unable to locate Sir Achilles Vratsides.

In quick succession he put through the calls.

First to the offices of Achilles Vratsides Investments in the City. There, someone told him that, as far as she knew, Sir Achilles was abroad. She suggested he call a New York City number.

He dialled New York.

From there he was told to call the headquarters of World Child Survival, only to be passed on to the caretaker of the Vratsides home in Washington, who suggested he call Palace Mansions.

Back at square one, he thought.

He decided to try Verity Cavallero's extension at Vauxhall Cross.

There was no answer. Perhaps she's at home, he thought.

But when he telephoned the *Manchester Madonna* he found the line permanently engaged.

He dialled 100.

'Can you test a line for me, please?' he said. 'I'm getting a continuously engaged tone.'

The operator said, 'Can I have the number?'

He gave it to her and waited, looking at the wall-clock.

Come on. Come on. Come on.

Finally, the operator came back on the line. 'I'm sorry, caller, but the subscriber has apparently failed to replace the receiver. I suggest you try again later.'

God, what a waste of time.

He hurried downstairs.

The car had been delivered to him at the front of the building. He put his handgun on the passenger seat alongside his mobile telephone. He drove off at speed, still fastening his seat belt.

20.55

Driving fast to Kensington, Celeste lowered the sun visor against the setting sun.

Five minutes later, as she showed her ID to the gatekeeper at the south gate to Kensington Palace Gardens she saw the police cars. Three of them, together with a van. Outside the main entrance to Palace Mansions the police were stretching out a cordon tape.

'What's this about?' she asked the gatekeeper.

'Suspicious death,' he said.

'Whose?'

'I don't know,' he said. 'What's your interest in all this?'

'I've come to visit someone.'

'A resident?'

'Yes.'

'Who?'

'Lady Vratsides.'

'You have? Then you'd better talk to one of the coppers over there.'

A group of police officers stood outside Palace Mansions. One seemed familiar. Blonde. Fresh complexion. She walked towards her.

As she got nearer, she recognized the face of WPC Helen Cliff.

'Celeste Quinceau,' Helen said. 'We met at that dinner, didn't we?'

'Right.'

'How's Alan?'

'He's okay,' said Celeste. 'You?'

'Fine. What are you doing here?'

'Just checking out a place.'

'What, here?'

'Right.'

'Who is it?'

'A woman called Lady Vratsides,' said Celeste.

'You know her?'

'Sure.'

'When did you last see her?'

'This morning.'

'What time?'

'Around one this afternoon.'

'You know what's happened?'

'No, what?'

'Celeste,' said Helen, 'you may be able to help us.'

'With what?'

'She's dead.'

'Lady Vratsides?'

'Lady Vratsides, that's right. She's been murdered.'

Celeste fingered the crucifix at her neck. 'Oh, sweet Jesus Christ.'

I'd better get on to Alan.

'Do you mind,' said Helen, 'if we ask you some questions about her?'

'Fine,' said Celeste. 'After I've made a call.'

21.04

Celeste tried three times to get through to Rosslyn and failed. She decided instead to tell Gaynor what had happened.

Gaynor, a few minutes from the *Manchester Madonna*, took her call on the move.

Celeste: 'Lady Vratsides is dead.'

Gaynor: 'When?'

Celeste: 'In the last hour. Murdered in her apartment, it seems.'

Gaynor: 'Jesus.'

Celeste: 'I can't get through to Alan. Can you?'

Gaynor: 'I'll try. Do they have any idea who did it?'

Celeste: 'No.'

Gaynor: 'How was it done?'

Celeste: 'They weren't giving much away. Pretty grue-some. A knife attack.'

Gaynor: 'I'll tell Alan.'

Celeste: 'Hold on a minute. I want you to tell him I saw WPC Helen Cliff. She was the one he brought to the party. You weren't there. She's seen the body. Tell Alan it's important. She reckons she's seen Lady Vratsides before.'

Gaynor: 'Where.'

Celeste: 'Near Angell's flat in Bayswater, she says. On the night that Slaemann and Park got killed. She can't swear to a positive ID. But she's ninety-nine per cent certain that's who it was. Apparently, she thought Lady Vratsides was a high-class whore of some sort. Didn't connect her with the killing in any way. But the SOC officers have found a gun in Lady Vratsides's apartment. Obviously forensics are going to have to go over it. But it could be the weapon.'

Gaynor: 'The weapon may not mean that much. Anyway, as you say, we'll have to wait on forensics for that one. Let me try to get hold of Alan. You might as well get back to Custom House. I'll see you later.'

21.15

Except for an eerie creaking in the pipes, the Porchester Spa was silent.

Angell watched the small Japanese Vapac gauge that showed the steadily increasing temperature produced by the steam generators.

The steam room had reached scalding point: 50°C.

His mind went back to the last time he'd been here with Kim. Last Friday. Grief welled up as he remembered.

You promised me you'd pay Rosslyn back for what happened to my face.

His Nomex fire coat and leather boots afforded him a firefighter's protection against the heat that would soon be unbearable and finally prove lethal. The Siebe Gorman breathing apparatus was in place. The oxygen cylinder on his back. A rubber mask dangled from his neck. He adjusted the flash hood to protect his eyes. Soon it would be time for lights out in the Spa. He checked his torch. He slowly unfolded the canvas pouch containing the Japanese knives. Selecting the *sashimi bocho*, as Kim would have wished, he heard the ringing of the entry bell.

Before he left the boiler room he sucked deeply on his Ventolin inhaler.

The moist air reeked of chlorine.

In the supervisor's office, where his make-up and woman's change of clothing were arranged neatly on the desk, he looked out of the window.

With a surge of excitement, he saw Rosslyn outside.

He was standing on the pavement by his car. Talking on his mobile phone. With his back to the building. Looking across the street. Wondering, Angell thought, *where Lady Vratsides has got to. Or if he's been followed here.*

He went to the front doors. Unlocked them.

My way out. I'll use his car to leave.

Then he began to turn out the lights. To keep the faith for sweet Kim.

Death by being boiled alive was the worst fate he could arrange for Rosslyn.

He relished the feeling of control.

If only Kim were here now.

21.29

said the clock on the dashboard of Rosslyn's car.

Over the telephone, Gaynor summarized what had happened at Palace Mansions.

And from Gaynor's description of Lady Vratsides's corpse, Rosslyn recognized the signature of Angell.

'And I'm sorry to have to tell you, Alan. He got Verity.'

'Where is she?'

'I'm sorry,' said Gaynor. His voice sounded dry. 'I hate having to be the one to tell you.'

'What's happened?'

'She's dead, Alan.'

Rosslyn shivered.

'I can't talk now,' Gaynor said. 'The police are all over the place.'

'Who found her?' Rosslyn asked.

'Daisy,' said Gaynor.

'Daisy?'

'Daisy and her grandmother,' Gaynor said, his voice cracking. 'I wish I'd got there before them. No kid should ever see what Daisy's seen. I don't know how she's going to deal with it. She's going to need a hell of a lot of help.'

'Who's with her now?' Alan asked.

'Her grandmother. But she's totally shaken up too. There's a WPC looking after them.'

'Can I rely on you to make sure Daisy's okay?'

'Yes. Leave it with me. And, Alan, listen to me. Don't you go into those baths. You saw what happened to Straub. I've just seen even worse. Even though it was two to one.'

'Two?'

'Vratsides was in there too, Alan. Same thing.'

Rosslyn stood in silence. Staring across the street. At the entrance. *Bloody doors will be locked.*

'Do you hear me, Alan?' Gaynor was saying. 'Do not, I repeat, do not go in there. I don't have to tell you, he couldn't be more dangerous. The bastard's off his top. Do you hear me?'

'I can hear you,' said Rosslyn.

'I'm coming over,' Gaynor said. 'Let the police handle him. I'll call them.'

'Don't do that,' said Rosslyn. 'If he sees them he'll do a runner.'

This one's all mine, Rosslyn vowed silently.

'Alan,' said Gaynor. 'I'm telling you, DON'T GO NEAR

HIM. That's an order. Can't you bloody hear me?'

'I hear you,' said Rosslyn. 'But this is my operation. I give the orders.'

'Alan,' Gaynor said. 'I am begging you. KEEP AWAY.'

'Mr Gaynor,' Rosslyn said coldly, 'do not, I repeat, do not call the police until you hear from me. That's an order.'

Rosslyn pressed the OFF button on his mobile.

21.40

Trying the entrance doors, he was surprised to find them unlocked.

Inside, the place was in darkness. He remembered some of the layout from his visit with Celeste and the meeting with Helen Cliff. The long passage to the supervisor's office. He tried to recall the rest of the layout. But he was unsure of it. He heard the creaking of the water in the pipes. Chlorine stung his eyes. He felt his way along the walls in the darkness. Already, after less than a minute, he was drenched in sweat. He tried to read his watch but the digits merged into a single green blur. He walked faster, the tiled floor slippery. He stumbled against tables and chairs, cursing the noise they made. From below there was a glimmer of light. A moving speck.

Holding the handrail, he came to the top of the stairwell which curved back on itself until he was in the basement. The light at the end of the passage moved. Like the beam of a pocket torch.

He could just make out an illuminated sign: STEAM ROOM. The pipes moaned. Boiling steam came from beneath the door. There was a small observation window in. Touching the glass, he immediately withdrew his hand. The glass was boiling hot. Inside the steam room, a light glowed red. He felt his blood pounding behind his eyes. Inside the steam room, he could make nothing out.

Where the hell is he? Maybe Gaynor was right. *I shouldn't be here. Someone else should be handling this.* He stepped backwards and tried to activate his mobile phone. His hands were soaking wet. His mobile wouldn't respond to his touch. *It's so hot. The place feels as if it'll explode.* He took off his jacket and loosened his shirt. Dropped his jacket on the floor. Stood and listened, his eyes straining, his heart racing. He stepped back a little further.

There was a metallic clang. Like someone hitting a steel cylinder.

Jesus. He's somewhere above in the dark. His eyes on me. I can't see him. HE CAN SEE ME. Gaynor was right. *Why didn't I leave this to the police? How long do I wait? I can't see to shoot. To kill.* The steam boiled beneath his shoes. *The floor is so hot. GET OUT OF HERE.* He felt for the walls to guide him back the way he'd come. *OUT OF HERE.* He took the handgun from the holster, freeing the safety catch. The steam door was thrown open.

A scalding cloud of steam hit him in the back as he raised his gun, spinning round. A beam of light half-blinded him. He saw the blurred, coated figure. Hooded. Masked. The blade lit suddenly by the light piercing the steam.

He fired once. Back away.

The figure kept on advancing.

He fired four shots in succession, then realized he must have struck home in Angell's chest. The figure fell sideways, the torch rolling across the floor.

Rosslyn blinked. Swallowed sweat. He retrieved the torch and shone it into the masked face. Saw the blood spreading through the white balaclava mask. Heard the wheezing from the bleeding chest. A rattle in the throat. Slowly he drew the rubber mask away from the face. The eyes were wide open and lifeless. Blood was still flowing from the mouth. He tried to find a pulse. Holding the wrist, he saw there were only four fingers on one hand. the other hand was still clamped around a *sashimi bocho*.

Somewhere overhead he heard the sound of a door thrown open violently.

And then he heard the screams, as if carried by the wind, of approaching police sirens.

23.00

Drew showed off her talent for debriefing until Rosslyn insisted he'd had enough. 'Tell the police they can keep their interviews till the morning.'

The telephones in Gaynor's former office rang continually. Again and again Drew told the press, the TV and the news agencies that, as Chairman, she would make an appropriate statement 'at noon tomorrow'.

Rosslyn asked, 'Who leaked the story?'

'The police,' said Gaynor angrily. 'They're claiming credit.'

'They won't get it,' Drew said.

'Let them keep it,' said Rosslyn.

Drew continued drafting the statement she intended to make to the press. Asking for contributions from the others. Saying it must be composed to reflect a co-operative and team spirit within Customs. Insisting that reference be made to the police and security services.

'You tell us what help they were,' said Rosslyn.

'I depend on you to provide me with the operational details,' Drew snapped.

'I wish I could be more help to you in that respect,' said Rosslyn. 'But unless you're going to credit Aiko Holland and the Americans, we've no one else to thank.'

'The Americans will want to be left out of it,' said Drew.

'I don't blame them,' said Gaynor. But you have to hand it to them. They were bloody good. Thank God Almighty that someone's listening in to the bastards upriver.'

'There's Helen Cliff,' said Celeste.

'I'm not thanking some little girl plod,' said Drew.

'With respect, Chairman,' said Celeste, 'if you weren't a woman, I'd say that was a sexist criticism.'

'It's an observation, Ms Quinceau,' said Drew. 'I am very tired. Let's not lose our heads.' She began to read out a passage from her draft statement: 'We cannot hope ever to eradicate the evil trade in pornography.'

'Her Majesty won't like that,' said Gaynor.

Drew ignored him and continued: 'But above all, in so far as *Operation Celeste* and Team E involves the safety and protection of children and the war against wealthy and organized interests who manufacture paedophile pornography on an ever-increasing scale – ' she paused for breath – 'we will wage war against it.'

'I'd leave the war bit out,' said Gaynor. 'We need the support of the chattering classes. You'll offend the peace brigade.'

'I want to mention my officers,' said Drew. 'All of us who bear the burden of budget cuts.'

'I think, in the circumstances,' said Rosslyn, 'that's a tasteless phrase.'

And for the third time since they'd returned to Custom House, he turned to Celeste. 'Have you called Daisy's grandmother again at St Mary's Hospital?'

'She'll call,' said Celeste.

'Don't you think it'd be better for everyone to get a good night's sleep before you see Daisy?' Drew said.

'I need to know she's holding up,' said Rosslyn.

'Alan's right,' said Gaynor.

The duty security guard telephoned to say there was a group of photographers outside.'Tell them to go away,' Drew told him. She was losing her temper. 'You heard what I said.' And she slammed down the telephone. 'Those people want a photograph of you, Alan. "Would you pose, for Christ's sake, beneath the traces of that graffiti?" They're sick.'

'You could always pose, Drew,' said Gaynor.

Drew began to write on her yellow pad. 'It's no laughing matter,' she said. 'Let's get this over with.'

While Drew wrote, Rosslyn turned to Gaynor. 'Where are you staying tonight, Chief?'

'In my own bunk,' said Gaynor. 'My Pauline's left a cold

supper for me at Lapwing End.'

Celeste, who had been writing something on a green Post-it sticker, opened her eyes wide.

'Just cold supper, Ms Quinceau,' said Gaynor, with the hint of a sparkle in his eye. He was about to say something when the call from St Mary's Hospital came through.

'Alan,' said Celeste. 'It's for you.'

Rosslyn took the telephone.

'Alan Rosslyn?'

'Speaking.'

'I am Daisy's grandmother.'

'Thank you for calling,' said Rosslyn. 'How are you both?'

'Perhaps you can imagine.'

'I think so,' said Rosslyn. 'I think so.'

'Just bearing up. In the circumstances. Bearing up.'

'Please let me tell you how very sorry I am,' said Rosslyn.

'Thank you.'

'Tell me,' said Rosslyn. 'How's Daisy?'

'She's asleep at last. They're keeping her in overnight. The shock and so forth. I do want to ask you something, however.'

'By all means. Go ahead.'

'Daisy's been asking to see you. She's dreadfully anxious to know you're all right.'

'Tell her I'm fine,' said Rosslyn, 'and when she wakes, say I'll be in to see her at nine.'

'She thinks the world of you.'

'I wish I'd done more.'

'I know you did your best.'

'I tried,' said Rosslyn. 'We all tried.'

'Daisy wants to know if you like her present.'

'The CD-ROM?'

'The video.'

'Whatever,' said Rosslyn. 'Yes, I like it a lot. Please tell her –' It was too much for him. 'Tell her –' He struggled to continue. 'I'm sorry. Please tell Daisy I love her.'

'I'll tell her,' said the grandmother. 'It'll make her very happy. Please –' She hesitated. 'Don't cry, Mr Rosslyn.'

But he couldn't stop.

Celeste took the telephone. 'I'll visit Daisy with Alan in the morning,' she said. 'Nine prompt. Good night.'

She held Rosslyn in her arms. 'It's okay, Alan. Let it out. You're okay. Cry. I'm here.'

Gaynor motioned to Drew. 'Shall we finish your statement down the corridor?'

He led Drew to the door and left quietly.

Rosslyn stared out of the window. At the Thames. The tide on the turn. The lights illuminating Tower Bridge. At the edge of the river where he'd seen the children hunting treasure and the dog with the rat. The blind girl. Her white dress. A police launch was turning in the river not far from the disused jetty. Its searchlight beamed at Custom House. For a passing moment it shone directly into Rosslyn's eyes.

'It'll be news tomorrow,' Celeste said quietly. 'Then it'll all be forgotten.' She held him close in her arms. 'By the way, Duggie Milo called. Said well done. He's over the moon. Even had Satomura call Aiko Holland. And he asked if you had any comment to make for *The Times* obituary on Vratsides.'

'What did you say to him?'

'That anything you might say about Vratsides would be unprintable. Oh, and there are two other messages.'

'Not now, Celeste. I want to get home to bed.'

'I want you to hear them,' she said. 'Drew asked me if I thought you'd consider reapplying for promotion. To take on Gaynor's job.'

'And you said?'

'That she should ask you herself.'

'She can forget it.'

'Think you might change your mind?'

'No.'

'Not even if I'm to be made your deputy?'

'She offered you that?'

'Yes.'

'There are better things in life, Celeste.'

'That's what I told her, as it happens. Here. Your other message.'

She was holding out the green Post-it sticker she'd been scribbling on a few minutes before.

Rosslyn read it:

I don't mind being your shadow. I believe in going on. I am not going to tell you, but I am inordinately in love with you. I will tell you that I am wearing a great big Zulu smile. Because of you. It's still Thursday now. But come Friday you will heal. I promise. You are my Achilles Heel. Please tell me it's the same for you. Tell me tonight. In your bed.

Friday 28 July

79°F/26°C. After a damp start to the day clear weather
will spread during the late morning. Wind southerly
to south-easterly, light. Hot.

00.05

'It's already Friday,' said Rosslyn.

Celeste was fingering the crucifix at the end of the gold
chain around her neck for good luck.

'Are you going to tell me?' she asked.

'Can you keep a secret?'

'Yes.'

'Then that's your answer.'

ACKNOWLEDGEMENT

Thomas Putt gave me invaluable help in the preparation of this story. I owe him a great debt of thanks.

R.G.
London, 1996